The Stepn

Ros Carne was born in London, and following university she worked in magazine and newspaper journalism including as a theatre critic on the *Guardian*. She later retrained as a barrister, practising for 13 years before moving to a university teaching job. She has two adult sons and enjoys playing the violin. Ros now lives in Somerset where she writes full time.

Also by Ros Carne

The Pupil
The Stepmother

ROS CARNE

THE
STEP
MOTHER

1℃ CANELO

First published in the United Kingdom in 2021 by

Canelo
31 Helen Road
Oxford OX2 0DF
United Kingdom

Copyright © Ros Carne, 2021

The moral right of Ros Carne to be identified as the creator of this work has been asserted in accordance with the Copyright, Designs and Patents Act, 1988.

All rights reserved. No part of this publication may be reproduced or transmitted in any form or by any means, electronic or mechanical, including photocopy, recording, or any information storage and retrieval system, without permission in writing from the publisher.

A CIP catalogue record for this book is available from the British Library.

Print ISBN 978 1 80032 398 8
Ebook ISBN 978 1 80032 397 1

This book is a work of fiction. Names, characters, businesses, organizations, places and events are either the product of the author's imagination or are used fictitiously. Any resemblance to actual persons, living or dead, events or locales is entirely coincidental.

Look for more great books at www.canelo.co

Printed and bound in Great Britain by Clays Ltd, Elcograf S.p.A.

Prologue

It was a good choice. The spot where the soft estuarine deposits had been dredged out of the riverbed. The sky glittered with stars and the sliver of moon gave off just enough light for them to see each other's shapes.

Both women were fit, both had occupations that called on their strength, and at first their spades sliced easily through the fresh mud and clay. But progress slowed as the hole deepened and the ground became more compacted. Every few minutes they stopped and leant on their spades, sipping water from a shared bottle.

When the hole was deep enough they returned to the car for the body, tried and failed to heave it over the gate. The older woman felt for the bolt and metal clasp, and managed to swing it open. A loud squeak rang through the night. Back at the grave they unwrapped the blanket.

'Wait,' she said. 'Let me hold his head. I haven't said goodbye. Not properly.'

He was already stiffening. She leant forward and kissed the point of his forehead between his closed eyes. In the near dark his face looked perfect, as if he were only sleeping. Then she pulled off her jacket and T-shirt, dug her teeth into the thinly woven cotton, ripped off a sleeve and placed it by his head.

Together they lowered him into the makeshift grave.

Part One

Chapter 1

This was the place. Where the path widened and sloped towards gates on each side, where her dog, Timba, habitually turned off into the field, where a month ago she had felt the cool liquid trickling down her legs, stuck her hands down her leggings and pulled out a blood-wet finger. Kate took a deep breath and sprinted on. She would leave those demons behind. Her fault. Unmotherly. Too thin. Too selfish. They battered her ears in a volley of irrational guilt.

She was running along the disused railway path, the pure air sweet in her lungs. On each side creamy blossom frothed over branches flecked with pale green leaves. Ahead she could see the outline of the ruined abbey.

For days she had been unable to move or work. She could only lie on the sofa, staring at daytime TV, a shadow on her heart. Gradually, she'd returned to the world. To the studio, the workshops, talking to friends, to students. To the counsellor at the hospital, who told her she must be gentle with herself. It happened to many women. It was just bad luck. Talking to Michael was more difficult.

'We'll consult the experts. See what they say. Whatever you want. I'll go along with it.'

He looked down at her with his long, patient gaze. She sensed his commitment. But in the weeks that followed, his support faltered. He had been unwilling to join her in counselling.

'I'm not talking to a stranger about my feelings.'

You don't talk to anyone about your feelings. The space between them felt very wide.

They had breakfasted to the sound of the morning news, Kate barely hearing as one horror piled on top of another. In the evening, Michael slumped in front of the TV, too tired for conversation. He was involved in a big case, a young woman brain damaged during surgery. It was intense, detailed work and if he didn't need to go to court or chambers, he would bury himself in his study for hours. At other times, when conferences and meetings ran on later than expected, he would stay over in the Bristol flat. It was a relief to Kate to have the house to herself.

A breeze swirled up and she was running into the wind. Some impulse propelled her to go faster, headlong into each angry gust. She could hear her father's voice: 'When the going gets tough, the tough get going'. Life came at you and you fought it. Playground spats. Carrot top. Ginger minger. Their taunts had fired her, and she had braved her enemies with hard cold looks and words as sharp as theirs until they scattered. The three miscarriages were the only truly bad things that had happened to her. And were they that bad? She was thirty-six and otherwise blessed. Work she loved, money to pursue it, a beautiful house. There were too many children in the world. She would be doing her bit for the planet. And yet…

The abbey ahead was growing larger. She flicked back her head to check on Timba. He was close behind her, snuffling about in the margins of the path. She took a step towards him, decided to take the shortcut back to the house, grabbed his collar and pulled him down the slope and through the gate.

They set off along the edge of the rhyne, the narrow drainage ditch that served as a boundary with the next field. In the distance, under willows misty with new growth, a herd of brown cows stood chewing grass. They reminded her of the little plastic models she had played with as a child. Though these would not be cows but bullocks, this being the season when farmers put them out to grass to fatten for meat. You had to watch out for bullocks. They weren't aggressive but they were curious, frisky, playful, could do damage. Still, it was a big field and she had plenty of time.

Timba was trotting in their direction. When she called his name, he carried on, but she repeated the call and eventually he looped back towards her, like a child half-avoiding, half-obeying instruction. She glanced towards the willows. The dog had unsettled the bigger beasts, piqued their curiosity. Four legs like them. A fellow creature. Smaller, but similar colouring. Could they see colours? Kate had no idea. They were heading towards her dog now, a leader setting the pace, the herd trundling behind him. Most were walking, but a couple at the side jumped on the spot, kicking out their back legs as if eager to cut loose. One darted off in pursuit of a straggler, scrambling onto its enormous square back, clasping it with gawky front legs. A ton of beef. An adolescent mating game. Kids fooling about.

Last year a local woman had been trampled to death by cattle. She had been holding three dogs on leads. Standard advice when confronted with livestock was to let your dog off. The woman had failed to heed the advice, which was curious because it turned out she was a dog breeder. She was found by the farmer later that afternoon. The cattle were clustered at the gate, the dogs circling her body, their leads trailing behind them.

Timba wheeled back to Kate and barked. She swivelled round. The animals were close, too close, the one at the front was staring at her. From where she had stopped a few metres away she could make out the dark rims of its soulful eyes. If it broke into a run, it would reach her in seconds. A run could become a stampede.

She powered on, conscious of her quick breath, the thump of her heart, the sensation of bumpy ground through the soles of her running shoes. The track across the field, though marked as an official footpath, was little more than a strip of flattened grass that had been crushed by dog walkers. Here and there it disappeared into patches of mud and clumps of sedge. You could easily twist an ankle. Kate skirted puddles and tussocks. Her legs, strong only seconds ago, felt weak and shaky.

Then came a rumble behind her, moving towards her, rising from the earth through her body like a drumroll. She flicked back her head. Tons of hefting bone and muscle were thundering towards her.

Her heart was banging against the wall of her chest now and something lodged in her throat as she carried on running. She needed to get out of this field, and she was only halfway there. Timba was supposed to draw them away, but the stupid dog was clinging to her heels.

Breathing in short bursts she leapt across the lumpy ground, willing herself to go faster. The gate was in view, but could she reach it in time? The herd was moving and unable to stop. It would not be deliberate. An accidental killing like a hurricane or an avalanche. The rhyne on her left was an option, though a cold, dirty and possibly dangerous option. Beautiful as they looked from a distance, these waterways were murky, stinking, thick with scum and run off from the fields. She had seen what the dredgers fished out: old fridges, tyres, metal bedsteads, smashed shopping trolleys.

The gate was close now. But not close enough. There was only one way. They were big and powerful, but they were domestic beasts, subservient to humans. Anyway, it was better to know your killer.

She whirled round and faced them. And, as she turned, she realised the drumming had already stopped. There was only a faint breeze and the piercing song of a blackbird. The herd stood motionless, its leader fixing Kate with sad brown eyes. They confronted each other and she noted the vestigial horns on each side of its square face, the ridge of curly hair between each tiny lump. A handsome brute. She had done it.

'Hi!' A cheery male voice rang out.

She turned towards the sound and there, a few metres to the side of the gate, stood a young man in a white T-shirt and blue jeans, a dark jacket knotted around his waist. There was a bandage on his lower left arm. Two dogs were sitting quietly at his feet, one was a small grey lurcher, the other, Timba.

The young man grinned. 'You OK?'

She leant forward over her knees, recovering her breath, waiting for her heart to slow. 'I thought I was going to get trampled.'

'They're big beasts.'

'I never believed they'd stop.'

'Best thing. Facing them. Well done.' He opened the small gate at the side of the main barrier, holding it back for her as she climbed over the low bar into the next field. 'Mind you,' he added, 'lucky I was here.'

Kate was tempted to point out that it was she who had turned to stop the charge, but she let it rest. It crossed her mind that he was more pleased with himself than the situation warranted. But she didn't know the man and could let him enjoy his miniature triumph.

'Thought they were getting a bit close. Time to scare 'em. Wave of the arm. That's all it takes.' He demonstrated with a wide gesture and she took in the smooth, muscular limb, decorated with swirling tattoos, deep blue touched with green and red. 'There's ways. Same with dogs. They need to know who's boss.'

'I thought of jumping in the rhyne.'

'Wouldn't recommend it. There's all sorts in there.'

Thickening clouds had shut away the sun. It felt like rain. The bullocks stood motionless in a crescent on the other side of the gate. Kate wondered what they were thinking. Did they resent their domination by these small pale humans? The air had a sudden cold edge.

'You running on?' he asked. But the shock had exhausted her. She was still shaking and there was no way she could run now. 'Don't let me stop you.' His smile was wide, bold.

'You won't.' Realising she might sound abrupt, ungracious, she added, 'By the way, thanks.'

They headed off, without speaking, towards the river and the track that would take them back to her house. As they walked, she took in his shape and build. It was her job to take in shape and build. It was what she saw in people. Michael teased her about it, telling her she regarded people as little more than skeletons clothed in flesh, raw materials for clay and plaster. Not satisfied with mentally undressing them, she liked to strip off their skin to see what lay beneath. Her sculptures were bold, anatomical.

'Do you have to stare like that?' he'd once complained. 'It's embarrassing. People think I'm married to a predator.'

'You care too much about what people think,' she'd laughed. But she tempered her behaviour in his company. In his absence there was no such need. Looking was what she did, how she lived, whether overt or covert. And so, without staring, from the corner of her eye, she studied the young man who walked loosely beside her. She was sure she had seen him before.

He was a little above her height, average for a man, and beneath his white T-shirt she sensed he would be taut and strong, not bulky, not a gym goer. Just a young and active man in that wonderful decade before the body heads downhill. She thought of Michael, more than ten years older than her, still slim, but despite his personal trainer, with loose, thinning flesh that was beginning to drop on his torso. As a sculptor she could find beauty and fascination in bodies of all shapes and ages. But as a woman, she liked young men. She had said as much to her friend, Jen, who ran the local cafe. Jen had laughed and said Kate was sex-obsessed and what was she doing with an old guy like Michael.

'He loves me. I can't race around forever. Plus, he won't leave me.'

Jen had raised an eyebrow. Kate had gone on to reassure her that for all her interest in bodies, male and female, she would never cheat on Michael. When she met him seven years ago, it was as if she had come home. She had travelled and experimented and shagged too many people; she was worn out by it all and wanted a man she could rely on, like a springboard, so she could do what she really wanted, and that was sculpt.

'Lucky he's not poor,' Jen had said.

'You think I want him for his money?'

'Helps. Part of the package.' It was the kind of caustic comment Jen was prone to making. But Kate let it go. Jen was a loyal friend. She meant no harm.

'I guess so,' she said.

Kate would think about Jen's comment in the weeks ahead when everything started to fall apart. Had she been right all along? What Kate had thought of as security, was it nothing more than money?

But at this moment, out on the moor in the spring breeze, under the clear sky and buffeting clouds, her desire for a younger man was well controlled and confined to looking. And this one was good to look at. She wondered if he would sit for her. The sense that she had seen him before returned and she tried to place him, socially. The voice announced Somerset, no strong accent, but a West Country lilt: the diphthongs, the turns of phrase. Kate had an instinct for tribes, and it was clear he was not of hers. She was an incomer. Born in London. University in Bristol. Odd jobs, sculpting, travel. And now here. She wondered what his job might be that he could afford to be out walking with his dog on a Thursday afternoon. Shouldn't he be at work?

'What happened to your arm?'

'One of their mates.' He gestured to the bullocks.

'I thought you were an expert.'

'Not always.'

'So, what do you do? Are you a farmer?'

'You know what I do. You've been in my shop.' And then it clicked. The butcher's in the town. 'Plus, I help out

II

at the abattoir when they're stuck. One of the big buggers took against me. Butted me up against the ramp. Smashed my wrist. Could've been worse.'

They were approaching the house. Kate realised that despite not running, for the last fifteen minutes she hadn't been thinking about her lost child. She had been studying her young companion and she didn't want him to disappear.

Chapter 2

Soon after moving into Kilver Farmhouse, Kate and Michael had employed an architect to redesign the ground floor. The enhanced space became a kitchen diner with an extension into the garden. They gave up cooking for weeks, managing with a tiny fridge and a microwave. Meanwhile, the double garage was converted into Kate's studio, complete with plumbing and electrics. After three months of what Michael called 'hell', the old kitchen and dining room were transformed into a vast, light expanse with granite worktops, an electric Aga, double sink, an island with refrigerated wine rack, a new kitchen table of reclaimed oak and sliding glass doors onto the terrace.

'Nice,' said the man as they walked in from the garden.

'It was a nightmare getting it done. They had to pull down a load-bearing wall and put in steel joists. We lived on ready meals while the work was going on, eating on the sofa. Sorry, you don't need to hear about my kitchen woes. What can I get you to drink?'

'Tea would be good. Two sugars, please.'

His dog settled in Timba's bed, leaving Timba to lie on the floor. Kate made tea, talking more than she wanted to, telling him about the move from Bristol, how they'd fallen in love with the house, the area.

'Everyone said it was too far from a station, too remote. But that's what we loved about it. They warned we'd get flooded. But we're above sea level here. We've been OK so far, touch wood.' He said nothing and when she turned towards him with the mugs, she sensed his eyes had been waiting for her. 'But tell me about yourself. I've never met a butcher before. I mean, apart from over the counter.'

He picked up the mug and she noticed that his broad, blunt hand was covered in tiny scars. His bandaged left arm rested on the table.

'People don't understand about butchery. They reckon it's just a job in a shop. Maybe worse than your average shop. Blood and mess and all that. But butchery's a skill. There's detail, precision, an eye for shape.'

'I never thought of it like that.'

'You look at any master butcher. Watch him cutting. Straight line between fat and muscle. A nice chop's a piece of art.'

Not quite, she thought. Though she didn't contradict him, only responding, 'I'm an artist. A sculptor.'

She would sculpt his head. The outline of the nose was always her starting point. His was long and very slightly bent near the top. Her gaze ran to his jaw, the soft curve of his lip. His hair was close-cropped, curly, dark like his eyes. Even in clay she could capture their intensity. As she told her students, it was a question of depth. You didn't need colour; contours and planes were enough to suggest degrees of light and shade.

Kate had abandoned painting when she found she was using so much paint it fell off the canvas in great wet dollops. That was when she realised that she should be working in three dimensions. It felt instinctive to her, the placing of objects in space.

The man seemed larger indoors. The body that had appeared loose and easy was more cumbersome. He was the kind of man who was better suited to being outside.

'Not many people ask about my work,' he said.

'Go on. I'm interested…' Not so much the content as the way he looked when he spoke, the light from the low sun falling in a ribbon of brightness across his strong features.

'People have got funny ideas about butchery. They think it's cruel. Chopping up dead animals. Happy enough to eat the meat, though. Way I see it, killing's fine if it's humane. We know the farmers who supply us. They give their animals a good life. That's the important thing. The animals don't suffer. As soon as they walk into the plant they're stunned.'

'I suppose that would be a good way to die.' She wanted to pick up a pencil and start sketching.

'I'll choose the abattoir any day. 'Course I won't be in the shop forever.'

'What are your plans?' She offered him a biscuit which he took, speaking quickly as he munched.

'We're moving to New Zealand. Plenty of space there. Did you see the film, *Lord of the Rings*? Those mountains. We'll be off soon.'

She would not ask about 'we'. He had a partner. Of course. Maybe even a family. There was no ring but that meant nothing.

He carried on speaking, 'Got to sort out Maxie. Easier to take a couple of kids than a dog. She'd leave him behind, but no way I'm abandoning Maxie.'

He leant down and stroked the little lurcher lying obediently at his feet. Then he turned to Timba. 'Nice dog. Where d'you get him?'

'He's from the shelter. Part German Shepherd, part something else. They weren't sure, bit of collie, maybe a bit of lab. They reckoned he'd had a tough first year before he was dumped. Michael wasn't keen on taking him, but I fell in love right away. He wasn't an easy dog, wouldn't even go out at first. After we got him out it was months before we could let him off. We lost him a few times, but he always came back.'

'He's very gentle.'

Timba was licking the man's outstretched hand.

'As long as no one raises a stick or anything large in front of his face. It freaks him out.'

The man was listening hard and it all came out. The long hours of training, the delight when Timba began to respond, that one terrible night of waiting when they didn't know if they had lost him forever, her joy in the morning when she opened the front door to find her beloved dog waiting patiently in the porch.

'Sorry, I'm wittering on.'

'That's all right. I get it.'

He smiled that wonderful smile again. She caught his eye and realised he did get it. Unlike Michael who showed only detached concern, this much younger man seemed to grasp instinctively how a dog could creep inside your heart. She carried on.

'He's calmed down a bit. Doesn't run off any more. He can be jumpy with people he doesn't know. But he seems to like you.' Suddenly she stopped. She was talking too much, opening up to a near stranger.

'Best be off.' He unfolded his body from the chair and reached for his jacket, slipping in the injured arm, apparently struggling to find the other sleeve.

'I'll help,' she said. And she held it out for him as he slid in his good arm. Her hands were on his shoulders and for a moment she thought he would turn around. But he stood motionless with his back to her as if he were thinking, contemplating a move as his body's warmth rippled through her hands to some place deep in her stomach. When he turned and met her eyes, the look was unmistakable, and she felt a quiver of anxiety and quickly moved away. But even as she wanted to shout at him to get out, she heard herself saying, 'Come again.' And she was pulling open the drawer in the kitchen table, taking out her business card, the one with her phone number and email, advertising her workshops.

'Here,' she said, handing him the card.

His smile widened. 'So, what does your husband do?'

'He's a lawyer. A barrister.'

'Interesting work.'

People assumed Michael spent his days in court defending criminals. In fact, he spent most of his working life sitting at a computer assessing how large insurance companies and hospital trusts could wriggle out of compensation claims. It was detailed, remunerative work and he was good at it.

'He's in chambers today. In Bristol. But he works at home quite a bit.'

He was staying over in the flat tonight. Out at some dreary drinks do for someone who'd got silk. He'd asked her to join him and stay over, but she'd have had to find someone to look after Timba and anyway, she hated that kind of thing.

'Any kids?'

The familiar pain shot through her like an arrow. He must have sensed the shift in atmosphere, but he only waited. Eventually she was able to speak.

'Not yet,' she said, reminding herself it was she who had invited him here, she who had plied him with questions. But now he was the questioning one, studying her as she had studied him. Was he thinking she was too old to start a family? Something uneasy had arisen between them and she wanted him gone.

He continued, looking at her steadily as he said, 'Thursday's early closing. I usually walk the dog. He doesn't get out enough. Tamsin never wanted a dog.'

'Oh.'

Tamsin. A real name. A real woman.

'She's not a dog person. But she came around. Had to if she wanted me. Maxie's soft as butter – but she never really lost it – that distrust…' he said. 'Maybe see you again.'

'Yes. Maybe.'

He continued to linger by the chair. 'I'm back in the shop tomorrow. They reckon I can serve if someone else does the cutting. Come on, Maxie.'

The small dog jumped up and Timba slunk back to his proper bed. Kate stood up and led the man to the back door which opened onto her disordered garden, running down to a wall and gate. He crossed the lawn and unlatched the gate, turning back to catch her eye before disappearing onto the moor.

For a few moments she stood watching the space where he had been. Then she crossed the drive to her studio. Once inside, she drew up the blinds. The warmth of the late afternoon sun poured in through the large windows as she went over to the store cupboard and pulled out a new bag of clay. It was heavy and cold to touch, and she heaved it on her worktable, peeling off the polythene and slicing out a couple of long brick shapes with her wire garrotte. An unused head-size armature stood on one of the modelling stands. She kept it for demonstration purposes, but she could make another tomorrow. Tearing off lumps of moist clay, she forced them into the spaces in the frame of wire and metal. How good it was to start again, like diving into cool water on a hot day. For the first time since losing the baby, she had an urge to make art.

Usually she worked from a model or at least a photograph, but the profile she had studied over the cup of tea was clear in her mind. Having fashioned the rough outline of the skull she began to shape the brow, recalling how it jutted slightly forward above the bridge of the long nose. The gesture of the nose was not quite right. She would perfect that when she saw him again. Now the philtrum, the line between nose and lips, the thinner upper lip and fuller lower lip curving to the firm chin. It was sketchy, but it was enough to let her move on, to build up the back of the skull. Then the bones and muscles of the head and face. The eyes were mere sockets. They would wait.

After about two hours of uninterrupted concentration, she stood back and stared at her work, walked around it. She needed more time, needed him here in front of her; needed to understand what happened behind those eyes. She gulped down a glass of water, sprayed the beginnings of the head and covered it with a bin bag. He had mentioned Thursday afternoons. But she would see him before that. She would leave it till early next week then go to his shop to remind herself of the detail. She realised she hadn't asked his name.

In the corner of the studio stood an old dresser. At the back of one of the drawers, behind a collection of postcards, she kept an old pencil case containing a lump of dope. She rarely used it. It interfered with her sculpting. But she made sure she never ran out, dropping in on her old mates when she accompanied Michael to Bristol. Her stash was modest, but it seemed to mature with age. Occasionally, as now, she needed a little smoke to help her calm down. Michael didn't approve. Apparently nicotine was an OK drug, but marihuana was out of the question. But Michael didn't need to know.

Chapter 3

In the harsh white light of the hospital waiting area, seated on a straight-backed blue chair, Kate was pretending to read a thriller on her tablet. Inches away, Michael was scrolling through messages on his phone. A younger couple sat opposite them, hand in hand, the woman a pink-eyed bottle blonde, the man's face square under a fuzz of cropped brown hair, his features lost in misery. But the set of their bodies spoke of shared understanding. This was a couple who wept together, laughed together, planned together. When had she lost this with Michael? Kate felt a stab of envy as she studied their sad faces.

'Mr and Mrs Leonard,' called the nurse.

In their early start for the hospital, Michael had left his hair unbrushed and his shirt collar was twisted. There was a time when that slight dishevelment would have touched a tender spark in her, she would have smoothed his hair and turned down the collar. Today the tender spark was absent.

They'd made love last night, if you could call it love. It was the first time for weeks. He'd taken her from behind, clutching her breasts and moaning as he pumped into her. He'd come quickly and she had followed with a brief rush of pleasure, nerve ends fizzing, heart unmoved. She'd reached for him then, but he had curled away, saying he was tired, and she had lain awake much of the night, conscious of an unmet yearning to be comforted, held.

And now, exhausted, pulling herself up from her seat, the yearning had become a dull ache. A touch from him would have soothed it and yet something stopped her reaching for his arm. Michael pocketed his phone, and they followed the nurse into the consulting room.

The consultant was a tall, thin woman who seemed to be folded into a chair that was too small for her. Her face was scored with wrinkles and her features too large for her narrow face. But her eyes were kind. The explanation was complex, and though Kate tried to follow she was assailed by weariness and found it hard to concentrate. Michael was tapping on his tablet as the woman spoke. With his familiarity with medical language, Kate trusted him to follow better than she did. She heard the consultant speak of tests, a possible weak cervix, genetic factors, older couples and finally something called 'sticky blood'. When the woman had finished, they both sat in silence. It was a lot to take in.

'You may want to go away and think about it. You have the clinic number. Opening hours are eight till eight, five days a week. If you call reception, they can put you through to me if I'm not seeing patients. If I am, I will ring you back. Or you can email my assistant. Is there anything you'd like to ask now?'

Kate wanted to speak, but the words would not come out. The big questions: Will it happen again? What's wrong with me? – had not been answered.

Michael had a question. 'You mentioned older couples. How old?'

Kate was thirty-six, Michael forty-eight. The age gap had once felt like a good thing. An older man, settled in his work, his needs. There was baggage, of course. A string of girlfriends whom he insisted remained friends. Not that there'd been much evidence of them. And an ex-wife and daughter who lived in Canada, only now the girl was in London on some dance course. Michael had been to see her a couple of times. Kate thought about the blurry photo in Michael's studio. Immy. An overweight adolescent in a baggy dress. The girl must have changed a bit if she was thinking about becoming a dancer. Kate wondered what she looked like now. Curious that he didn't have anything more recent. She jolted herself back into the present. The consultant was speaking.

'We normally consider a couple to be older when the woman is over thirty-five and the man over forty-two.'

'Why forty-two?' asked Kate.

'It's research-based. Forty-two is the average age when the viability of sperm becomes compromised.'

Michael tapped on his tablet. It was the kind of expression he might use himself. Viability compromised.

'So, Mr and Mrs Leonard, Kate, Michael, perhaps you would like to go home and think about it. If you are interested in the test, please call my secretary in the morning or whenever you like. Do take your time in deciding. Obviously you will want to discuss this further. There's no rush.'

But there was. Every day was a wasted chance. He must have felt the rim of the contraceptive cap last night, but he'd said nothing; neither then, nor later. She wished he had. She could have explained, confessed her fears. Losing another would break her. She wanted him to know. That way they might bear this together. Better to have nothing than another wasted hope. Or had he failed to notice, wrapped in his world of private sensation?

There was a long pause. The consultant was waiting for one of them to speak but they remained silent.

'Do either of you have anything you'd like to ask?'

'Would you need to test us both?' asked Kate.

'We test the woman first. It's a simple blood test. As to when we test the male partner, it depends on the result of the first test. In the short term, we usually advise some barrier method of birth control. It can be an upsetting time to try to conceive.'

The consultant's long face softened as she looked at Kate. But it was a look that invited departure. Kate stood up. Michael thanked the woman for her time. When Kate tried to speak nothing came out but a short exhalation of breath.

'And thank you for coming,' said the woman, standing up. Kate didn't move. She had more questions. She was sure she did. But at that moment she couldn't remember what they were. The woman took a step forward and held open the door. Kate waited for Michael to touch her, a simple pat on the arm would have been enough. But there was nothing.

'Are you all right?' she asked as they left the department.

'Yes. Fine.' He was striding towards the exit.

'Want to grab a coffee?'

'I'd rather go straight home. I need to prepare for a conference tomorrow.'

'OK.'

If he didn't want to talk about what was happening to them there was nothing she could do.

'There's a management committee meeting. It could go on late. I'll probably stay over in the flat.'

'Right.'

Did he want her to object? He had always valued the freedom she gave him. It was as if both of them were speaking in a code that the other could not read.

'You don't mind, do you?'

'No. Of course not. Why should I mind?'

She was suddenly relieved by the prospect of his absence. If he had tried to approach her earlier, she would have welcomed him. If he had come for a coffee they might have discussed the consultant's advice. But the distance between them was becoming heavier each moment and it was beginning to feel like an immoveable weight. And there was something else. The young man with the laughing face. His image had drifted into her mind as the consultant had been speaking, sticking there, refusing to disappear.

A voice in her head tried to reassure her. It was an innocent preoccupation. Nothing more than a desire to look at him one more time. The sculpted head had still to be completed. She would arrange for him to sit for her, perfect the detail, fire the finished work in her kiln. Job completed, she would set him aside, try harder with Michael, call the consultant's office to arrange the test.

But for now, she needed to remind herself of that slightly bent nose, those full lips and smiling eyes. And the memory of his loose-limbed youthful body was enough to put a new bounce in her step, as they passed through the sliding doors of the hospital and into the bright spring sunlight.

Chapter 4

He was not there. She had been holding herself taut with expectation and something firm inside her collapsed.

From the back of the queue she eyed the slabs of beef behind the glass counter, figuring out what to buy, remembering a radio programme she'd been listening to on the way into town. The message had been that we should all eat less meat. The presenter had taken it as a given. Was that what was causing the tiny shift in her stomach, the hint of nausea as she scanned the display? Had the programme unsettled her? Or was it the sad gaze of the leader of the herd lingering in her mind, prompting the heave of her stomach as her glance ran along the bloody cuts? The deep red was unsettling. If she must eat flesh, would pale flesh be easier?

When it was her turn, she pointed to a tray of plastic-wrapped drumsticks. Free range. She imagined happy chickens pecking for grain in a farmyard. Then she remembered the other point in the radio programme. We should all have fewer children. Or no children.

She handed over cash and asked, 'The other guy who works here. With the tattoo? I heard he had an accident. Is he OK?'

'Steve. Yeah. He'll be in tomorrow. Want me to pass on a message?'

'No. No message. I was just concerned he was all right.'

'Steve's all right. Take more than a frisky heifer to hassle him.'

Was she imagining it, or was there the hint of a leer in the assistant's smile as he handed over her meat and change?

Chapter 5

The following day was Thursday. Early closing. A week after she had first seen him. Michael was working at home. She stood at the door of his study in her running gear.

'You going in the rain?'

'It's only a shower. Timba needs to get out.'

She lingered, giving him a chance to speak. Then, when he didn't, she asked, 'Is there anything you want to say?'

'About what?'

Was he really that obtuse?

'About the hospital?' She couldn't say the word, baby. 'We haven't talked about it.'

'There's not much to say. It's tough for you. I get that. Tough for both of us. I assume you'll be having the test.'

'Yes.'

But even as she spoke the doubts were building. She had longed for a child. But something had changed. Now she longed for him to hold her, to beg her to stay at home with him. Couldn't he stop working even for a moment? They could sit on the sofa with coffee and talk everything through. He could offer to take the day off, come with her to the hospital when she took the test.

He seemed about to speak, but he only bit his lip, screwed up his face and turned back to the spreadsheet of figures on his computer screen. She sensed him holding something back. Was it an affair? It was the obvious thing, yet it was impossible for her to imagine Michael with another woman. He could flirt, she'd seen him in action, but that was no more than a game. He'd once announced, laughing, that he couldn't understand how any man could manage the stress of two women. One was enough. But people changed. People lied. That drinks party last week. It was only a drinks party, yet he had stayed overnight in Bristol. He often stayed overnight. Once, when he'd hinted that money was tight, she'd suggested renting out the flat. Increasingly, he worked at home when he wasn't in court. The rest of the time he could commute. But he'd been adamant. He wasn't prepared to give it up. And if there was someone else, it would explain why he didn't want to talk about the miscarriage.

She stared at the familiar, tired face she had once thought so distinguished. Other women might think that too. And even as the thought of other women crossed her mind, Michael swivelled his head back towards her and threw out a smile.

'Have a good run,' he said.

—

Cattle had gathered under a grove of lime trees near the railway line. Sensible dog walkers would be waiting in their homes for the shower to pass. But Kate loved running in the rain, cool water streaming down her face, splashing against her ankles when she hit a puddle. Running loosened the ache inside her. The lost baby. *Whatever was happening to her and Michael?*

A recent conversation with her friend, Jen, bubbled up in her mind. They'd been drinking coffee in Jen's cafe at the weekend. Kate had complained, not for the first time, about the lack of support from her husband.

'I'm sure he's doing his best,' said Jen. 'He's a good man at base. And men are like that. They find it hard to show their feelings.'

'Don't give me that cliché. Something's up with him.'

'Like what?'

She hadn't mentioned an affair. The idea was no more than a seed at that stage and not something to be alleged without evidence. According to Jen, infidelity was akin to treachery, a hanging offence. Jen would never forgive a cheat. In the end, all Kate had said was, 'Dunno. Maybe something at work. Law can be pretty stressful.'

Jen had replied, 'Did he ever tell you what happened with Simone?'

'Oh, that was years ago. They were both so young. It didn't work out.'

'But she was his wife. She had his child.'

'I wasn't about to contact her for a reference.'

Jen had raised her eyebrows and gone silent. But her eyes were full of questions, questions Kate had sometimes posed to herself and set aside, pressing them tight in a small, locked compartment. What had happened between Michael and Simone? Why had he lived alone for so long? Why did he appear to have no friends other than work colleagues? He had no other family, no mother who could laugh with a wife about her son's little weaknesses. But, as Kate told herself, it was Michael she had married, not his family, not his friends. And why was this all circling in her mind now?

She ran on, speeding beyond thought until there was only the rhythm of her pounding feet, the deep reassurance of her flowing breath. Timba was racing ahead, and she turned off the path onto the field, slowing a little on the rougher ground, her long legs dropping into a comfortable pace. The cool rain splatted against her face, and she laughed out loud at the absurdity of her preoccupations. None of it mattered. There was no point in dwelling on the past or fearing the future. What mattered was this moment, the bliss of movement, the joy of possessing a body that could smell and see and hear and run. It was time to stop moaning. She was lucky.

Within minutes she was at the gate where she'd met the young man last week. Despite her resolution to be grateful for what she had, she was disappointed not to see him, pushing her feet harder into the soft ground, propelling herself forward, laughing again, this time at her own stupidity. Not at the gate. What had she expected? A flirty youngster with plans to go to New Zealand?

Without stopping, she scanned the field for Timba. If he chose to disappear after prey there was nothing she could do but wait. There'd been rabbits, pheasants, even hares, though there were fewer hares around this year. But as her eyes returned to the path ahead, she heard a bark, two barks. There he was, far out in front, running in circles with the little lurcher. And standing by, watching them both, was Steve.

The rain had grown heavy and she stopped under a line of poplars, their pale spring leaves giving scant protection.

'Hi,' he said, walking easily towards her. He wore a hooded jacket and seemed unbothered about the down-pour.

'Hi,' she answered, adding, 'I was about to turn back.' But something in his gaze was stopping her.

'Don't do that,' he said. 'Come with me. I'm on my way to the church.'

Kate stared through the rain to the ancient church, a few hundred metres away at the top of the sloping field. Like so many Somerset churches, it was built above the flood plain but, unlike most other churches, this one was cut off from the village. The nearest house was a farm with a long garden. On the other side there was nothing but heavy yew and lime trees. Kate had been in only once, to inspect the carvings, an ancient Christ figure in crumbling Hamstone and a more recent King Alfred in wood. As far as she could recall there was not much else of interest. But it would be shelter. They could dry off.

There was no break in the mass of cloud and the rain looked set for some time. She should call Michael. If he cared at all, and in her heart she still believed he did, he might wonder why she was still out on the moor in this weather. But it would be impossible to hear in the wind and rain. She would call from the quiet of the church.

Steve was heading straight up the slope, avoiding tussocks with his long, easy stride. The two dogs were scampering from side to side. The storm had sent them into a frenzy. It was hard walking with the wind against them and the rain was lashing now, stinging Kate's cheeks.

When they reached the churchyard Steve stopped under one of the enormous yews and said, 'My mum does the altar cloths. They're in here.' He reached over his shoulder tapping his small backpack. 'I promised I'd drop them off. We can wait inside till it stops.'

In the church porch, Steve ordered his own dog to sit while Timba gave Kate his doleful, don't leave me alone look. 'Stay with Maxie,' she said. And he sat. He was a good dog, a loyal dog.

Steve lifted the latch of the heavy door and it swung open with a sustained creak. They stepped into the hush.

Kate took a long breath, the cool, dry air filling her lungs, stroking her nostrils with the sweet, overarching scent of incense and lilies.

She followed him across the wide grey flags, two pairs of footsteps echoing around the ancient stone until they reached a small wooden door set deep into the wall behind the altar. He unlocked it, swinging it open and holding it back for her as he flicked the light switch. They were in a tiny room, about eight-foot square, the vestry, where priests prepared for the service. Vestments were hanging from one wall. Bookshelves lined another. In the corner was a long cupboard.

Kate stood close as he eased off his backpack, bent down, took out a key and unlocked the cupboard door. She could smell the hot sweat from his back. He lifted some folded linen from the bag and started to arrange it on a shelf. She watched, imagining how it would be to touch him. There was a precision and beauty in his movements that spoke to her, as if organising linen were his special skill. But now her phone was ringing. She unzipped it from her belt bag. Michael. She stepped out of the little door into the space by the altar.

'I'm in the church,' she said, explaining about the rain and the need to take shelter. He offered to pick her up and she told him not to bother. It was a spring shower and would soon pass. She would look at the carvings and come home when the weather improved.

'Don't be too long,' he said. 'I've got something to tell you.'

Her heart gave a jolt, though she managed to keep her voice level as she asked, 'What is it?' She realised she was trembling, and immediately wished she could take back the question. She didn't want to know. Not

33

here. Not now. While she was sheltering in the rain with another man. What was going on? And when had he ever announced in advance that he had something to tell her? It was totally out of character. 'Will I like it?'

'You might. You might not.'

Her throat tightened.

'So what is it?' Her whispered words echoed around the heavy stone walls.

'I'd rather tell you to your face.'

Emotions swirled. She might like it. She might not. Then it could not be another woman. Her fear melted in relief. But there was growing anger. What was he playing at? Ignoring her for days, then summoning her home because he had something he wanted her to hear, something he couldn't explain over the phone. She felt like screaming with irritation, but instead she called on every instinct of suppression, managing a casual – 'OK then. See you later,' – before hanging up.

She was tucking the phone in her belt bag as Steve emerged from the vestry. 'I should get back,' she said. The words sounded forced, as if coming from outside herself.

'Yep.' He nodded.

He wasn't going to dissuade her. This would be her decision. But as she met his eyes the constriction in her throat loosened and she could not walk away. Not yet.

'I was in your shop yesterday,' she said. 'I thought I might see you.'

'Disappointed?'

'A little.' And she felt herself smiling as she added, 'I'm Kate.'

'Kate. Nice.'

His eyes were fixed on hers, feeding off her with a look so powerful that for a moment she thought she might topple over onto one of the wooden choir stalls. She tried to focus on Michael, who might be distant but who still cared enough to worry about whether she might be wet and cold. Who had something to tell her... Perhaps he had decided to join her in counselling. Perhaps... But there were so many perhapses. She would find out soon. But now there was something else she needed.

'Would you do something for me?' she asked.

'Depends.'

The gaze was unashamed, blatant. No one had looked at her in this way for seven years. She should walk away now. But she was glued to the spot.

'Would you stand there in that light while I take some photos?'

'What's that for, then?'

'I told you, I'm an artist. I'd like to sculpt your head.' She didn't tell him she had already started.

'All right.'

She pulled out her phone and circled him, taking repeated shots. Front view, side, three quarters. She wished she had brought her better camera, but these would do for now. Whatever her resolutions about Michael, she couldn't help feeling she would see this man again. And before she could stop herself the words spilled out.

'I wonder. Would you be able to come to my studio? To sit for me. Just for an hour or so.'

'Why me?'

'It's the shape of your face, the bone structure, the profile. It's what I'm looking for.'

He replied as if it was the most normal thing in the world.

'OK,' he said. 'When do you want me?'

'Whenever you can make it. I guess it's more difficult for you. Work, family and so on.'

They had crossed the nave and arrived at the heavy outer door. He pulled it open and they were back in the porch, their two obedient dogs standing, ready to go out into the world.

'So, when are you free?' she asked. He looked doubtful and she wondered whether 'free' was the appropriate word – 'To come to my studio. I could pay you.'

As soon as she had blurted out the offer, she realised this was madness. He was not a professional model. What was she thinking? But he seemed unfazed.

'Tamsin's taking the kids over to her mum and dad next week. She'll be gone a few days.'

'How old are the kids?' she asked. It was not simply politeness, she needed to know, needed to picture this young man's life.

'Four. They're twins. Archie and Logan.'

Two four-year-olds. He could probably use the money.

'Would it be OK? I mean of course you should ask her. See what she thinks. Like I said, just the head.' He looked serious. She imagined his brain sparking in his skull.

They could fix a time when Michael was in Bristol. He'd mentioned a big case starting next week. He'd be away a lot. Steve said nothing, only smiled. She took the smile as assent, as she heard herself speak. Unlike the hard, brittle words she had used with Michael, these poured out like water.

'Give me your number. I'll text you some possible times. Maybe you could come after work?'

Even now her head was telling her to stop, reminding her she could still pull back. Steve was looking at her steadily, pausing a little too long before putting his hand in his back pocket and pulling out the card she had given him.

'No need,' he said. 'I'll text you.'

Of course. She had done it without thinking, from a sudden urge to connect to this little-known man. She could still pull back. If he did text her, she could always change her mind, let him know things were too complicated. Away from the magnetism of his presence she might feel different. And she would delete anything he sent her. Just in case.

Years ago, Kate had given Michael her PIN. His own phone had been broken and he'd wanted to check the route while she was driving. Apart from that one occasion, they'd never looked at each other's phones. They weren't that sort of couple.

She realised Steve was still waiting for her to speak.

'OK,' she said.

They walked out of the porch and crossed the grave-yard.

At the road they both hesitated preparing to go in their separate directions. She wondered about shaking hands, but that would feel wrong and so she offered a jerky nod of the head. He took a step towards her and placed two fingers on the same spot he had touched a week ago, setting off the same sweet ripple down her arm.

Chapter 6

Her quick feet beat against the tarmac as she listened to the warning voice in her head. What are you doing, Kate? What are you doing? He was an ordinary young man. Simple. Uneducated. They had nothing in common but their love of dogs. However, his physical presence had hurled her into a place she had forgotten existed.

She pounded on towards the house, telling herself this was lunacy, a flash of lightning. Like all storms, it must pass. But as she sprinted through the fine mist of rain, Timba trotting at her side, she couldn't deny what was happening to her. Wet, cold, exhausted, her body was tingling with excitement. When had she last felt so alive?

Pushing open the heavy front door, she felt the blast of warm air from the hall radiator. She kicked off her trainers and stood motionless for a moment, listening to the regular ticking of the grandfather clock. Its sound was soothing, she needed to be soothed. The clock had belonged to Michael's parents and he wound it every week. At first it had been kept on the upstairs landing, but the chimes woke Kate from sleep and Michael had agreed to move it.

'I don't know why you want to keep it,' she'd argued. 'We don't need it. It only takes up space.'

But he had insisted and now she was glad. The gentle tick-tock was reassuring, a reminder of her other life, her proper life. Anything else was madness.

Their cleaner, Sally, had been in that morning, as she was every Thursday, and the old farmhouse smelt of furniture polish tinged with woodsmoke from last night's open fire. Her house was taking her in its comfortable arms, welcoming her. She shook out her wet hair and stared into the mirror at her flushed face, her shining eyes. Who was this woman? And suddenly she thought about her oldest friend, imagining what Jen would think about her recent behaviour... Jen must never know. She could not risk losing Jen.

Michael's voice rang out from his study.

'You're back!'

'I'm going for a shower,' she shouted, running upstairs and into the bathroom. She wasn't ready to face him yet.

Ten minutes later, refreshed, and wearing a new silk shirt she knew he liked, she carried two cups of tea into the study. His attention was locked on his screen. Words and numbers, calculations, legal submissions; a mind-spinning world she had never tried to enter. She occasionally wondered what he found so fascinating in perpetual argument. On the few occasions he had started to talk about it, she had found herself switching off. He'd noticed, accused her of being wrapped up in herself. Since then, they both avoided the topic. But today she walked up to his desk, put her arm around his shoulders and asked, 'How's it going?'

He caught her eye and smiled. 'You wouldn't want to know.'

'Try me.'

'Not now.' And then, still smiling, he added, 'You look nice.'

'Thanks.' She smiled back, but the smile felt strained. Why now? When he hadn't offered her a compliment for months. 'You wanted to talk about something.'

She stood looking at him, holding her tea, waiting for him to speak. The pause felt very long, and she moved to a nearby armchair. His earlier words rang in her head – 'You might like it. You might not.'

'I heard from Simone,' he said.

The name was a shock. He spoke about her so rarely. Yet only this afternoon Kate had been thinking about her. All she could say in reply was, 'Oh.'

'She rang about Immy.'

'And how is Immy?'

'Not great.' His voice dropped and his eyes shifted to a spot somewhere to the side of her forehead. 'She's had an accident.'

'Shit! Is she all right?'

'I don't think it's serious. She's young and fit. But it'll take a few weeks. She fell. Hurt her knee.'

'So, when did that happen?'

'Just over a week ago.'

'You didn't tell me.'

'I had no idea how serious it was. Simone went to the hall of residence yesterday.' His gaze moved back to meet hers. 'Immy was in a bad way. Not just the physical thing.'

'How d'you mean a bad way?'

'Simone seemed to think she was having a breakdown.'

'Poor kid. So, she'll have to go home?'

'That's the thing, she can't go home. Simone's rented the house in Toronto.'

'So, where's Simone living?'

40

'Paris. I told you.' Had he? Kate had a vague memory of him talking about Simone changing jobs. 'Only Immy can't go to Paris. Simone's in a tiny flat with some new bloke.' He hesitated, looked down at his desk and said, 'She says it's my turn.'

'I don't get it. What does she mean? You've been paying out, haven't you?'

'She wants Immy to stay with us.'

'What! Without consulting us?' She sat up straight.

'It happened so fast. Immy was saying she didn't want to come. I was waiting to see if Simone could persuade her. We both decided she shouldn't be left alone.'

'Why didn't you speak to me earlier?'

'The moment was wrong. You'd mentioned the hospital and... I thought I'd wait till you were back from your run. You're always calmer after a run. Plus, we still weren't sure if Immy would agree to come.'

She thought, *we*. But all she said was, 'Go on.'

'Simone rang again when you were out. She sounded desperate. She was about to hire a car and drive Immy down. I persuaded her to wait. I needed to speak to you and we both needed time to prepare. I asked for one more day and I'd come up and get Immy myself.'

His eyes were on her now, imploring, and she saw something new in him: anguish, concern, something she had not seen before. Had he loved Immy all along? If so why had they never seen her?

Soon after they married, they had taken a holiday in the States. He'd flown up to Toronto for a couple of days. She'd offered to go with him, but he'd persuaded her to stay in New York with her friends. It was always tricky with Immy and Simone, and he'd rather handle it alone. She hadn't pressed him, sensing a raw nerve. Looking back

41

with hindsight she could see she should have accompanied him. But she'd been a coward, nervous of the awkward meeting with the ex-wife and teenage daughter. And now Immy was about to move in. She couldn't speak.

'There's loads of room, Kate. She's my daughter. I can't abandon her.'

He'd abandoned her for eighteen years, hadn't he? But she swallowed the thought. She didn't want a row. Not now.

'Plus, there's mother–daughter stuff. Simone reckons Immy will be better away from her. A new environment. Away from the city too. We both thought the countryside might be, you know, healing.'

Healing? What had got into him? No way was that Michael's language.

'You mean she's dumping her with us.'

'Not dumping. Not at all. It'll only be till after the summer. We could take a couple of weeks' holiday. Maybe Greece? We haven't planned anything yet. The idea is Immy can recuperate somewhere quiet, go back to the dance school in September. At least the college have agreed she can. They would, wouldn't they? Another £16,000.' He looked vexed as he often did when talking about money. But the imploring look returned. 'I realise it's a shock. It was a shock to me.'

'It's a bit bloody sudden isn't it? What's she going to do? There's nothing for young people here. No transport, no jobs, no entertainment. Most of the locals are over sixty. Apart from the young families. God knows where the singles are. I assume she's single?'

'No idea.'

'Why doesn't she stay in the Bristol flat? Kids love Bristol. You and I had a good time.'

They had moved to the country as people did, to have a family, a quieter life, only the family hadn't happened, and all the other women she knew had children and she had never felt so alone. And now her husband's troubled daughter was being brought to live with them and the girl didn't even want to come. Kate gulped down an urge to scream. Michael was still talking.

'You know what it's like. I'm in and out of chambers and court. The flat's tiny. I'd have to sleep on the sofa. Anyway, Simone doesn't want her left alone. Immy's flatmate said she wasn't eating properly. I suspect there's more to it. Simone wouldn't tell me everything. Don't look so cross, Kate. It could work out well. You're around a lot. We thought maybe Immy could model for your workshops.'

'We?'

'We. Her parents.'

'And what does Immy want?'

'I've no idea.'

Chapter 7

Kate hated housework. After two years of marriage, fed up with the mess around them, Michael had offered to pay for Sally. But that night, Kate stayed up late, preparing the room for her stepdaughter, anything to delay the travesty of intimacy that was seeping into their marriage. She had come to fear bedtime. Would she and Michael lie on opposite sides of the bed? Would he move towards her? If he did, how would she respond? How could she reach for him when her mind was filled with images of another man? Whatever she did would be wrong.

When she finally got to bed, he was almost asleep.

'What happened to you?' he murmured.

'I've been cleaning Immy's room,' she said.

'She won't notice,' he muttered, turning away to face the wall.

She lay awake, relieved yet restless, reliving the touch of Steve's hand on her arm, the scent of his sweat, his dark eyes shining on her. Fantasies were sweet. Innocent. If Steve did contact her, she would ignore him.

–

Fifteen hours later she was standing in her studio, listening to the rattle and creak of the old printer, watching the photos tumbling one by one to the floor. She picked them up. Two profiles, two three-quarter views and one from the front. Enough for her to finish the head. He could never sit for her now. It sounded like Immy would be here twenty-four seven. She and Steve might meet again on a dog walk, nod and smile and say 'Hello!' as country people do. His image would linger in her mind a little longer, a pleasing memory. Nothing more.

As she crossed the drive she heard the ping of a notification. She pushed open the door of her studio and, having placed the prints on a shelf, pulled out her phone. There were two messages. The most recent was from Michael.

Just passing Stonehenge.

It had been sent an hour ago, which meant they would be here very soon. The other was from Steve.

WHEN U WANT ME?

Kate had no idea how long she had been staring at the small screen when she heard the scrunch of tyres on gravel. She spun round. Through the open window she could see Michael reversing his Audi to a halt outside the front door. Taking a deep breath, her gaze reverted to the crude language of the text. There was no time now. Later she would send a polite apology.

She put away her phone, placed the photos on the shelf by the wall and stepped out onto the drive to witness Michael lifting a large suitcase onto the front porch. A slim dark-haired young woman was following him across the drive. She carried a backpack and was pulling a small wheelie. There was a faint asymmetry in her gait but not enough to extinguish the grace with which she moved. Indeed the injury, if that's what it was, only added to her interest. Close to the front door, she stopped, gazing up at the big old house. Kate studied her.

She was not pretty. Her features were too irregular, too heavy, too shadowed by the ghost of her father. But she was striking. The eyes were a surprise. Blue-grey, like Michael's, with a hint of East Asian heritage in the shape. He had not mentioned Simone's origins. Kate was startled by a stab of jealousy as she found herself picturing the absent ex-wife.

It was a chilly spring day, yet Immy was stylishly underdressed in ripped jeans and a dusty pink T-shirt, cut diagonally to expose one delicate shoulder. A serpentine flower tattoo curled up the side of her long neck. Her heavy, almost black, hair was loosely wound into what looked like a pair of chopsticks. Her complexion was uniformly pale. No obvious make-up but for the thick pencil that accentuated the straight line of her brow. Kate recalled the photograph of the plump child on Michael's desk. This could be a different person.

Timba was already running towards her, barking, and Kate was about to shout the usual reassuring, 'Don't worry, he won't bite,' when she realised that Immy showed not a trace of nervousness and was waiting for the dog to approach. When he drew close, still barking, she held out a hand for him to sniff and smiled. A good sign. At least she liked dogs. Swallowing her apprehension, Kate put on her best friendly stepmother face and strode towards her, spreading both her arms.

'Welcome.'

Immy made no move to approach, so Kate took another step forward and wrapped her in a hug. There was no obvious reaction. Clearly she found animals easier than people. Kate held her just long enough to feel the firm line of her back and shoulders before withdrawing.

'How are you?' she asked.

Immy offered a tepid smile and muttered something that sounded like a cross between 'Hi' and 'Hey'.

Michael stepped out of the front door onto the shady patch of gravel.

'So, you two have met?'

What did he think they'd been doing?

'How was your journey?' she asked. Immy had no chance to answer before her father began a detailed description of roadworks on the A303.

'Come on, Immy,' Kate broke in, leading the girl inside, 'I'll show you your room. Give me one of your bags.' She grabbed the little wheelie and carried it through the front door and up the wide staircase.

Kilver Farmhouse was a long two-storey building with two separate attic spaces. Immy would have a room at the front, overlooking the drive, the studio, and a small wood. At the top of the stairs Kate turned right, checking that Immy was behind her and leading the way down the corridor to the final door. She pushed it open and switched on the overhead light. The room faced east and according to Kate's earlier visitors, artist friends from Bristol, it was a wonderful place to wake, with loud bird-song and sunlight edging around the curtains. But in the afternoons it was dark.

The friends had also reported scratching sounds and scurrying footsteps from the uninhabited attic above. Rats? 'No,' Kate had replied, 'definitely not.' Mice perhaps. Or a trapped bird. Wasn't it more like fluttering? The friends weren't sure. Whatever it was, it had unsettled them.

47

The room was papered in ancient green Laura Ashley dating back over thirty years. Kate had put fresh lily of the valley in a little vase on the chest of drawers and the air was sweet with their scent.

'Enter!' she announced, holding back the door, proud of her efforts: the clean towels and fresh soap, the vacuumed carpet and polished furniture.

Immy stood at the threshold for a moment before walking in slowly, sitting on the bed, bouncing a little to test the mattress. She inspected her surroundings, taking in the old wooden wardrobe, the washbasin and desk before standing up and stepping over to the sash window. For a few seconds she stood looking out towards the wood. Then she turned back to Kate with a grin.

'Cool.'

'Yes, it's a nice room.'

'Big.'

'I suppose your room in the hall of residence was quite small.'

'It was shit.'

It was the longest sentence she had uttered. In it, Kate could detect the rhythm and pitch of Canada.

'Yes, student residences aren't great. This is a bit old-fashioned but...'

'It's awesome.'

Her smile widened. At the same time, she yanked out the chopsticks, letting the mass of hair drop to her elbows. Then she kicked off her flat shoes, flopped backwards on the bed and shut her eyes.

Kate stared at her strong features, the pale skin and dark hair contrasting with the faded pinks and blue of the quilted bedspread. She had never seen a picture of Immy's mother. Michael had few photos of anyone. As far as she knew, there were none on his computer or phone. He had kept some faded prints, stuffed into a drawer along with other relics of the pre–digital age: paper clips, staples, rubber bands. Kate had glanced through them. His father was there in his RAF uniform; the brother who died at fifteen. There were several ex-girlfriends, class pictures, graduation photos, tourist shots of Paris and Florence, some with smiling young men and women at the fore. Kate had no idea who they were. There were none of his mother. And she would have remembered a woman with eyes like Immy.

'I don't keep photos. I'm not a photo sort of guy. I prefer to live in the present,' Michael had once said. But Simone was both past and present. As the mother of his child there would always be a link.

Immy lay still, her chest rising and falling. Resting, at peace, she looked almost beautiful.

'We eat about seven. Would you like to sleep?'

Immy nodded.

'OK, I'll call you in an hour.'

At that moment, Kate heard the scratching sound. It was unusual to hear it in the daytime. She ought to get into the attic to have a look. But the ceilings were high, and it would be a difficult swing from the top of the stepladder. Michael was a few inches taller than she was and might manage it. And though he was useless at anything practical or domestic, anyone could put down poison. Squirrels might have got in from the branches of the yew tree that brushed the side of the gable. Nibbling rodents had been known to chew on electric cables, causing fires. Ideally, they should convert the space into another spare room. The attic had never been used, not even for storage and it was always a bad idea to leave empty spaces in a house.

Michael was in the sitting room, feet up on the coffee table, drinking beer from a bottle, watching the news. This loutish behaviour was uncharacteristic, Kate swallowed the urge to tell him to remove his feet and get a glass. Instead she sat down next to him and said, 'She's sleeping.'

He carried on watching the news. Irritated, she picked up the remote and turned down the sound. 'What's she going to do here, Michael?'

He sighed. 'We'll take it day by day. Let her hang out. See what comes up.'

'At least she likes Timba.'

'There you are, she can take him for walks. Don't stress, Kate. It'll work out. You're always racing for an answer. Now can I watch the news?'

He stretched out a hand. Kate was still holding the remote and was about to hand it over, but something was niggling. She might as well ask it now.

'Michael... you never told me what happened with Simone. I mean why—'

'For God's sake, Kate, you're not going to bring all that up are you? It was years ago! Why does it matter what happened? I was young. She was young. I don't ask what you were up to in your early twenties. Frankly, I'd rather not know.' His words were like a punch in the face. Her answer stuck in her throat as he snapped, 'And don't look at me like that.'

'Like what? I could say the same of you.'

There was a fire in his eyes that she had never seen before. She expected him to revert to the TV, drown her out with the sound, but he jumped up, staring down at her for a few long seconds before spinning around and disappearing out of the room. She heard the backdoor slam behind him.

She waited for her breath to still. Patience. She needed patience. He was reaching out to Immy now, which was the important thing. His outburst was shocking but clearly her question had stirred up painful feelings. Nothing could be gained by pressing him. Whatever had happened with Simone was long past.

In the kitchen, she threw together a sauce of garlic, bacon, courgettes, and olives, and put on water for the pasta. At least there was someone else to share the meal. She had no desire to be alone with him. Maybe another woman in the house was what she needed. Even a troubled young woman who was little more than a girl. There was something in Immy's enthusiastic appreciation of her bedroom that gave Kate hope. She was a sensitive creature. One day they might even be friends.

Fifteen minutes later the three of them were seated at the long kitchen table. Michael opened a bottle of Merlot and started to pour. Immy covered her glass with her hand.

'No?'

Kate handed Immy a glass of water and let Michael refill her own glass. The wine would help. She still had no idea how to play it. If you knew your role you could adopt it, but stepmothers hadn't been given many useful precedents. She watched his face as he savoured the wine. It was as if the outburst had never happened.

Immy was picking at the sauces, pushing the bacon to one side.

'Gosh sorry, I didn't know. You should have told me.'

'Dad knows.'

'Christ, Michael why didn't you mention it?'

'Calm down, Kate. It's not a disaster. We'll remember next time. Are you OK picking out the meat, Immy, or do you want a plate without sauce?'

'Better without.'

Kate scooped up the plate and put it to one side. She hated food waste. But Immy had only fiddled with it. She would pop it in the fridge and eat it herself for lunch tomorrow. Would Immy expect lunch? Lunch was whatever Kate had left over from the night before. And the big question had still not been answered. What would Immy do?

She thought of Steve, not much older than Immy, preparing for New Zealand. The people in town were mostly old. The few young ones she had spoken to were already parents. Where were the singletons? In the pubs? It was ten miles to the nearest club. Then she remembered Jen was looking for help in her cafe. But Immy didn't seem the extrovert type. Kate couldn't imagine her chatting to strangers.

She laid out a plate of unadulterated spaghetti.

'Parmesan OK?'

'Sure.'

They ate in silence. She watched Michael and Immy. Physically they were father and daughter. But there was no obvious bond between them. Each appeared wrapped in their separate world.

'How's the knee?' asked Kate.

'Oh, it's OK. Not that bad.'

'Your father said there was other stuff.'

'I guess.'

'Give the girl a break, Kate. She's just arrived.'

'I'm being sympathetic.'

'No worries,' said Immy, reverting to her slow progress, chopping the spaghetti with her spoon.

'You must be exhausted,' said Michael, when they had both cleared their plates and Immy was still pushing bits of spaghetti around hers.

Exhausted? Why? According to Michael she had slept most of the way. For the last hour she had been resting on the bed.

Immy laid down her spoon and fork in reply, though she accepted a large helping of Kate's home-made coffee ice cream. Then she stood up and announced, 'Guess I'll crash.'

No offer to help clear up.

'Of course. Go on up,' said Kate. 'Let me know if there's anything you need. Sleep well.'

'Thanks.'

Thanks. It was better than nothing.

Kate left Michael with the washing up, explaining she needed to finish what she'd been doing in the studio. He mumbled a reply. She topped up her wine glass and carried it across the drive.

The security light shed a glow across the gravel as she crossed to the long, low building that had been a double garage before it was converted into a studio. It was perfect for sculpture; one of the reasons they had bought the house. Large windows had been installed in all the walls, sky lights in the roof and, during the day, light streamed from every direction. Spotlights had been mounted along the beams. Kate often sculpted here in the evening, a single spot on her work, blinds left open onto the creeping dusk, the drive and the lights of the house at the front, the grey of the garden to one side, the gloom of the woods at the back.

The door was unlocked, and she walked in, switching on a line of spots, scanning the space around her. The tables were ready for tomorrow's class. Her model Miranda was heavily pregnant, but she'd promised to make it for one more session. Kate needed to construct another armature, but it was too late now, she had drunk too much wine to be fiddling with wire cutters and hammers. Early tomorrow would have to do.

There was a thrumming, banging in her head that would not subside and though she was on her third glass, she knew it was not the wine. She thought of Michael's reaction. It was not surprising he was stressed. He must feel some guilt for the wife and daughter he'd left or who'd left him. It was never clear what had happened. But he was right. Few of us could bear examination of the crazy things we did in our twenties. And he'd always supported Immy financially. Maybe that was the problem – money. For all Kate's rationalising, the thrumming continued.

A joint would help. But she'd run out of weed. So, rather than smoke, she sat on a wooden chair and stared through the window into the blackness, waiting for the turmoil to subside.

It was quiet. She walked over to the light switch, turned out the light and returned to sit in the dark so she could better see the shapes of trees or, if she looked out across the drive and up to the starlit sky, bats flitting out from the box in the gable. The window was open, and she inhaled the soft night air. An owl hooted. Crows cawed from the canopy of the small wood. She loved this place. Alone in her studio, deep in her work, she felt less isolated than she did in company, when she was the only woman in the group who couldn't talk about her children. After the bustle of Bristol, it had been a dream to move to the quiet of the countryside. The woods belonged to them and it was half a mile to the nearest neighbour. Behind the garden lay fields. She waited until her heart stilled and the banging in her head had eased. Then she opened her messages, looked back at the most recent and tapped a reply.

Hi Steve. Thanks for the message. I'll be in touch.

Chapter 8

The class had just begun. Four elderly women and one man were sculpting Miranda's head.

'Modelling's my favourite,' she said. 'I get into a kind of trance. It's great. I don't mind people looking. I'm not stripping off though.'

At the start of the course, Kate had given a short talk, explaining the anatomy of the head, the major bones and musculature, illustrated by a life-size replica of a female skull. Afterwards, she had circulated, advising on skeletal structure, relative distances, how every feature in a profile could be measured from the lower depression of the ear, what she called the 'point of truth'.

She'd started offering classes soon after moving to the farmhouse. The students came for two hours twice a week and one full Saturday a month. There was not much profit after she'd paid for materials and Miranda's fee. Michael advised her to keep a log of heating and lighting for tax purposes, but she had never got round to it. He'd also suggested she start another class, perhaps run summer courses.

'I'll think about it,' she'd said. But she had no desire to do more. Teaching was draining, and she needed the mental space to create her own sculpture. So far she'd only managed to exhibit small pieces at art and craft fairs. What she needed was a gallery to show an interest in her work.

Her sculpture was finely detailed, naturalistic. One gallery owner had hinted it was too realistic for current fashion.

'Maybe if you can give it a new twist.'

'What kind of twist?'

'Not for me to say. People are looking for something different, original.'

The man's comment was deflating. It took a while to find your own style. Some women artists had no success until they hit fifty or even sixty. Not that she intended to wait that long.

Moving between her students' tables she studied their work, offering advice where sought, using her favourite wooden tool to adjust the line of an eye here, the curl of a lip.

Every half an hour Miranda needed a break, and the hushed quiet gave way to chatter, the making of tea and coffee, the crunch of biscuits, the exchange of compliments on the different heads. Kate kept the breaks short. These were good people, eager to know her, but she preferred to preserve a distance. Once, one of them had asked if she and Michael planned to have a family. Kate had mumbled something noncommittal and the woman reflected aloud on whether the artistic vocation might provide either explanation or consolation for childlessness. Kate nodded in response and was relieved when the woman chose not to come back to class after the holiday. She had not mentioned the miscarriage, having no taste for the rush of sympathy that would doubtless follow. When anyone asked after Michael, her habitual response was, 'Fine, wrapped up in his work as usual.'

The women would smile and say, 'Men!'

After five minutes the bell would ring, Miranda would climb back onto her chair, the students would return to their tables and silence would resume.

Shortly after the second break, Kate was moving between the tables when she sensed a presence behind her. She turned. Immy was leaning against the door jamb, the hint of a smile on her pale face.

'Hello, Immy.'

'May I stay and watch?'

'I don't see why not. Anybody mind an audience?'

'Not at all.'

'Delighted.'

'Hi.'

There was another hour of class, and no reason why Immy shouldn't observe. Boredom would soon seep in. At the end of the next half-hour stint, Kate turned to the doorway expecting her stepdaughter to have moved on, but she was still there.

Miranda heaved herself down. She and Immy would be close in age. Perhaps they could get to know each other. But Miranda was on her phone within seconds and Immy was busy responding to the queries of the participants. With the simple confidence of older women, they insisted she introduce and explain herself.

'You're a dark horse, Kate, you never mentioned this exotic creature.'

'She's just arrived.'

'How delightful. And how long do you plan to stay, Immy?'

Used to Immy's monosyllables, Kate was surprised by her easy responses. The more they gushed, the more artic- ulate she became, smiling and answering their questions with disarming frankness, explaining her dance injury, her difficulty in adjusting to London, the expense, the overwhelming size of the place, the complexities of city transport. Kate was surprised to hear that her stepdaughter was looking forward to exploring Somerset, though she was mostly here to 'chill'. The women extracted more from her in five minutes than Kate and Michael had wrung out in twenty-four hours. Immy appeared pleased, and asked if she could remain for the final session. Afterwards, the students lingered to chat.

'Do bring her over, Kate dear. The girls would love to get to know you, Immy. They're all crazy about dance.'

Kate listened in admiration as Immy countered every enquiry with grace.

'Thanks for being nice,' said Kate, after they had left.

'I can do nice,' returned Immy with a grin and a flick of the head. 'When I want to. Shall I help you clear up?'

Surprised and pleased, Kate handed her a broom. While Immy swept, Kate checked that the heads had been properly sprayed and wrapped in plastic, before wheeling the high tables into a corner and carrying her toolbox into the storage area. Here she kept her miniature kiln, bags of clay and metal for armatures. Tools were methodically stored in a cabinet of narrow drawers. Old casts, moulds and discarded work lined the shelves that covered the inside wall. On the middle shelf, under a bin bag clipped on with a clothes peg, she had left the half-finished head of Steve. Gently, she removed the bag. Seeing his face again sent a jolt through her body.

She scrutinised her work. The eyes were still hollow sockets, though she had managed to capture the curve of the lower lip from the photograph. She picked up the water spray, doused the head and replaced the bag.

Looking down, she realised that her phone was in her hand, already open on the message page. She must have pulled it up without thinking. He had replied to her last text.

OK.

It meant everything and nothing. She paused a few seconds, looked through the window into the studio where Immy had put down her broom and was studying the students' work, and then typed.

I'll be in touch.

Back in the workshop, Immy had emptied the dustpan and was studying the charts and posters attached to the walls between the large windows, bones of the skull in vibrant orange, green and purple, graphic illustrations of the muscles of neck and shoulder. Then a shelved display of model animals, quarter and eighth-sized dogs, cats and horses, some fired in the kiln, others cast in bronze and plaster.

'I like these,' said Immy, picking one up and studying it.

'They're commissions. People pay to have their pets done. To remember them.'

'You should do Timba.'

'I might.' There was plenty of time. Timba was only four.

'He's a beautiful dog. And these are really good.'

'Thanks.'

Immy moved on, pausing by the full-size human skeleton dangling from a hook in one corner. It was useful for demonstrating the precise action or shape of a limb. In the past, Kate had sculpted her own half-size figures. She was considering offering a life class to more advanced students. But she would need a professional model. And with that thought, her eyes rested on Immy who was circling the room like a cat in a garden.

'Who's this?' asked Immy, holding up one of the photographs.

'Oh, just a guy I was sculpting.'

Why had she left him there? Stupid.

'Nice-looking.'

'Yes. Good bone structure.'

Immy put down the photo and carried on until she had reached the end of the wall, when she swivelled round to face Kate, addressing her with a new clarity and confidence.

'May I have a go? I mean make a head?'

Immy was gazing at her, waiting for her answer. The late afternoon light fell across her unmarked skin. The blue in her eyes seemed more intense than before. The contrast with the heavy dark hair was extraordinary. For a moment Kate thought about bringing out her old paints. But Immy hadn't asked to be looked at, to be admired. She wanted to make her own art. She would expect feedback, encouragement, praise. Yet there was something touching in the way the girl was reaching out and Kate heard herself say, 'Of course. Why not join the class next week? The group seems to have taken to you.'

'Do I have to wait a week? They're already way ahead of me.'

'It's not a race. It doesn't matter where they are. I could lend you a couple of anatomy books in the meantime. You might find them useful.'

Immy looked perplexed and Kate thought she glimpsed the beginnings of a pout. Of course, she reminded herself. Generation Z. Immy could not be expected to open a book, particularly for the purpose of research.

'Can't I do it now?'

Kate studied the hopeful face. At least the sullenness had disappeared. And there was something the girl wanted. Desire, any desire, was preferable to apathy. And what could be more therapeutic than the desire to make art? Why shouldn't Kate offer the one gift she had?

'I guess I could give you the quick version. Then you could try again with the model next week.'

'That is so cool.'

'Only I'll have to disappear and cook supper for Michael.'

'No worries. I'll just get on with it.'

'OK.'

'You're very kind.' Immy took a step towards her. 'Having me stay. I mean you could have said no.'

Could she? It hadn't seemed an option. She was contemplating how to frame some words of reassurance, when Immy looked hard in her face.

'I nearly died.'

Kate's heart skipped. The words were shocking, but the girl's expression was clear and open, and Kate realised she had been chosen as a confidante. Before she could say anything, Immy continued.

'It's not like it was a cry for help. I didn't want to be found. Only my flatmate got back early. All I can remember is her shouting and shaking me, and pink muck, blood and stuff, all over the bed.'

Kate was horrified. Why was this girl chucking her crap all over the stepmother she barely knew?

'You don't want to hear this,' said Immy, reading her mind even as she edged closer.

'Sit down,' said Kate, pointing to one of the wooden chairs. 'Tell me.' Immy sat, looked at the floor, drew a breath and started again.

'Dana cleaned me up a bit...'

She paused and stared at her hands, clenching and unclenching her fists, as her body began to sway backwards and forwards. Kate had no idea how to react. Should she hug her stepdaughter? Tell her she was safe now? Tell her she could stay as long as she wanted? She said nothing and after a while, Immy stopped swaying as if waking from a trance. She looked at Kate.

'Thanks for listening,' she said. 'It means a lot to me.'

'So, then what?' asked Kate, caught up in the girl's story.

'Dana said there was no way I could stay in the flat now. She got Mum's number off my phone, told Mum I was depressed, not eating, shit like that. I made her promise not to tell her about the pills. Not that Mum would want to know. It was like I was in everyone's way.'

'And your dad?'

'I couldn't tell him either.'

'But you're telling me.'

'You look... kind... you don't mind, do you?'

'Of course not.'

'People don't want you if you're like that. Not you though. You're different. You're prepared to help me.'

Help? Even before this messy confession she had not wanted to help. Immy had called her kind. Was she kind? Could Immy see something she herself couldn't see?

'So why... why did you do it?'

Immy was staring at her hands again. Kate stood up and walked over to a cupboard, took out a bottle of brandy and two glasses. Without asking whether Immy wanted one, she poured them both drinks and said, 'Only if you feel you want to talk about it...'

Immy held her glass and took a large gulp. Then she let out a breath and started to speak, looking straight into Kate's eyes.

'I'm a dancer.' She stopped, gulped. 'Was a dancer. Dancers are supposed to fly. Only I lost it. It used to be easy, but when I got to London my head clogged up with other stuff. The focus went. At first it was the balance. I couldn't rely on it any more. Then the memory. There were too many mistakes. Everyone was watching me, judging me. I couldn't bear it. I started to miss classes, rehearsals. My teacher called: I had to go in or I'd need to do the year again. I forced myself – walked into that room full of dancers, real dancers, beautiful, talented. And it was like I was a fake. A nothing. Everyone could leap and turn and do anything they were asked to do. Except me. I couldn't do the one thing I'd always been good at, the only thing I ever wanted to do.'

The girl's face was taut as she relived her pain. Kate could see her throat swell and constrict.

'So, what did you do?' she asked.

'I walked out.'

'Didn't anyone follow you? Try to stop you? Find out what was the matter?'

'No way. They've got thousands of kids after that place. They're not going to worry about one messed up Canadian who can't hack it. Later I found out my tutor had been trying to contact me. But I wasn't picking up my

phone or looking at emails. I'd already decided. I felt
better when I'd decided.'

'You make it sound so simple. Almost rational.'

'It was rational. Only it didn't work.'

'Did you even think what it would do to people? Your
parents?'

'No.'

'What if you'd succeeded?'

'Mum'd be angry with me. But she's always angry with
me. I think she'd feel sort of relieved.'

'And your dad?'

'Might wake him up a bit.'

The studio was warm, but Immy's words were a blast
of cold air. Kate shivered. 'How did you do it?' she asked.

'Paracetamol. Diazepam. I was a coward. I told myself,
next time I'd do it properly. A weapon, a rope. That way
I'd know I meant it. Maybe swallowing a load of pills was
too easy.'

Kate wasn't ready for this. The girl should be talking to
a counsellor. A therapist. Not a self-absorbed artist who
was dealing with her own fractured marriage, her own
private loss.

'Did you see anyone afterwards? A doctor?'

'No.'

'You might have damaged something. I mean, intern-
ally.'

Immy shrugged. 'I'm fine.'

'What about the knee?'

'There never was a knee. It was… like… an excuse.'

'So why here?'

'They decided between them. Mum wouldn't have me.
There was only Dad.' She gulped her brandy. 'This is nice.'
Her face broke into a grin. 'I might get to like it here.'

'We need to tell your father.'

'No.'

'He should know.'

'No, he shouldn't.'

Immy was adamant, and Kate sensed a strength of purpose that reminded her of Michael.

'Immy, we'll talk about this again. I won't tell Michael what you've told me. I'm no expert, but you've had a horrible time. You need to be gentle with yourself, take things slowly. You could help in the studio. You might like to model when Miranda gives up. The weather's getting better. You can take Timba out for me. The countryside's lovely.' Everything Michael had suggested. Everything she had scoffed at.

'Sure, I could model. I don't mind being stared at, as long as I don't have to move.'

'You won't be allowed to move.' Kate grinned.

'Brilliant.' Immy grinned back.

'And right now, you can start on your own piece. It might help.' Kate waved her arm around the studio, offering Immy an entry to her world. 'Working with clay can be very restorative.'

'Show me.'

Chapter 9

Kate set down her brandy, picked up the skull and began to explain the basics of facial anatomy. After a shortened version of the usual lecture, she wheeled out one of the prepared worktables, cut open a new bag of clay and sliced off a thick oblong. Immy listened and watched in silence.

'So, here's the thing,' Kate told her. 'The starting point is like a fish, flat from the nose to the back of the head. You need to draw out a profile. Use a photo from the book. There's a good one of a female head. I'll prop it up on the lectern. Then on Saturday you can adapt it to Miranda. Or start again. It doesn't matter. All good practice. If you've still got energy after supper, I can show you how to work up the bones and muscles.'

And she picked up the lectern with the open book and placed it nearby.

'Is the male skull the same as the female?' Immy asked.

'Pretty much. The female is a bit smaller.'

Immy was heading for the display shelf where she picked up the photo of Steve, carried it back to her table and placed it on the lectern on top of the open book.

'I'll copy this,' she said, her focus narrowing as she studied first the picture and then the profile Kate had started for her. A few seconds later, with intense absorption, she began to mould and shape the first stages of Steve's head.

Working from a photograph was no substitute for the real thing, but Kate's initial reluctance to let her start now felt unkind. If Immy enjoyed working with clay, if it took her out of her own difficulties, let her pursue it.

It was six thirty. She should go and put on supper. But having heard something of her stepdaughter's story, Kate felt disinclined to leave her alone. She would pursue her own work for half an hour. Then they would close up and go to the house together.

It was light enough to work without spots. The clarity of early evening was perfect for sculpting. Michael knew that and would be happy to eat later. After last night's outburst he had done what he always did when things got difficult, disappeared into his work. Now he seemed engrossed in some new case, rarely emerging from his study.

In little over half an hour, Immy had made remarkable progress. The outline of the nose and lips were detailed along the edge of the flattened surface.

'It's good,' said Kate, taking a step towards her.

'Thanks. Doesn't look much like the picture.'

'Not yet. You wouldn't expect that in half an hour. Certainly not from a photo. Most people take days. Even with a model. But the proportions are good. You've got an eye. It's a recognisable man.'

The words of praise struck home. Immy was aglow, and Kate recognised the rapid mood shifts she knew so well in Michael. The girl had inherited some of her father's temperament.

'It's amazing. Like, when I was doing it I wasn't thinking of anything else.'

'Sculpture's good for that. But that's true of anything you're absorbed in. Law does it for your dad. Dance must be the same.'

'I'll never dance again.'

'Of course, you will. You're going back in September, aren't you?'

'Too late. I'll never be a dancer. Not now.'

'Why not? If your knee's fine. If the problem's in your head.'

'You think it's nothing.'

'I don't think it's nothing,' said Kate and she stepped towards her stepdaughter and laid a hand on her arm. Immy was slim, but even through the T-shirt she could sense the arm was strong. And the eyes that looked at her as she spoke were filled with gratitude. For all her beauty and creativity, perhaps Immy hadn't had much appreciation of her own gifts, her hard work.

'You won't tell anyone, will you? You won't tell Dad?'

'Of course not.'

And she opened her arms. Immy walked into them and Kate held her in silence. The girl was trembling. Kate sensed she was about to weep and she wrapped her close. Immy's head was against her shoulder, the thick hair soft against her cheek. The sensation was sweet, but was quickly followed by a quiver of anxiety. Her stepdaughter was fragile, unpredictable. Kate needed to be careful. Just as she was wondering how to pull away without upsetting her, her thoughts were interrupted by her husband's voice, deep and steady.

'Won't tell Dad what?'

They jumped apart. How long had he been standing there?

'Nothing important,' said Kate. She glanced at Immy. There were tears in her eyes. 'Girly stuff. Immy and I are making friends.'

'Good,' he said. But it didn't sound as if he thought it good. 'I've made the supper.' Without waiting for a reply, he turned back through the door and crossed the drive to the house.

Chapter 10

They were standing close, Immy's tear-filled eyes were fixed on hers.

'We freaked him out.'

'He'll be OK,' said Kate.

'He's weird, my dad. Never says what he means.'

'He finds it difficult to show his feelings. It's an English thing.'

'I guess.'

'Come on. We better go to supper. See what he's managed to rustle up.'

Michael was setting places on the table, lining up the knives, forks and spoons with care. A casserole had been placed in the centre, the air was heavy with the odour of garlic and chilli, and the colourful salad looked like something out of a celebrity cookbook.

'Amazing,' said Kate.

'Wow! Thanks, Dad.'

'Pleasure.' But his voice sounded flat as if preparing their supper had been the opposite of pleasure. 'It's only vegetarian chilli. I got the recipe from the paper.'

Kate wished he would lighten up. He was behaving like a schoolboy who'd been left out of a gang. She said nothing. He served the food and they ate in silence.

'Delicious,' said Kate, though the chilli was too strong for her and he had forgotten to put out the water. She stood up to get glasses and filled a jug from the tap.

'I should have remembered you can't take chilli,' he said, as if it were a failing on her part. Immy glanced from her father to her stepmother and returned to her food.

'It's fine,' said Kate.

'I like it,' said Immy.

Michael watched them eat for a few seconds, and then asked Immy how she had enjoyed the sculpture.

'It was great,' mumbled Immy through a mouthful of food. Kate reached for her water. 'Kate's a brilliant teacher.'

'So I've heard,' said Michael.

It should have been a compliment. Why then did it feel like another dig? As if nothing she could do or say was right. She felt like throwing her food at him.

'I'm going to model for her,' continued Immy.

Michael gave her the tough, questioning look that Kate knew so well and used to find strangely attractive. And yet it was he who had suggested the modelling in the first place.

'I might do the life class too.'

Kate couldn't recall talking to Immy about the life class. Had one of the students mentioned it?

'Don't look like that, Dad.'

'Like what?'

'Like it's some kind of blue movie. I'm only sitting on a chair.'

'Naked.'

'So?' Immy shrugged.

'When is this class?'

'A couple of weekends away,' interposed Kate. 'Three of my portrait students asked me to arrange something. Immy's happy to model and it would save me contacting the art school.' She almost added, '...if it's OK with you...', but held back when she remembered Immy was twenty-two years old and could make her own decisions.

'I'm cool with it,' said Immy, putting down her fork and looking up. 'I'm used to being looked at. Anyway, it's just a one-off to help Kate.'

'I forgot to mention,' said Kate. 'Jen says there might be a job in her cafe.' To her surprise, Immy's face lit up.

'Awesome!'

'Is that what you want?' queried Michael. 'Work in a cafe?'

'How hard can it be?'

'That's not what I meant. How are you going to get there?'

'She can borrow my bike.'

'That road's lethal.'

'For God's sake, Michael, what's she supposed to do? She can't hang about here all day.'

'What about the knee?' he asked.

'It's fine. Much better,' said Immy.

'That's not what you told me in the car.'

'What is this, Michael? Cross-examination? If Immy wants to work, isn't that a good thing? What's the matter with you tonight?'

'Nothing's the matter. I'm simply asking. It's not just the knee and the journey to town. A cafe seems an odd choice after all that work at the dance conservatoire.'

'It's only a holiday job,' retorted Kate.

The air was heavy with silence and then Immy said, 'Thanks for the dinner, Dad. Reckon I'll go and hang out in my room.'

And she jumped up. No attempt to suggest an injured knee.

'Night then, Immy,' said Kate.

'Night Kate, night Dad.'

Immy hovered by the door. Michael grunted something incomprehensible and she left the room. Kate stood up and started to clear the plates.

'What's up, Michael?'

'I paid thousands for that bloody dance course.'

'Then you should be glad she's going to earn some money. As for the modelling thing, you're being ridiculous. It was your suggestion as I recall.'

'Don't let's argue. I can't talk about it now.'

'So, when can you talk about it?' she snapped.

'When I'm ready. I'm going to watch telly.'

He disappeared through the door to the hall and she started to wash up, lowering her hands into hot suds, trying to empty her mind as she slowly wiped each plate. After she had finished and stacked the dishes, she felt calmer. She dried her hands and picked up her phone. A message had arrived three hours earlier, immediately after she had sent her own.

2pm. Church.

But she had made her decision. She wouldn't go. She didn't need another complication in her life. Whatever was going on with Michael needed to be resolved. Immy was just an excuse. He would be having a tough time at work and taking it out on his wife, the one person he could trust on whom to vent his fury. Classic stuff. She would try to talk to him again later.

But even as she was thinking this, she found herself opening up her settings. For years she'd used the same PIN. There was no reason to suspect Michael would open the phone, but it would be better to be safe. She tapped in a new number. Timba's birthday. No one but her would know that.

Two hours later, Kate and Michael lay together in the queen-size bed that had once been the site of so much pleasure and excitement, and now offered plenty of space to be separate. Michael was curled away from her, his face to the wall. Kate reached towards him and traced a line down his spine with her fingers. There was no detectable response.

'I can't do it when she's down the hall,' he said.

'We can be quiet. Anyway, she's twenty-two. She knows what married people do. Not that she'll hear anything down there.'

He didn't reply. But, after a few seconds, he said, 'What was going on in the studio?'

'What do you mean – going on?'

'That hug looked pretty intense.'

'For God's sake, Michael! We were talking.'

'What about?'

'Does it matter? – OK. We were talking about what happened in London.'

'So, what happened?'

'Pretty much what Simone told you… She needs to take it easy.'

He swung round to face her, and the words came out hard and short.

'So, she's known you for two days and she tells you everything. She can barely speak to me.'

'It sometimes works like that. Women prefer to speak to other women.'

'So it would seem.'

'And father–daughter relations are often…'

'Often what?'

'Tricky… What's up, Michael?'

'I can't talk about it now. I'm too tired.'

'So, when?'

'Stop interrogating me, Kate. When I'm ready.'

'Won't you tell me anything?'

He reached for the light, switched it on while propping himself on one arm, and stared at her hard as he said, 'This house, this life. Don't take it for granted.'

'That sounds ominous.'

Was he about to announce he was leaving her? No, that wasn't it. It was something else. The contours of his face looked hard in the bright light of the reading lamp. She could make out the bones beneath the skin, a nerve twitching on the side of his cheek. His reaction to her friendliness with Immy was absurd. She had never seen him like this.

'Has something happened? Is it work?'

'I told you. I can't talk now.'

It was always too early or too late. He was tired or she was tired. He was busy or she was busy.

'Maybe you should take a break from work. You mentioned a holiday.'

Something snapped in him.

'Did I? I must have been mad. How can I take a break? I have to keep this bloody show on the road.'

And he turned out the light, leaving her ignorant and feeling vaguely guilty, though she was not sure what she was feeling guilty about.

She lay awake in the dark wishing she could roll back time. They'd been happy once. But he was pushing her away with his anger and distrust. All the ease and pleasure they had once known seemed to have evaporated, leaving a void which was rapidly being filled by the image of a young man with laughing eyes. It was a long time before she could sleep.

Chapter 11

Timba tore across the open fields, racing into the swirling wind, stopping at times to sniff the air. They were heading up the slope to the church, Kate grateful for the blustering weather as it blew out the tensions of home. At least Immy seemed to enjoy waitressing. She had been in the cafe just over a week now, biking there and back, staying over a couple of nights in Jen's spare room.

At the top of the slope Kate turned towards the church-yard, pushing wide the gate, and entering the dark tunnel of yew. Timba had leapt on ahead and was sniffing around the gravestones. The canopy of branches swayed in the wind as she snaked around tumbled gravestones towards the front entrance.

It was Thursday afternoon, two weeks since she had last seen him. There had been so many texts. Asking, imploring. At first she had ignored them, driving to Taunton last Thursday for fear he might turn up at the studio unannounced. A week on, her resolve had weakened.

After Michael and Immy had left for work she'd texted him.

Today?

Soon after she heard the ping of a message.

2pm. Church.

OK, she'd replied.

It was just after two now, but there was no sign of him. If he were here, his dog, Maxie, would have been waiting. Unless he had taken Maxie inside.

'Stay, Timba,' she murmured. The dog lay down on the cold stone. A rush of affection caused her to kneel beside him and wrap her arms around his head. He turned his face away. Someone once told her that dogs don't feel love, only trust. Timba trusted her. He let her kiss him and hug him, tolerant, but apparently bemused by the sudden display of warmth.

She straightened, pulled up the latch on the heavy oak door and pushed it open. The church remained unlocked all day, locked each night by the local farmer.

Inside it was cool and quiet, only the sound of Kate's footsteps as she crossed the echoing flags towards the little room near the altar. The small door was locked. It was five minutes past the appointed time. Perhaps he wouldn't come. Perhaps it had all been a stupid game. Better that way.

She turned back to the nave and sat in one of the pews, enjoying the peace and stillness, closing her eyes, wondering what it would be like to pray, breathing gently in and out, letting the breaths lengthen until she was floating on a wave of calm. It wasn't prayer, but it was the nearest she could get to it. Time passed. She had no idea how long she had been sitting there, conscious only of the hard pew beneath her, the faint scent of incense in her nostrils, the echoing quiet, the slow rhythm of her breath.

A loud bark rang through the silence. Timba. Another bark, higher pitched, more insistent. Then the church door swung open and she turned to see him walking slowly towards her down the central aisle.

Everything about him was the same, though sharper than she remembered, as if he had moved from the far distance into high definition. His hair, which was longer on top, was shaved around the sides. His jeans were close fitting, his white T-shirt looked clean, freshly ironed. A denim jacket was slung over his shoulder and the long, easy strides of his walk triggered a deep, physical memory.

'Hey,' he said.

Her heart thumped. She wished she had told him not to text. Wished she could tell him now. She would explain that any future meetings would be wrong. Instead, she felt her smile spread from her mouth to her eyes, heard her voice, low and welcoming.

'Hi.'

'You waited for me.'

He was smiling too. She looked at her watch. He was fifteen minutes late. Why? Had something, or someone, delayed his departure? Had he rushed here? He didn't seem to be rushing. In fact, the contrary. Was the slow pace deliberate? Did it give him a sense of control to know she had waited for him?

'Why wouldn't I wait?' she said.

'You said it's been difficult.'

'My stepdaughter's staying.' His smile broadened as she continued. 'She's a dancer. Only she's had some trouble.'

'Sounds interesting. Am I going to meet her?' He grinned. She felt a flash of irritation. All women were potential objects of desire for this young man. He was already fantasising about a girl he had never met.

'I don't think so.'

'She might come in the shop. What's she look like? Got a picture?'

He was teasing now. Deliberately.

'No picture, and I don't expect she'll be in your shop. She's vegetarian.'

The smile collapsed into a pout.

'Too many of them. Bad for business.'

'You don't need to worry. Not round here.'

All the time they were speaking he was looking at her with the same bold unwavering gaze. He hardly blinked. Why were they talking about Immy and meat eating? The words were irrelevant. It was clear what he wanted. What she wanted.

'I thought you'd bummed me out.'

'I wanted to finish your head.' He narrowed his eyes, his eyebrows shifted, tiny muscles transforming his expression. This was how she would finish the head, with the hint of a question. 'The photos, remember? After you left I started work. I need you to sit for me. I don't like to leave things incomplete.'

'OK,' he said. 'I'll come now.'

The wind was rising as they left the church, a storm predicted. They passed a couple of dog walkers on the footpath back to the house, older women whom Kate knew by sight, nodding to each other and shouting, 'Hello!' through the angry gusts. The women glanced with interest at Steve. Of course, he would be familiar from the shop. It was crazy, reckless. Walking with him in daylight with their two distinctive dogs on the edge of this small village. Too late now though. And what had they to hide? It was not as though her thoughts were plastered across her chest.

Fifteen minutes later they were inside the studio. Steve sat a few feet away from her on the high modelling chair. Maxie was asleep in Timba's bed. Timba, uncomplaining, was lying near him on the bare floor. The wind had abated, and clear afternoon light streamed from the windows and skylights, striking the man's cheekbones, prominent brow and long, straight nose. Her gaze blurred and refocused, swinging from the clay head to her model. His skin was unblemished, smooth, as if it had been oiled. His jaw and chin were well defined with just a hint of stubble. Stubble was hard to effect without a textured clay. She would ignore it.

After half an hour she suggested a break. Steve shook his head and limbs, stretched, descended from the chair. Kate could not shift so quickly. There was a phase at the end of each session, when she felt herself hovering between the heat of creation and the cool detachment of the everyday human world. It was like waking from sleep, those moments of vulnerability, when the body was unguarded, open to strange sensations, fantastical thoughts. Picking up a thin wooden tool with a metal tip, she leant in to finish the detail of one eye.

She was carving out a tiny piece of clay inside the iris when she sensed a pressure on her waist. His hand was running down the curve of her buttocks. Very slowly, she lowered her arm, placing the tool on the worktable.

Her brain whirred. Immy was at the cafe and would not be back until six. Michael had said he would be home for a late supper, though in the past he had surprised her and turned up early. Law was unpredictable. Cases collapsed, settled. Conferences were cancelled. The hand moved on. She was wearing a baggy shirt and loose trousers, her work clothes. And now the hand was moving down inside her waist band.

'Wait,' she said, pulling away. She still hadn't looked at him. 'Follow me.'

There was nowhere to sit or lie except hard chairs or the battered and threadbare two-seater sofa under the window. There was the wooden floor, but the workshop was ablaze with sunlight. And though she could have pulled down the blinds, it felt too public. Someone might venture down the drive, knock on the studio door. People had been known to walk straight in: puzzled delivery drivers, men wanting to read a meter, women delivering the parish magazine. Any number of strangers could turn up at this out-of-the-way place.

She was avoiding his eyes. Not yet. She needed a moment. Her right palm was dusty with dry clay and she stopped at the sink to wash it off, all the while feeling the warmth of his body close behind her. After drying her hands, she reached for one of his. It felt strong and cool. She led him through the narrow doorway to the storeroom.

The space was cramped but private. Sculpted heads, busts and animals filled the shelves. There was an old kitchen cupboard stuffed with bags of clay and armatures, drawers for tools and a miniature kiln. Between the kiln and the doorway there was a window and next to the window a narrow strip of bare wall. Kate pulled down the blinds, leant back against the wall and faced him at last.

His body was pressed against hers. For a moment she could barely breathe. He was moving too fast. She had wanted him, but not like this. A blast of wind tore through the trees in the wood outside. A long, leafy branch of the ancient yew flapped against the window, and a draught of cool air whistled through the gap between the blind and the glass beside her. She shivered and pulled away.

'Don't move,' she said, raising her hand to his face and tracing the line of his lips. 'Wait.'

She stepped away from him across the tiny space, opened a cupboard door, stretching upward, pulled down an old, soft blanket she used during the winter to wrap nude models between sessions, laying it over the thin strip of floor. Meeting his unwavering stare, she started to remove her clothes. He did the same. He reached for her, but she shook her head. Grey light filtered through the loose weave blinds. She wanted to see all of him.

'Not yet,' she said, helping him take off his T-shirt. 'Socks.' She smiled.

He bent down. When he straightened, his body looked so beautiful she thought she might faint.

She lay on the blanket and waited for him. He was scrabbling around now, reaching for something in the pocket of his jeans which he had thrown on the floor. As he took it out she realised it was a packet of condoms. He was careful where she was not. But she knew it was not simply carelessness on her part. Her longing for a child was so deep that it wouldn't matter whose it was. She shook her head and pulled him towards her.

'It's fine,' she said. It then crossed her mind that she knew almost nothing about this young man – his habits, his sexual history. But she wanted him skin to skin and it was too late. He had tossed away the packet and was deep inside her, touching a point of pain and pleasure that made her cry out in the quiet.

He finished first. It took only a few seconds more for his touch to bring her off. She lay still, staring at the skylight, floating on a wave of physical contentment. Then she shifted onto her side and began to trace her fingers down his spine, realising as she did so, that this was how she had caressed Michael last night. And she had the ludicrous idea that Steve knew what she was thinking because instead of turning to face her as she hoped, he pulled away, leaving her with the shock of estrangement and emptiness. And now he was standing up grabbing his clothes, stepping into his jeans, pulling his T-shirt over his head, no longer fixed on her but onto some different time and place, somewhere else he needed to be.

'I'll text you,' he said.

'OK.'

She stood up and threw on her clothes and they walked out into the studio. She wondered if they would kiss again, but he only touched her arm, catching her eye for a second before turning away. Then he whistled at Maxie who roused himself from sleep and stood up to follow his master out of the studio door. Timba ran out after them as far as the edge of the garden, then stopped. Kate watched as the man and his dog crossed the lawn towards the river path. She expected him to turn around and wave, but he continued to walk straight ahead.

She sat on the wall that bordered the garden, gazing over the moor. The last hour felt like a dream from which she was slowly waking. Had it really happened? Her body felt light as if it might float away and she stared past the trees and fields to the enormous sky, her hands pressing on the cool stone as if to remind herself where she was, who she was. Minutes later, she had no idea how many minutes, still recovering, she stood up, walked back to the studio, picked up her small wooden tool and began to work on the young man's eyes.

The crunch of gravel roused her from concentration. She glanced at the clock. More than two hours had passed without her noticing. Immy was pushing her bike across the drive. Kate wiped her hands, took a deep breath, put on her best smile, and stepped out to meet her.

'Hi, Immy. How was your day?'

'Ace.' The lovely face was beaming. 'I'm good at this job.' She started to wheel her bike towards the bike shed. Kate followed, marvelling at this bright young person, so different from the forlorn creature who had arrived at the farmhouse two weeks ago.

'So, what's Jen getting you doing?'

'All sorts. Serving tables, coffee, tea, cake, taking the money. She even taught me to use the coffee machine. I'm a qualified barista! Chatting to people. Everyone is so friendly. Not like London. Everyone knows everyone. It's amazing.'

'How's the bike ride?'

'Scary. I might try to find a place in town. Only it's nice being with you.'

It was nice for Kate too. How long was it since someone had expressed the simple pleasure of her company? Steve didn't count.

Immy went on, 'I like your hair that way. It's cool.'

After Steve had left she'd slipped on a scrunchie to keep it out of the way when sculpting. Strands had come loose, dropping around her face.

'Oh. I just bundle it up like that for work.'

Immy smiled at her and held her eyes, Kate felt a rush of panic. What if the girl could read her mind? What if she knew what Kate had been up to? What if she had come back earlier, seen Steve, and said nothing? But all that was absurd. Immy was just in high spirits.

Talking to strangers. Serving coffee and tea. Friendly customers. Small town life. For all the anguish about dance, Kate began to wonder if her husband's daughter was, after all, just a simple girl who liked to be liked.

'Can I see what you've been up to?' asked Immy. Without waiting for a reply, she bounded up the three steps into the studio and stood facing the head of Steve. 'You finished it.'

'Yep. I've been working on it this afternoon.'

There was a curious pleasure in the ease with which the lie came. When Immy smiled, how lovely she looked. Kate wondered about her sexuality. Immy had never mentioned a boyfriend, though she seemed acutely conscious of her own body. It was not so much vanity as an awareness of her own desirability. Perhaps that's why she enjoyed the cafe, admiring glances all day long. Attention lifted her from her shell. Was there someone special? Kate herself started young, but she was almost thirty before she had learnt to enjoy sex. Perhaps Immy hadn't got there yet.

What would Steve think if he saw her? He might go into the cafe to have a look. He and Immy might meet on the moor or in the woods when Immy took Timba out. But he wouldn't meet Immy here. He wouldn't come to her studio again. It was too dangerous. And despite his promise to text her, she wondered if he even wanted to return. There was nothing to suggest his heart was engaged. It had been simple lust. He had taken what he needed and now would stay away. She too had taken what she wanted. Like an inhalation of breath held too long, she would let it go.

Chapter 12

But it didn't turn out like that.

Three days after the tangle on the floor of her storeroom he left a text.

Thursday. Church. 2pm.

Brief. Peremptory. Shockingly devoid of affection or human feeling. Yet its very absence of emotion appealed to her, excited her. It was simple, uncomplicated. And despite her promise to herself, she knew she would go.

He appeared even more beautiful than she remembered, taller, straighter, his eyes more intense, his skin darker. The weekend had been exceptionally warm for May. Perhaps he had been to the beach with this family like so many others. He looked as if he would tan easily, unlike Kate whose pale skin burnt at the slightest hint of sunlight. She was not a mirror watcher. Michael once called her the least vain woman he had ever known. But yesterday she had studied her own complexion. The freckles across her nose and cheeks that had looked charming in her teens, acceptable in her twenties might now be seen as blemishes. As the sun heated up she habitually wore invisible sunblock. Today she had masked some of the darker patches with a light foundation, and as this much younger man approached her down the aisle of the church she felt uncharacteristically self-conscious about her looks.

Without speaking he wrapped her in his arms and kissed her, pushing her back against one of the heavy stone pillars that supported the ancient building. His hands were on her shoulders, her neck, her breasts. It was impossible to release herself without a struggle. She wanted him, but not like this. Not here. Kate was not religious, but for many people this was a holy place. Was it the faith of others that made the air feel different, purer? Or was it just the lingering scent of incense and flowers? If they'd lived in a city they could have chosen the anonymity of a hotel. In a small village there was nowhere to go. She was relieved when Steve drew back, took her hand and said, 'Come on.'

They left the church and crossed the fields to the old railway path where she had first seen him. It was a beautiful day, and the dog walkers were out in force. He was no longer holding her hand, just walking beside her, a small gap between them. Apart from her sculpting students and Jen, Kate had few friends in the area. But Steve was the local butcher. He was well known. As he greeted strangers with a smile, their questioning glances felt like tiny darts. His recklessness was shocking. Surely someone would notice he was walking with a woman who was not his wife. But he didn't seem to care.

At a gap in the bushes he said, 'Down here.'

It was no more than a small opening in the hedgerow, the waymark sign covered in brambles and ivy. He held back the growth for her, treading down the nettles as they emerged into the open. Without speaking, they crossed the field towards the far ridge and the railway line, the dogs darting from side to side in pleasure at the wide expanse.

The fresh spring air brushed the bare skin of her legs under her loose skirt.

Trains used to stop at all the small towns. But those stations were long closed, and now the Intercity tore past ghostly platforms on tracks raised high by bridges and viaducts above the low-lying pastures. After a few minutes, the footpath cut under one such bridge, towering walls of Victorian brickwork, a roof of iron girders and an echo that amplified their slightest breath.

He stopped.

'Listen,' he whispered. His voice reverberated around them, bouncing back to them in a clear reply.

It was cool under the bridge, water dripping through moss and lichen. A train thundered along the track above them and he turned towards her.

She leant back against the cold damp brick. His lips were on her face and neck, his hand under her skirt, tugging at her knickers. She helped him, yanking them down one leg and stepping out so she could open up to him. Without speaking, she handed him a condom. She had bought a packet in Taunton, too self-conscious to ask for them in her local chemist. After the heedless unprotected sex of the first time, she had reconsidered. If this were to continue, she needed to be careful. He took one without comment and managed to put it on without interrupting the seamless flow of their contact. And she was ready for him. She'd been ready since she'd spotted him half an hour earlier in the church. Since she'd woken that morning and known she would see him.

Steve moved fast and today she wanted it fast. The effort of staying upright accentuated the sensation until pleasure was fanning through her body in uncontrollable waves. His arm pushed her against the wall, and she hung onto it to stop herself collapsing, hearing herself gasp, then cry out. His broad hand clamped her mouth. Too late. The gasp and cry were bouncing off the brickwork, echoing through the cavernous space below the track. He took his hand off and laughed. And another echo sounded off the walls, ringing out across the field like a peal of bells, up to the path where the cyclists pedalled, and dog walkers strolled.

She almost said, 'I love you'. But managed not to. It was ridiculous. She didn't love this man. She barely knew him. Couldn't even say whether she liked him. She just loved the way he made her feel, the way his wild, abandoned laughter made the world seem bigger and more brilliant than any world she had ever known.

The laughter died down. He was holding her shoulders, looking serious now. She pulled up her knickers as she heard him say, 'Next time we'll go somewhere better.'

'Where? There's nowhere we can go. It's…' Words formed in her mind. We can't. There won't be a next time. We need to stop it now.

But the words wouldn't come out and he said, 'How about yours?'

'That's impossible.'

It hadn't been impossible last week. Not when she was sculpting his head and lay down with him on the floor of her storeroom.

'OK. I'll work something out,' he said, zipping up his flies, looking around across the empty field. She looked away to the muddy ground, a smashed beer bottle, old crisp wrappers, a used condom which could have been their own. She could not do this again. 'Wait here. I'll go first…' And he untied Maxie who had been sitting quietly tied to a fence post next to Timba.

She stood watching as he strode across the field away from the railway line to the river path. Like a child in a game, she shut her eyes and started to count to fifty. Three… four… fifteen… twenty-five… forty-nine. At fifty she untied Timba and walked back to the railway path. An elderly couple walked past her with a cheery nod and a 'hello'. She was conscious that her own 'hello' was a little brighter, a little louder than usual.

Chapter 13

The air lay heavy and thunderous on the dry land, but no rain came. Inside the house, another storm was brewing. Immy appeared to be avoiding her father. She was friendly to Kate, helping in the studio, modelling on Sundays, but when Michael was around she'd withdraw to her room, saying she was bushed. She'd joined the local gym and spent much of her spare time working out. Michael was gloomy and preoccupied, barely speaking at meals, disappearing into the vegetable garden or his study at weekends. In bed, at night, he turned to face the wall. Once again Kate wondered if he had found someone else. With the thought came a throbbing sensation, starting in her temple spreading through her body. She was shocked at her distress, her hypocrisy.

'Is it me? Are you fed up with me?' she asked.

'It's not you. It's me. Work stuff.'

'Tell me,' she said.

'You wouldn't be interested.'

'Try.'

'Not now. Anyway, it's too late. One day I might have to talk about it.'

He was shutting her out, as if communicating with his own wife would be a burden. He seemed to be harbouring some inexplicable anger for which there was no outlet, other than his nightly conflict with the TV as he ranted at the stupidity of politicians.

He hadn't asked about the hospital and she hadn't made the appointment for a blood test. Life seemed too complicated to contemplate any kind of medical intervention or even advice. And there was another anxiety that ran like a constant vein through everything else. She'd had unprotected sex with a man she barely knew. He was married, with two children. She told herself he was unlikely to be carrying anything unpleasant. But what if she was pregnant? And what if, this time, the baby clung on?

Kate, Immy, Michael, each in their separate bubble. Perhaps that was family life. But it hadn't always been like that. She thought about the early days in the house when they had planned improvements, organised holidays, studied architect's drawings for the new kitchen and studio. Shared endeavours. The next shared endeavour should have been a child. Michael's child.

Steve was texting every day. Brief messages. He needed to see her. When could he see her? She left them unanswered, telling herself she would stop this madness, though with no firm idea as to how she would do it. Drafting a reply proved impossible. Everything she attempted sounded cold, dismissive. He didn't deserve that. She deleted texts without sending them, knowing she would have to meet him one more time, tell him face to face. She would make a little speech. That way she could be gentle but firm, gauge his reaction and respond accordingly.

The weather had broken that night. After the morning rain it was a fine, warm afternoon. Michael and Immy were both at work. Kate was in her studio, trying to prepare for a class the following day. All effort felt mean-ingless. After constructing two of the five armatures she needed, she gave up the task, swung around on her high stool and stared through the window towards the wood. The proposed wording of her text turned over in her mind. Next Thursday? After work on Tuesday? Keep it simple. No sentiment. No hint of what she was thinking. But each time she started to tap out the letters, her hand froze. Anything she wrote felt duplicitous, furtive. Even though the aim was to end it. Conflicting thoughts battered her skull. The inside of her head was like a boxing ring.

A drink would help, but however bad things might be, Kate drew the line at drinking alone at three in the afternoon. Then she remembered the fragment of dope at the back of her drawer. A smoke wouldn't help her draft a message. In fact, she would be wise to stay clear of her phone. Useful or creative work would be out of the question. But an hour or so in a different mental space might resolve the present impasse. She would allow herself one weak joint and then take Timba for a walk. That should sweep out the mental cobwebs. By the time Michael and Immy were home the drug would have worn off, she would have got through the afternoon and be able to see and plan more clearly.

Before she could change her mind, she was rummaging in the drawer for her little stash. There it was, squashed into her school pencil box. Savouring every second of the ancient ritual, she stuck three Rizla papers into an oblong, sprinkled a river of tobacco, crumbled in the resin and rolled up. Then she flicked on her lighter and drew in deeply. The paper glowed. By the third inhalation, the world was slowing down, tension melting like ice to

95

water. Her gaze drifted across her studio, stopping at one of her newly glazed heads. She had used a combination of blue, green and cream slips. Standing up and moving closer, she noticed for the first time the tiny darts of silver in the mottling. The effect recalled the breaking waves of a dark sea. She stared, mesmerised. Smoking might interfere with creation, but it certainly enhanced appreciation. Her eyes swept along the shelf past the glazed head to a brightly painted biscuit tin. Suddenly she was ravenous. A handful of biscuits and she would take Timba for a walk. She was staring at her dog snoozing by the door, wondering whether to go now or give in to the biscuit urge, when he leapt up, barking. Seconds later she heard the sound of a car and the scrunch of gravel.

A battered four-by-four pulled up outside the house. The driver's door swung open and slammed shut. Kate stared in amazement as Steve walked around the front of the vehicle. He was wearing a proper shirt and chinos instead of his usual T-shirt and jeans, and a rush of electricity tore through her as she took in the familiar body, the set of his head and shoulders. Unable to stop herself, she slid off the stool, flung open the studio door and descended the steps to the drive, her heart pounding. Timba ran out ahead of her, and Steve stooped down and ruffled the dog's fur. When he straightened up and stepped towards her, Kate felt a smile spread across her features. Her arms opened wide.

'That's nice,' he murmured when, at last, they separated. 'I thought you might be pissed off, me turning up.'

'I am,' she said, still tasting his kiss, breathing the scent of his warm skin. 'Wait a sec, I'll stick Timba in the house.'

He waited as she pulled the reluctant dog away, shutting him behind the front door and returning to Steve who was waiting at the base of the studio steps. Without a word she took his hand and led him up and through the open door. What was left of her functioning brain was struggling to work out how much time they had. Michael wouldn't be back for at least two hours. Immy would be away even longer.

She said, 'What happened? Did you just walk out of the shop?' It was hard to get the words out. Cannabis usually made her chatter. Not this time.

'They sent me on a course. It finished early. There was only one thing on my mind.'

Her body was ready, tingling. It was so good to be wanted. And yet...

'What if...?' But she couldn't finish the sentence, couldn't utter Michael's name in Steve's presence.

'I'd think of something,' he said. 'Anyway, he's not.'

He drew her close. She tried to remember her little speech, but there were no words left. All she knew was the touch and smell and taste of him.

He sniffed.

'So, what you been up to?'

'All gone now,' she replied, pulling away from him with a little laugh. Then she circled the room, letting down the blinds. No way would she offer him any. She was nicely chilled, didn't want to be off her head. And she dragged the old blanket out of the cupboard and laid it on the floor, conscious of his dark-eyed gaze following her every movement.

'Take off your clothes,' he murmured. She shook her head, and he added, 'I've never seen you properly.'

'I can't. We can't...'

But as she hesitated, his hands were on her breasts and she heard herself laugh again as he started to undress her.

For a few seconds she stood naked before him, enjoying the look on his face.

'You too,' she said. 'Everything.' And she helped him remove his own clothes.

She had forgotten what it was like to make love when stoned, how time slowed, how pleasure lingered. Nothing but him and her. It went on and on until she thought she would explode with the joy of it. But then something shifted, sensation began to fade, and a curious numbness was stealing through her nerve ends. Her body seemed to be breaking up, disintegrating, until she was nothing but mist. Where was she? Who was she? What was happening? Somehow she willed herself back to earth and reached out to him. But he was no longer beside her. She opened her eyes and looked up.

He was standing over her, staring down and as she registered his young, strong body, faintly grey in the shuttered light, everything felt wrong. He shouldn't be here. He was not her husband. She caught his eye, he grinned and looked away to the phone in his right hand.

Realisation surged through her and she jumped up. 'What the hell!' she screamed, trying to grab the phone as he held it away from her.

'Hey! Cool it.'

'Give me that phone,' she said.

'You took plenty of me.'

'That was different. I asked first. And I'd never take you naked.'

'OK. No need to freak out.' He was still holding the phone away from her as she threw out her best basilisk stare. He lowered it then, appearing to study the picture he had taken.

'Delete it,' she insisted.

'Are you sure? You look great. Don't you want to see it?'

'No. I want you to delete it. Now.'

He shrugged and swiped his finger across the screen, saying, 'Pity. It was a good shot. Artistic.'

'Give me that phone,' she demanded.

'Not if you're planning anything criminal.'

'I need to check I'm not on it.'

He passed the phone over.

'I thought it'd be fun to look at them when you're not around. You don't believe I would actually show them to anyone.'

'I don't know what I believe...' She inspected the phone. It appeared almost new. The only photos in the gallery were a series of snaps depicting cuts of meat which she assumed he had taken for his course. She handed it back. All she could think now was how quickly she could get him out.

They dressed in silence. When she turned to him he was standing in the same place. And at that moment he reminded her of Michael. The same pleading look when he had done something to upset her.

'I thought you wanted it,' he said.

'Please, Steve. Don't come here again.'

But he only moved closer, laid one hand on each side of her waist, and looked hard into her eyes. There was a tenderness there. She had not seen it before. Once it might have touched her heart, but now everything inside her recoiled as he said, 'What we have. It's special.'

The dope was wearing off and she felt weak, too drained to speak. What was she doing with this man?

'We're good together, you and me.'

'You think so?' she mumbled.

Her little prepared speech was coming back to her, but the words stuck in her throat. And now he was leaning towards her, stroking her hair, running his finger down her cheek. She shivered, though she let him kiss her again. Only this time his tongue felt too large, too rough and the kiss tasted sour.

'Tamsin's away with the kids next week. You can come to mine.'

'It won't work, Steve.'

'I'll pick you up.'

'I can't. We can't.'

'I'm not letting you go,' he said, gripping her wrist and smiling. And she wondered if she had misread his tenderness. There was a brittle edge to his smile. His eyes were no longer warm but burning. The grip on her wrist was growing tighter and she was about to tell him he was hurting her when he let go, spun round and out of the studio door. She pulled up one of the blinds and watched as he turned his car on the drive and roared up the lane.

Relief washed through her as she walked around the studio, pulling up the blinds to the low afternoon light. Then she sat by an open window, looking out to the garden and the moors beyond, as the sun dipped behind a long, pink cloud. The air felt cool on her neck and throat, her bare arms. She waited for the trembling to cease.

Chapter 14

Her period was late. Only by a few days, but enough for Michael to notice. He was quick with numbers, keen on calculations and he would soon work it out. She decided to say nothing. A late period was not unusual. Stress could do it. Anxiety about a further miscarriage. She'd been pushing her runs and eating less. All were possible explanations. She prayed he wouldn't say anything. Not until she knew and had worked out what to do. Though even as she tried to blot out the thought of what it would mean, she knew in her heart that if she were pregnant she would keep it. Steve might be the father, she might lose Michael, but she could not wilfully destroy her chance of having a child. Her own child.

Two days after the stoned session on the studio floor, a text arrived.

Thursday 2pm at the church.

She didn't reply. Even if he had fathered her child, she could not see him now, not in the way they had done. She did the one thing she always did when the world crashed down on her – she threw herself into her work.

She was preparing a selection of sculptures for a local summer fair. It was an annual event with stalls, a bouncy castle, face painting and races for the children. Her work would be displayed for sale in the village hall. She would be sharing the space with four other sculptors and carvers. It would hardly be the exclusive exhibition she aspired to. But it would be a start. For years she had meant to exhibit at the fair. At last she had the beginnings of a collection, mostly small animal figures which were easy to transport and sold well. And she hoped, too, to give an indication of her more ambitious work with a view to obtaining commissions for portraits or life figures.

One more piece was needed – a reclining nude. Immy had agreed to model. The life class had gone well. Immy had sat easily and was unself-conscious. Michael had spent the afternoon watching sport. She'd hoped nothing would be said, but over dinner he'd interrogated his daughter in a way which seemed to Kate almost prurient. It would be easier if he were out of the house next time.

It was a Monday morning, Immy's day off from the cafe. Michael had left for Bristol on the seven-thirty train, and morning sun was pouring through the windows of the studio. Just after nine o'clock, Immy clomped up the steps from the house, still in her pink-and-black-spotted pyjamas, both hands clasped around a large mug of coffee.

'Hi Immy.'

Kate had already run up the hill with Timba, showered and made sandwiches for lunch. Her worktable was set out with tools, and a bag of new soft clay rested on the floor by her feet. She was eager to start.

'Bit chilly in here,' muttered Immy, looking around her.

'It'll soon warm up. There's a pile of blankets next to the cupboard in the storeroom. The heavy brown one is probably the warmest. And I brought some pillows from the house. Get what you want, spread them out on the platform.'

The heavy brown one was the one she had used with Steve. It was too big for the washing machine, so she had simply folded it afterwards and placed it back on the pile. She'd checked last night, and it looked and smelt fine.

While Immy pottered about in the storeroom, Kate prepared her worktable, heaving out lumps of damp clay. The piece would be quarter-sized, a reclining nude, her subject facing the artist, propping herself up on one arm. Immy would find it easier than standing. She glanced at Immy organising pillows on the platform, the blanket hanging over her head and shoulders as if she had just stepped out of a prison van. Suddenly she threw it back and stood naked, displaying her lovely young body. She was smiling broadly, nothing self-conscious in her stance or expression, as if standing unclothed in front of another woman was entirely natural for her. A moment later she was spreading the blanket on the platform.

'How about a mattress?' she asked.

'It won't work. I don't want you sinking down. Just use the pillows behind you. Best if you lean on one arm.'

Immy lay on her side. Kate studied the pose and walked over, touching Immy's shoulder to adjust the line.

'That's nice,' said Immy. Surprised and a little shocked, Kate pulled her hand back. 'You can touch me. It's not a problem. I like it.'

What should she say? She had no wish to upset Immy.

'You don't find me attractive?' asked Immy, a cheeky smile creeping from her mouth to her eyes. It was disarming, and Kate found herself smiling back, relaxing, and able to speak.

'That's not the point, Immy. You're here to model. Anyway,' – she laughed quietly – 'we're already treading on ice with your dad. It wouldn't be a terribly good idea would it?'

'Guess not,' grinned Immy. Kate grinned back and the air felt clearer.

'So, we'll just get on with it. I won't touch you again. But if you straighten your back a little that would be good.' Immy complied. 'Great. Now bring your top leg over the knee. Perfect.'

She walked back to her table and took a deep breath. Immy was staring into space as if the brief flirtation had never happened, and Kate reminded herself that her step-daughter was only twenty-two years old, barely more than a girl. She would be larking about. Or maybe desperate for affection. Offering her body might be her way of finding it. Kate would ignore the exchange and carry on.

Standing behind her lump of unformed clay, she looked back at her model and began to shape the body.

'There's no way I can hold this,' moaned Immy after a few minutes.

'OK. Try to get a bit more comfortable. I can get you more pillows if you like. Only I need the line of your hips on the platform...'

'How about using a photo?'

'I'll do that too.'

'That's how you do the animals, right?'

'The animals won't stay still for me...' And she took out her camera and took a series of shots of Immy on the platform.

'Timba would stay still,' said Immy, looking affection-ately at the quiet dog who was slumped on his bed in the corner.

'True,' said Kate, finishing her series of shots.

'I'll try,' said Immy. 'And I'll take Timba out for a walk after lunch. He and I are good friends.'

Timba raised his head and cocked an ear at the sound of his name, dropping back onto his paws when there was no further show of interest.

Immy straightened her back, stretching her long legs along the platform, propping herself on her hip and elbow and letting her arm drop. Kate resumed the work, using callipers and a ruler to calculate the size of the torso and limbs.

'Brilliant. You can read a magazine if you want to. I'm not too worried about the face.'

'That's a relief,' Immy laughed.

'Here.' Kate stepped forward with a magazine.

'*Country Interiors*! Bloody hell!'

'Look at your phone if you prefer. Just keep to the same position.'

Immy began scrolling her phone with her thumb. Her hair was falling in her eyes and she started to twist it up.

'Have you got anything I can tie this with?'

'No. I need the hair loose. Hair's always interesting.'

'It itches. Gets in my eyes.'

'Stick it behind an ear. I want the length of it. The phone's fine, though.'

Eventually Immy settled, and for the next half hour she barely shifted. The studio was warm, and soon Kate lost herself in her work, smoothing out the line of each muscle, the sweep of the hip, the hint of bone where the sunlight glistened on wet clay. This was where she found happiness. Caught in her work, oblivious of everything else.

After half an hour, the alarm went off. Immy stood up and shook her limbs. Then she stood on tiptoe, effected a rapid twirl, and leapt across the cluttered room, one leg outstretched, narrowly avoiding stools, worktables and bags of clay.

Kate was transfixed. 'Fantastic. Next time I'll do you dancing…'

'That's not dancing. That's just moving about. Anyway, I don't dance any more.'

'But you will,' said Kate. 'Just stay like that.'

And she ran for her camera.

'Hey, I can't keep this up,' laughed Immy, her outstretched leg dropping to the floor.

'OK. I've got the camera now. Just do what you were doing before.' And Immy leapt and twirled, ending up once again in a perfect arabesque.

'Great. Now grab a drink of water and we'll get started again.'

'Bully,' laughed Immy. It was a joke, but Kate felt a flash of discomfort. Another model had once accused her of forgetting she was a human being. Of using her. The model had been a friend. But after sculpting her, the friendship had cooled. Was that why Michael had always refused to sit for her? Still, the photos were good.

'Are we allowed to chat?' asked Immy when she was back on her platform.

'If you like.' Kate preferred silence, but if it enabled Immy to keep still she wasn't going to object.

'I'll tell you about the cafe.'

'OK.'

'There was a row on Saturday.'

'Great.'

As she refined the tendons of the upper arm, she wondered if her morning's work might lead to a commission. There were plenty of wealthy people in the area.

People with big houses and space to fill, some of them second homes. Figurative sculpture was becoming more popular. The public was fed up with installations and slap-dash abstracts covered in political slogans telling you what to think. They wanted something beautiful, something to keep, to look at again and again. Maybe she just needed to find that special twist.

'That guy came in on Saturday afternoon,' said Immy.

'What guy?'

'The one you photographed. The butcher guy.'

Kate's hand stopped, slipping on the edge of the knee.

'Bugger.'

'What?'

'Nothing. Go on.'

'Yeah. He looks better in the flesh. Not that tall but fit. Well, you would know.'

Kate tried to focus on her work, the faint swell of the bicep, the curve of the elbow. It would be easier to fix the arm with a metal support, but she wanted to fire the sculpture without having to cut it open. And all the while Immy was talking about Steve, dwelling on the detail. More detail than Kate would have wished to hear. But she listened, transfixed.

'He was with some woman. About my age. Dumpy with a square face and thin blonde hair. Sort of pretty, or she might have been if she hadn't looked so pissed off. They had two little kids, boys. One was sitting at the table playing with a phone. The other was running in and out of the cafe towards the river. The woman was going crazy, chasing after him, dragging him back to the table. I remember thinking Jen should put up a barrier along the river. But she likes the way the bank sweeps down to the water.'

'So what happened?'

'I got their drinks, and the guy was grinning at me when I put them on the table. The woman didn't look too pleased. I don't know if it was the kid running about or her bloke shining on me. After I left the table I heard her lay into him.'

Kate picked out a wooden tool to define the hair. Individual strands would look ridiculous. Better to shape it in a series of masses.

'They didn't stay long. The guy comes up to pay and the little kid runs after him. Then when the guy turns, the kid slips away and hides under one of the tables. The cafe's gone quiet by this time, everyone watching.

'Next thing, the mother stomps over to the table where the boy's hiding, yanks him out and slaps him hard across the top of his leg. Thwack. Just like that.' Immy swiped her loose arm through the air.

'Hey! You're supposed to keep still.'

'Sorry. Like, he's wearing shorts and you can hear her hand on his skin. He goes quiet, like he's in shock, and then he starts bawling. That sets the other kid off and now the dog's barking. The guy just stands there like he doesn't know what to do. So, the woman grabs hold of the kids and drags them out and the guy sort of trails after her.'

Immy stopped. Kate continued to smooth the edge of the hair on the shoulder. The words were tiny pinpricks. The guy. The woman. The kids. Without looking up, she said, 'Must be difficult. Having twin boys.'

'Did I say twins?'

'I think he told me they were twins. If it's the same man.'

'Sure. It was him. And his wife's a bitch.'

'Maybe she was scared the boy would go too near the river.'

'He was nowhere near the river. He was under a table. She shouldn't have hit him. No excuse for that.'

'Still, it must be tough. Two little kids. Poor woman.'

'Why are you taking her side?'

'Dunno.'

At one o'clock they crossed the drive to the kitchen and ate the sandwiches Kate had made earlier. They were both ravenous. Afterwards she handed Immy a twenty-pound note. Immy looked pleased and said she would take Timba for a walk. She needed to stretch out. She was heading for the door when she stopped and turned. The light struck her eyes, glistening in tiny diamonds on her dark pupils. Her thick hair was twisted up now, accentuating her swan neck.

'If you change your mind,' she said with a shy smile. Kate's heart was beating fast. Not waiting for a reply, Immy ran out into the garden. Kate stood at the door and watched her disappear, wondering what game the girl was playing.

Minutes later, Kate was back in the studio, focusing again on her work. She uploaded the photos onto her laptop and checked the detail. The face was unimportant, but she needed to map out the hair over the neck and shoulder. It would have been easier to have it up. But long hair was a challenge she wanted to meet. And the dancing pictures were amazing. She glanced at her phone.

He had texted again.

I'll pick you up at the church Thursday. 2pm.

She left the text unanswered.

Chapter 15

Michael texted to say he'd be staying overnight in Bristol that evening. Kate was relieved. This thing with Immy would subside. But until it did she would rather not have him around.

She cooked cauliflower and spinach curry for dinner. Immy chatted easily, offering more snippets of cafe gossip. Who was sleeping with whose girlfriend; whose kids had been caught selling drugs; the date and location of the next illegal rave. Small town life was beginning to seem more interesting. There were no further flirtatious suggestions. Kate made no reference to what had occurred. Immy was not only unpredictable, but fragile, and Kate didn't want to hurt her.

The mice sounded worse than ever as Kate lay alone in bed that night, unable to shut out the image of Steve's deep-set, dark eyes, the sharp curl of the lip, the sour taste of that last kiss.

'Kate.'

A low whisper cut through her drowsiness and she pulled herself up on one elbow. Moonlight slipped through the gap in the curtains, and she could just make out the dark shape of her stepdaughter standing by the bed in her polka-dot pyjamas.

'Immy?'

'I can't sleep.'

'Can't you listen to music or read something?'

'Don't be grumpy with me.'

'Immy. You're an adult. You know how to sleep alone.'

'What's that noise?'

'Mice. Bats. I'm not sure.'

'It's creepy.' She moved closer and sat on Kate's bed. 'I don't like being alone.'

'No, Immy.'

'Can't we just talk?'

'It's the middle of the night.'

Immy said nothing, but she didn't move. Kate had already said, 'No.' Would she have to throw her off?

'I thought you liked me.'

'Of course I like you.' In the narrow stream of light, Immy was studying her as if waiting for an answer. 'Listen Immy, you're a beautiful, clever young woman. But you can't live your life just responding to every stray impulse.' Every stray impulse. The words lingered in the air, echoing back to haunt her. Was it a stray impulse that had caused her to strip off and lie naked on her storeroom floor with a man she barely knew? Were some impulses more powerful than others?

Immy was sitting close to her on the bed, her left hand inches away from Kate's shoulder.

'I get that it's a bit lonely for you around here,' Kate continued. 'But give it time. You enjoy working in the cafe and you don't have to stay here if it's difficult. You mentioned moving in with this other girl.'

'Jo. Her name's Jo.'

'And she works at the gym?'

'She likes me.'

Kate thought about reaching for the bedside light. She wanted to see Immy's face properly. The words were simple but revealing.

'That's good.' She almost added, 'You need friends your own age', but immediately realised it would sound patronising.

'I like her but...'

Kate tensed, sensing what might come. Quickly, she changed the subject.

'It's great she's offered you a room. You can work the summer and go back to the dance academy next year. They're keeping the place.' She was talking too much, too fast. Why invite conversation at this late hour? Why not just dive under the covers and tell Immy to piss off?

'I'm not going back.'

'Maybe not. But keep an open mind. See what happens. It's a difficult time for you. It can be a while before you find your way. I know it was for me.'

Half of Immy's face was illuminated by the moonlight, the other half in shadow. Was she going to leave? No.

'Immy, go back to your room.'

'I want to stay.'

And before Kate could stop her she was pulling back the covers and sliding into the bed.

It felt both strange and natural, staring into the darkness, acutely aware of Immy's slender, pyjama-clad body stretched out beside her. They lay motionless, inches apart. Kate had not the heart to throw her out, praying that Immy would not make a move. She was in no mood for embarrassing scuffles. Though as the seconds fell into minutes and she inhaled the soft scent of Immy's young, clean skin, she found herself wondering how she would respond if a move was made. But just as her imagination was beginning to spiral into scenes she would prefer not to imagine, Immy shifted. She now lay curled on her side facing the wall. Kate listened as the soft breath grew long and heavy. Soon, Immy would be asleep, and Kate would be the wakeful one.

She stared into the half dark. Thoughts floated through her semi-conscious mind as she hovered on the edge of sleep. Her husband's sad, tired face. This thing with Steve which had arisen from nowhere, had grabbed hold of her, shaken her out of her misery and was now over. There'd been no texts since that afternoon, and she'd left the others unanswered. By now he would have got the message. Or would eventually. She could only carry on breathing. In. Out. The breath grew slower and heavier as her troubled consciousness faded. And all the time her skin was pricking with the heat of Immy's beautiful young body lying motionless beside her.

Chapter 16

When Kate woke in the morning, Immy had gone. She scouted the house. The kettle was hot, and the bike had disappeared from the shed. It was evening before the girl reappeared and by then Michael was back, so it was impossible to speak of what had happened. As they sat down for dinner that night, Immy announced her intention to move in with Jo, the young woman she had met in the gym.

'Oh, we'll miss you, Immy,' said Kate quickly. Michael caught her eye then looked at Immy.

'What brought this on?'

'I've been thinking of it for a while. Not that I don't love it here. You've been very kind. But I'll get killed if I keep cycling down that road.'

'And who's this Jo person?'

'I told you about her, Dad. She works at the gym.'

'I don't recall you mentioning her.'

'Maybe you weren't listening.'

Michael let the comment go. 'What sort of age is she?'

'A bit older. Does it matter?'

'Just curious. But you're right. It matters not one bit as long as you and she get on. So, when are you leaving? Want me to drive your stuff over?'

'I thought tomorrow.'

'That's sudden,' said Kate, automatically. And as the words spilled out, there came a sharp twinge across her lower belly. She knew what it was. Her period was about to start. And with the sensation came relief, mingled with sadness, not unlike what she was feeling about Immy's departure.

Chapter 17

Kate was on the terrace when Michael returned from dropping Immy off. She had poured herself a large glass of white wine and set out a bowl of salted cashews. He joined her with a whisky, and they sat together without speaking, as the sun dropped behind the trees. Birdsong filled the air, punctuated by moments of silence as if the world had turned itself off, only to start again seconds later. Just like Immy, she thought, dumping herself on them with her moods and unpredictability, only to disappear and leave them with a vacancy. Kate had thought it would feel easier, simpler without her. But Immy's presence, demanding though it was, had deflected her own attention from the lie that stood between them.

'How was she?' she asked.

'OK. I think. There's no spare room. She's sofa surfing.'

'She didn't tell us that.'

'No. I guess she wants to be independent. At least from us.'

'What's this friend like?'

'Bit ordinary. Not the sort of woman you look at twice.'

His reaction was provoking, but she couldn't face a row and so she shifted onto easier ground.

'At least she likes the cafe. People accept her. She doesn't have to prove anything.'

He stood up, walked to the edge of the terrace, appearing to study his work in the vegetable garden before spinning round to face her.

'Thanks for being nice. I know it wasn't easy at first. But Immy appreciated it. She told me. She admires you.'

'She's a lovely young woman.'

It was true. Yet the words sounded false, inadequate. A cloud blocked the light of the orange sun and the evening was suddenly cold. 'Shall we go inside?' she asked.

'Let's stay here.'

It was phrased as a proposition, but it was more than that. If she suggested going in, he would accuse her of being difficult, making a fuss about a minute change of temperature. Might even throw in something about it being a typical female reaction. And she didn't want confrontation tonight. She stood up with her drink and walked away from him down the terrace.

'Come back, Kate,' Michael said. 'We'll sit here for a bit.'

She flinched in resistance, but she did as he asked. They faced each other across the table. She was conscious of his hand on his glass a few inches away, and wondered if he would reach out to touch her. They had made love again last night. Strange, she thought, that he could seek out the most intimate part of her in the darkness, but rarely touch her in the daylight. Once, emboldened by a couple of glasses of wine, she'd asked him why he found it so hard to show physical affection. 'It's how I am. Self-conscious, I guess. Anyway, I can't bear these couples who are all over each other in public.'

She understood what he meant. And yet. She longed for the warmth of touch, an arm around the shoulder, linked hands. There were more waking hours out of bed than in bed. She stared at the place near her wrist where Steve had held her so tightly a week ago. There'd been a red mark for a few days. She'd covered it with a plaster. If Michael asked, she planned to tell him she'd snagged her skin on a bramble. He hadn't asked.

For a few seconds they sat in silence, then Michael asked, 'Did you go back to see the consultant?'

'No.'

'And will you?'

'I doubt it.'

'What are your plans? Has something happened?'

So, the child had been a plan. For him at least. The word felt so wrong. His eyes were drilling into her, digging for truth. There would be one more lie. The last.

'Nothing happened.'

He stood up and walked away from her, gazing out over the flower garden. Summer growth was rampant. The hedges had not been trimmed since last autumn and weeds choked the flowerbeds.

'I thought you wanted a baby.'

'I did. Then. I'm not sure now.'

'What do you mean, not sure?' His voice rose and the words were coming faster. 'How can you be not sure?'

'I'm too old.'

'Thirty-six is not old. That's just an excuse,' he snapped.

Excuse for what? Why was he so angry? A baby should come from love. Not anger. 'I wasn't meant to be a mother,' she said.

'That's ridiculous.'

'I've got the wrong personality.'

'Don't be absurd.'

'I'm not motherly. I'll never be motherly.'

She thought of her lust for the young man, the unexpected stirrings of desire for her stepdaughter. Of her irritation when she'd heard the voices of children at the flat next door in Bristol. Her relief at moving into a house where there were no human sounds wafting across the perimeter fence. Her distaste for the pregnant women lumbering around the supermarket in front of her. Her own mother had been preoccupied with her drunken, irresponsible husband, losing herself in tranquillisers, admitting she was unsure how to manage her strong-minded, wilful daughter. There was a reason Kate couldn't hold a baby, why every foetus had dropped out of her in a pool of blood.

'If you're thinking about your own parents, stop now. You are not your mother.'

She was about to say, 'Don't tell me what to think.' But she bit her lip and swallowed the words, wondering how they would be in five years if there were no children. Was this marriage strong enough for childlessness? Did she even want it to be strong enough?

'You'd be a fantastic mother.'

The words were a shock. He'd been so distant, so unappreciative, seeming not to notice her for days on end. And now it was as if he could see something in her she hadn't even seen in herself. It might be wishful thinking, but it moved her that he thought to tell her. Her instinct was to deny it and then she remembered a conversation with Jen. They'd been talking about compliments. How Kate always deflected them, threw them back at the giver.

'It can feel like a rejection,' Jen had said.

Kate didn't want to reject Michael now, not when he was trying, in his awkward way, to come close to her.

'Thanks,' she said, even as she was thinking how wrong he was. 'I'm not sure I'd have much patience.'

'You're patient with your students. You've been patient with Immy.'

'They're adults.'

'I could look after it.'

'You?'

'No need to sound horrified. It's not unknown.' Before she could answer he said, 'It's getting cold.' And he picked up his drink and went in.

She remained sitting on the terrace, staring at the gold and orange sky, wondering at his rapid mood shifts. She appeared to have touched a nerve. Where it had come from, this sudden urge to nurture? What about his work? He was rarely at home. Was he planning to give it all up? How would they manage?

She followed him into the kitchen where he was sitting at the table staring into his whisky. When she touched his shoulder there was no response. She took a breath and said, 'I need a break after what happened. I'm not ready to try again. I'm going back on the pill.'

'The consultant spoke about barrier methods. She didn't advise the pill.'

'I don't need her advice.'

'You should have spoken to me.' She had come in to console him, but she bridled at his assumption.

'I'm speaking to you now.' There was a cold edge in her voice. She didn't like it, but she couldn't stop it.

'I can hear you,' said Michael, every word landing with a thump on her troubled heart, the same heart that was telling her, *Let it go*. But she couldn't let it go. And before she could stop herself, she had snapped again.

'Don't tell me what to put into my body.'

They were lying in bed, both on their backs, both staring at the ceiling. They had barely spoken during supper. She had apologised, but he had only grunted in response. Would he say anything now? As if in answer to her thoughts, she felt his hand on her thigh. She reached out and touched it. If only they could stay like that without moving. But she was already softening inside, her body asking for more. With practised movements he focused on her pleasure, knowing where and how to stroke her, leading her into a shuddering climax. Afterwards, with a few short thrusts he collapsed in a series of aching groans. He was soon asleep, and she lay beside him listening to his soft snore.

She had grown used to the sound. Had once found it a comfort. But now loneliness washed through her. Their relationship was like a dance. He took a step towards her, she backed away. She stepped towards him, he backed away. And the rows seemed to blow out of nowhere. There was so much talk about intimacy, but it felt like an unattainable goal. How did people get there? Those other couples who were all over each other in public. They must have something she and Michael lacked. Or was it, as Michael sometimes suggested, a performance, a public show to cover the emptiness, the undeniable fact that we are, each of us, alone.

She hugged her pillow. She could never tell him about Steve. That secret would live with her forever, a hard wedge separating her from her husband.

Thoughts whirled about her head just as they had two nights ago when she lay in bed with Immy. It was a clear, bright night and the light from the full moon gleamed around the edge of the curtain. Knowing she wouldn't sleep, she slipped out of bed, picked up her phone and walked to the window. She drew the curtains aside and looked out at the pale midsummer night. The quiet was soothing, so different from the city where traffic never stopped. Perhaps she would play a game. Something undemanding to bore her and make her feel sleepy. She skimmed the screen on her phone, looking for the app. But habit took her finger to the message page. She had avoided the church and the familiar places, taking Timba further out in the car for their walks. But whatever she told herself about avoiding Steve, her body's memory retained the excited expectation of seeing his latest text. And her heart lurched to see he had sent two more that evening. It was madness. He must realise it was over. She deleted both messages without reading them.

Chapter 18

A few days after Immy left, Kate received a voucher, inviting her to attend a free personal training and exercise session at the gym. It was followed by a text from Immy telling her she'd sent the invitation and they could meet there.

Indoor exercise was abhorrent to Kate. Even in winter she would rather run across frozen fields than workout in a heated room. And the idea of being shown how to adjust the electronic settings on a machine with the aim of improving muscle tone felt like sacrilege. But she wanted to see Immy, and it would be a chance to meet Jo who worked at the gym and had offered to explain the equipment.

Kate liked Jo immediately. She had a warm, wide smile and an open manner that inspired confidence. With friendly efficiency she showed Kate how to operate the equipment, how to attach herself to the sensor to monitor cardio and calorie burn, how to stop in an emergency. Each machine had a computer screen and headphones and, as you worked out, you could imagine yourself skimming across a mountain pass while you listened to your own choice of music.

Kate was following Jo's instructions for an effective warm-up, when a bunch of college kids came in, chattering. They moved in a pack, jumping on and off the equipment. Jo was firm.

'This is a gym not a social space. If you want to piss about you can go outside.'

The kids quietened down. Most of them left. A handful headed for the workout room and started exercising. Jo's calm authority was impressive.

After her warm-up, Kate mounted an exercise bike, working her thighs and buttocks as she tried to focus on the virtual landscape. Immy was on the other side of the room, pounding a treadmill, her lithe, young body sweating itself into oblivion. It wasn't long before Kate began to feel queasy from staring at the moving track, and she found herself looking past the screen to observe Immy. The girl's lovely face was aglow with effort and perspiration, and Kate felt a rush of affection as she reflected how easy it was for Immy to lose herself in physical movement.

Immy was slowing down now, panting. Kate continued to watch out of the corner of her eye as the girl's body slackened and her hands fell loosely across the bar at the front of the machine. And now Jo was walking purposefully towards the treadmill. Immy smiled. And, immediately, Kate knew.

They were in a public space. There were other people around. Yet the look between the two women was unmistakable. When Immy stepped down and draped her arm around Jo's shoulder, Kate glanced down at the metal handle in front of her, feeling as if she were intruding on a special and private moment.

She tried not to stare as Jo leant her face close to Immy's and murmured something inaudible. Her own heart was thumping. It was hard to know if it was the effect of intense exercise or the surprise of what she was witnessing.

But as she examined her reaction, lowering the gradient of her workout, she began to understand why her body was shaking, her brain whirring. It was anxiety. How little time had passed since Immy had tried to take her own life, since she had offered herself to Kate. She could only hope that Jo would be kind to her stepdaughter.

She turned back to the screen in front of her, noting their easy communication through the corner of her eye. And as she scanned their happy faces, her concern for Immy melted into a wider reflection. How would it be to experience a different kind of intimacy? Could she ever desire another woman as Jo and Immy did? She was pedalling up her mountain pass, keeping her eyes unfocused to avoid motion sickness. The answer came in the image that hovered beyond the blurred outlines of rocks and trees. It was Steve, and he was laughing in wild abandon as he had on their last afternoon together under the railway bridge. It seemed she was doomed to want men.

When she looked up, Jo had disappeared and Immy had moved onto the arm weights. Kate descended from the bike and said she would meet her in the coffee bar.

'Giving up so soon?' laughed Immy.

'Not my thing,' replied Kate with a grin.

She took a quick shower. There was no soap, and she couldn't get the water to the right temperature.

Twenty minutes later, all smiles, Immy arrived to join her. 'Thanks for waiting.'

'I wanted to see you. How's it going?'

'Great.'

'New place OK?'

'Well, it's kind of small. But we might get somewhere bigger. Depends on Jo's work. She's looking for something in Glastonbury.'

If there had been any doubt before, there was now none. Immy and Jo were an item. It had happened very fast. But, as Kate reminded herself, Immy was twenty-two. Life was like that when you were young. Kate remembered a swirling kaleidoscope of places and faces, different beds, different bodies. She was thinking of how to respond when Immy said, 'I had to leave, Kate. I think I was falling in love with you.'

Something lurched inside her, but as the shock faded, she realised she was moved. At the same time, she was grateful that Immy had the sense to absent herself from the farmhouse when she did. From Kate's vantage point of fifteen years, falling in love sounded extreme, even ridiculous. But, as Kate reminded herself, Immy was susceptible. Alone in a foreign country, it would be natural to let your guard down.

'Does Jo know that?'

'Of course not. You can love more than one person at a time.'

Kate thought of Michael. The long, slow build up before she could feel anything more than detached interest. Then the contrast, the rush of excitement with Steve. Immy spoke as if love was the easiest thing in the world. Right now, it felt like the most difficult thing.

'Stick with Jo.'

'I will.'

'And if you need help – money or anything – just ask.'

'You too.'

Kate reflected that it was unlikely that Immy would ever be in a position to help her, but it was touching to hear the offer. Nothing more was said about their brief flirtation. Immy sought affection. And now she had found it. When Jo passed through the coffee bar and touched Immy's arm, Kate felt a momentary twinge of envy. When had Michael last offered that reassuring contact?

They said goodbye, holding each other in a long, tight hug. They would meet again soon. Immy promised to join Kate for a dog walk on her next day off. She was already missing Timba.

–

The house was strangely silent. Something was missing. Then she realised. It was the clock. The place felt empty without its comforting tick-tock. Michael must have forgotten to wind it.

She walked into the kitchen where he was seated at the table with a glass of whisky. No paper, no tablet, no phone. None of the usual props. Something must have happened. Was it the work problem about which he had hinted? But when eventually he did look up to meet her eye, he was scowling and she sensed immediately that the thing that had happened, whatever it was, involved her.

'Hi,' she said, hearing the sharp edge in her voice.

'Sit down.'

'I'm going for a shower.'

'You take a lot of showers these days.'

'What's that supposed to mean? I've been in the gym.'

'Don't they have showers?'

'Yes. I'm having another. There was no soap.'

His eyes were glassy from drinking.

'So what exactly are you washing off?'

She felt herself grow cold. 'I don't know what you mean.'

127

'How long has this been going on?' he asked.

And the cold became ice, and she was shivering so much she could not speak. He stood up and took a step towards her and for one second she was afraid he might hit her. But he just stood in front of her, his body trembling with emotion. He had been waiting for her, drinking, and now she was in front of him he was unable to hold back his rage, giving her no time to reply.

'I wanted to believe you. All those excuses. Women hug. Women are more intimate than men. You were just getting to know her. Only she leaves suddenly. What if she couldn't face telling me the truth? What if she needed to get away from you?'

He was very close to her now, so close she could smell his sour, whisky-scented breath. 'You're a fucking octopus, couldn't keep your tentacles off my kid. No wonder you're back on the pill. No wonder you don't want my child. You're right. You're not fit to be a mother.'

But in spite of his fury, her icy fear began to melt as relief ran through her. She may have done wrong. And thank God he didn't know how wrong. But one thing she could claim. She was innocent of any designs on Immy. His face was red and bloated, inches away from her, but she didn't step back. Only tried to keep her voice calm and steady as she said, 'None of that is true.'

He held out a small stud earring. Immy's. And now his voice was lower, more controlled, as if he were offering evidence to a courtroom.

'Sally was here this afternoon. She asked if she should change our sheets. I said, yes, only faintly embarrassed to acknowledge that my wife's a slob. But that's why we employ her isn't it? Can't expect a creative artist to notice a detail like dirty sheets. As she was leaving she told me she'd found one of your earrings stuck between the mattress and the headboard. She'd put it on the side-table. When I saw it, I knew immediately.'

Kate struggled to maintain a neutral expression. Laughter was rising inside her and would surely inflame him further if she let it out. She should have been a better housewife, should have changed her own sheets. Thank God she had admitted nothing. She shook her head slowly.

'You are so wrong.'

'Don't speak to me in that supercilious tone.'

His manner was threatening, and he was still very close. There was nothing she could say in reply. He wasn't asking for explanations. She could only stand her ground. What she had done with another man was indefensible and he must never know. But how dare Michael accuse her of messing with his daughter.

'I've no idea what tone I'm using. All I know is that you're wrong.'

'OK, prove it,' he countered.

'How can I prove a negative? You need to talk to Immy. She's with Jo now. I saw them together at the gym. It's more than just sofa surfing.'

His head gave a little jerk as if he were trying and failing to take in this new information. Kate wondered whether it would trouble him to learn that his daughter was gay. Surely not as much as the suspicion that his own wife had tried to seduce her. His reply gave little away. And yet it was so outlandish she almost laughed.

'Jo's probably in on it.'

'Oh, for God's sake, Michael.'

'Give me your phone.'

It was in her bag with her sports kit. Had she deleted the messages from Steve? She thought not. But as he lurched across the table for her bag, she remembered. She had changed the PIN. She was safe. She took it out of the bag and handed it over.

He tried to open it and turned to her, glaring. 'You've changed your PIN.'

'Yes. It's what they recommend. I do it every few months.'

'What's the new number?'

'I don't need to tell you. I don't need to tell you anything. Not when you're like this.' She would have time to delete everything. If she blocked Steve's number she could give Michael the new PIN tomorrow. She could see him struggle with his anger. He couldn't force the number out of her. What could he do? 'But I'll tell you about Immy.'

'Go on.'

His face was still aflame, but she sensed his energy waning as she took the initiative. She wondered how long he had been drinking.

'She slept in our bed. It's true. One night when you were away. She'd heard that scuffling sound. Mice or whatever. You were going to put down a trap or poison, but you never did. I don't blame her for being scared. It can be spooky sleeping alone in this old house.'

He was watching her steadily, swaying very slightly.

'God, I hate it when you drink.'

'Then don't drive me to it.'

There was no point in arguing with him. She knew what he was like. It was everyone's fault but his.

'So, yes, we slept together. Women do that sometimes. They enjoy being close.'

She was astonished at her own effrontery, her double standard, yet what she said was true too. There had been an innocence in Immy's presence in her bed that night. Immy had been asleep within minutes. But what came out next was a step too far.

'They're not obsessed with sex the way men are.'

The casual comment flipped something in him. Nor was it correct in Michael's case. It was she who had pushed for sex with him when Immy was in the house.

'Fuck you, Kate,' he said, standing up and walking out through the open doors into the garden. She watched and waited as he paced the lawn. It was another spectacular evening, almost midsummer and it would be light for hours. Perhaps he would go out the back gate and walk across the moor. It might help him to calm down. They were surrounded by beautiful countryside, but Michael rarely went out except to mow the lawn or tidy the vegetable patch. She was about to go upstairs for her shower when she heard his voice behind her, stern, peremptory.

'Where are you going?'

'I'm going for my shower.'

He was standing in the open doorway, his face contorted with pain. She thought he might burst into tears, but the rage came out in a series of shouted questions. 'Can't you see I'm stressed? Don't you get it? Can't you even try to help?'

'How can I help when you're like this? You never talk to me, Michael. You never tell me what's wrong. Except this thing with Immy. It's all in your head.'

'You should know what's wrong. You're supposed to be my fucking wife.'

'That doesn't give me sixth sense.'

Maybe it was the way she said it. Another counter-attack when what he wanted was for her to turn to him, beg forgiveness, offer him her open arms. Whatever it was, she had tipped him over the edge. She was about to turn away and head upstairs when she saw him pick up a plate from the draining board, raise it above shoulder height and hurl it across the room. She ducked as it flew past her, smashing on the opposite wall.

'For Christ's sake, Michael. That nearly hit me.'

'Don't mess with me, Kate. Can't you see I'm at breaking point? I hope to God what you're saying is true, because if you're lying to me I think I could kill you.'

Could he see her shaking?

'You need to talk to someone, Michael. Not me, a friend.' A counsellor, a therapist was what she was thinking. But she wouldn't say that. It would only enrage him further.

'What fucking friend?'

'You've got colleagues, haven't you? You spend enough time in that place.'

He didn't answer. Only stood up, called Timba, and left the house. She picked up the dustpan and brush and swept up shards of white china, wrapping them carefully in newspaper before dropping the package in the bin. His violence had shocked her. The plate had been very close.

She showered and cooked. While she was waiting for him to return, she took fresh sheets and made up the bed in the spare room; Immy's room. It was almost dark when he returned. They ate in silence and went their separate ways.

Chapter 19

Kate woke soon after sunrise. For a few seconds she had no idea where she was. Then she remembered. She was in the spare room. And the events of the previous night raced through her mind. The accusation, her denial, Michael's anger and distrust, both building up to an anguish which seemed to have nothing to do with Immy, nothing to do with her, everything to do with some desperation of his own.

She slid out of bed and into their room, creeping past her sleeping husband, for fresh clothes from her drawers, trusting she would not wake him. The hurled plate had been horrifying, but surely it had not been aimed at her? If he really wanted to hurt her, he could do so easily. The explosion had been like a cloudburst, clearing the sky for a new, blue day, allowing space for something real, authentic. The only lingering cloud was Steve. What was he up to? He wouldn't want their relationship made public. She decided to read the texts. Maybe they needed one more meeting.

As she showered, dressed and went downstairs for coffee, she felt an unfamiliar wave of compassion for her troubled husband. She was beginning to see how abandoned he felt, how he'd looked for support she'd been unable to give.

All that would change. She would spend the morning in her studio and when Michael emerged she would suggest some joint activity, a walk out to the Polden Hills then on to Glastonbury, a visit to the abbey and the hippy magic shops. They would climb the Tor, look down across the Levels, those low-lying pastures that were once covered in water. Somerset reminded her of a soup plate. There were days when she needed to climb out of the flat base to stand on the rim and look down on their little world, to realise they were part of something bigger.

She let Timba out, ate breakfast and carried her coffee across the drive. The sky was clear, the day promised to be fine and warm again, and she was eager to start work. There were a number of sculptures that needed firing before the art fair. Some of the better ones had been sent to the workshop to be cast. But casting was an expensive process. Michael had hinted it was time to economise. Better to fire and glaze most of the pieces in her own small kiln.

Kate was carrying two of the animal sculptures into the storeroom, when her gaze alighted on Steve's head, swathed in black plastic. It looked eerie, a hooded prisoner. Telling herself it was just another lump of clay, she peeled off the protection.

She had captured his likeness, but you didn't need to know the man to appreciate the boldness and energy in the piece, the curl of the lip, the life in the eyes. What if she fired it? She might sell it. Not locally, of course. Further afield. She might take it to one of the galleries in Bath.

The cold clay was hard but still damp enough to work with. She hovered next to it for a moment, uncertain what to do, knowing she should get rid of it. Rejected pieces were easily recycled, smashed with a mallet, left to soak, reconstituted as fresh, usable clay. Steve would not be completely lost, only transformed into something new and better. But she could not let him go.

Despite years of practice there was always a mild tremor as she sliced off the top of a scalp with her garotte in order to hollow out the core. But it was a satisfying process. No longer creating, but refining the results of her creativity, like editing a book or varnishing a painting. Steve's head was stuck into the armature, and it took half an hour of burrowing before she could lift it off and rework the two pieces into a whole, ready for firing.

When he was ready, she looked again at the face and was carried back to the joy of their first encounter. This was how she would remember him. When she'd first seen him and been floored by his beauty, when all was unrealised, an innocent fantasy. Not as she feared he might be now, harbouring resentment, rejected and angry. She still hadn't read his texts. Kate lowered him into the kiln and set the timer. In twenty-four hours he would be ready.

Then she took Timba out, went to the supermarket, bought more food than usual and planned the meals. At lunchtime she went back to the house. Michael was in the kitchen with a coffee, scanning the news on his laptop. He looked drained but seemed calm. She wondered who would apologise first, telling herself she had nothing to apologise for, even though she knew she had everything.

The residue of the previous evening was settling like dust. After lunch, Michael said he had to work, but by the end of the afternoon he agreed to drive out for a walk. The sun was bright and the air still warm, as they set off up a grassy slope behind a car park on one of the hills on the Glastonbury road. Timba scampered ahead. It had been close all day, the heatwave showing no sign of ending. The summit of the hill was only 300 feet above sea level, but it was cooler here. They walked in silence, not companionable silence, the other sort, the sort where the unspoken hovers between you like a ghost.

Kate looked down to the criss-cross of drainage channels over the flat land, the black-and-white cows, dotted across the fields like a scene from a Dutch painting. Her head was filled with sounds, the faint breeze, the hum of traffic beyond the trees, the chattering of sparrows from the hedgerows. Michael was staring at his feet. From time to time she heard him take gulps of air like a hungry man gobbling food. When they got back to the car she suggested the pub.

As she set down their drinks, he said, 'I'm sorry about the plate.'

'That's OK.'

It wasn't OK, but she couldn't remember when he had last said sorry. And then, because for the first time in months he appeared to be ready to talk she said, 'What's troubling you, Michael?'

For a few seconds he sat drumming his fingers on the table in front of him. Usually he would brush aside such a question, but she sensed that last night's explosion had loosened something inside him. She waited, ready to listen. And he began.

'Work stuff. You'll find it boring.'

'Michael, just talk to me.'

'OK I'll try.' He gulped his lemonade and gave her a wry grin. 'You could have bought me a half.'

'We agreed no alcohol, remember?'

'Did we? OK. So, where to start? Maybe Matthew's silk party, yes that was it, the one you didn't want to go to.' She nodded. She remembered it well. It was the day she had met Steve. 'Something was going on and I wasn't part of it. Everyone knew about it. Everyone except me.'

What was he talking about? His grey-blue eyes seemed to have retreated into their sockets as if he was watching something; not her, not the people in the pub, but something invisible, something inside his head that was haunting him. He was beginning to sound paranoid. Should she be worried about his mental health? Was this pure fantasy? A mid-life crisis brought on by his suspicion about her and Immy? She held back her instinct to tell him his worries sounded ridiculous, or even to try to reassure him, knowing she must let him speak. And he continued.

'Eventually one of the pupils told me. A mature student. Attractive woman. Your age. No, I'd say a bit younger.'

Kate almost snapped that she didn't need the details. But she stopped herself in time. So what if he needed to feed her vulnerability? She had promised herself she would give him space and that was what she would do.

'Gillian. She'd been headhunted for some new partner-ship. Other people from chambers were moving there. Most of the civil team. That's where the work's been going.'

He'd mentioned a falling off in work, though she'd not given it much thought. Peaks and troughs. They were normal for any freelance.

'But you still have your own cases?'

'That's not how it goes, Kate. We all need colleagues. We cover for each other, pass work around. People won't instruct you if you're alone. Plus, solicitors are taking a lot of the work on themselves. Barristers will soon be extinct.'

He stopped speaking. His fingers were still tapping the table. It was irritating and Kate was swallowing the urge to ask him to stop. It was as if he could not control the tiny movements of his body, the muscles of his cheek shifting under his skin, the twitch of his jaw. She imagined his teeth grinding, forward and back, side to side. Under the table she felt one of his legs jigging up and down. She thought of the sophisticated, successful man who had wooed her ten years ago, wondering what had happened to him.

He said, 'If you're alone you quickly become no one.' His low voice sounded desperate. She had often heard him irritated, angry, frustrated, but never like this.

'You're not no one, Michael.' His hand was stretched across the table, inches from hers. She edged her fingers closer.

'It sometimes feels like it,' he said.

She smiled. 'We need to do more together. We were going to have a holiday with Immy. We could still do that. We might take Jo.' He made a face. 'OK, we don't know her very well and they probably prefer to do their own thing. But we could go together. Just us. I'll look up some places in Greece. And we'll start entertaining again. How about a dinner party? It would give us a chance to use all those gadgets we bought for the kitchen. I'll look out some menus.'

The haunted look was fading. 'I thought you hated that sort of thing.'

'Not necessarily. Not if we invite the right people.'

'Should be fine if there's plenty of booze.' He was already sounding more cheerful.

'I'm sorry, Michael. I know I've been distant, preoccupied. I'm not as sociable as you. But if you like it, I'll like it.' Where had this woman sprung from, this pliable wife? It was as if Kate had downloaded a Hollywood script from the 1950s. Even more so when she stretched out her hand and placed it on his. 'You don't really think I'd try it on with Immy do you, Michael?'

'I don't know what I think.'

'Please believe me. She was frightened. She wanted someone to look after her. It wasn't me. She seems to have found that someone in Jo.'

'I guess I'm just a jealous, old man.'

'No you're not. It was a normal reaction. Finding the earring. I totally get it.'

They sat in silence for a few moments and then he asked, 'What about the baby?' His eyes were boring into her head.

'Give me time.'

'How much time do you need? Last time I mentioned it you said you were too old.'

'I am too old. A woman is always too young or too old. But a few months won't make much difference.'

She held his gaze even as the enormity of her lie lay like lead upon her heart. Yet somewhere beneath the burnt-out wreckage of her marriage she could feel his love for her, the smouldering remains of her love for him.

Chapter 20

Come to my house. This week's good.

She stood for a moment staring at the letters. It was immediately followed by another text.

I need to see you.

The kitchen door swung open and Michael walked in, nodding at her and going straight to the fridge for a beer. Turning around, he yanked open the can and leant back against the worktop. She was still holding the phone. He must have read something in her expression because he asked, 'Everything all right?'

'Sure. Just one of my students. She can't make the weekend class.'

Quickly, she closed the page, returning to the dinner preparation, setting out the vegetables next to the sink. Michael didn't move.

'Can I help at all?'

'No, it's fine.'

She hoped he would leave to watch TV in the other room. Then she could reply to Steve, tell him to stop texting. But he remained leaning against the counter, sipping his beer, watching her. She was peeling vegetables over the sink when she glanced back at him out of the corner of her eye, noticing he had switched his focus to her phone. He'd said nothing about the PIN. Had he somehow discovered her new one? There would surely be ways to do it. You only had to look at YouTube. She and Jen had talked about it. You could do anything with a phone.

Kate picked up the small chopping knife and began slicing a large carrot into tiny pieces. When the pieces could get no smaller she pushed them to one side of the board and was about to start on a courgette when she found herself staring at the sharp knife, and then at the fleshy tip of the first finger on her left hand. The next moment a stinging pain tore through her and blood oozed out onto the chopping board, staining the carrot a dark vermillion. Was it a slip or was it deliberate? Perhaps a bit of both. She felt sick to look at it. But the bleeding was a relief, as if she had untied something very tight inside her.

'Now what have you done?'

He took a step towards her, sounding more weary than sympathetic, as if Kate's life was a series of preventable accidents. Without answering she wrapped her finger in kitchen roll, walked to the first-aid drawer, and took out an Elastoplast.

He was staring at the blood-soaked carrot on the chopping board then at her. She searched his eyes for any hint of tenderness. Nothing. Part of her wanted to pick up the first heavy object and fling it at him. Yet after she had stuck on several large plasters, his look softened and for one crazy moment she imagined falling on her knees, confessing. He would hold her in his arms, stroke her back, tell her he was there for her, tell her he would forgive her. But when she looked again, the warmth had gone and she knew she could never tell him. Unless he found out, she would carry this secret forever.

'It's fine. I'll clear it up. We can have courgette instead,' she said.

'OK. Give us a shout if you need anything,' he said, throwing out a casual glance and leaving the room.

Chapter 21

They ate on the terrace in the warm evening air, drinking red wine. Afterwards they watched the clouds banking in the darkening sky, and she listened as Michael talked about an item on the news and the latest political scandal. He sounded agitated, distressed, as if he were personally affected, asking for her opinion. She told him she agreed with him. She knew he would try to argue her down if she did not and she did not want argument tonight.

At the first spots of rain they went inside. It was still warm, and they drank more wine and watched a film on iPlayer, together on the sofa for the first time in months. If Steve would only disappear. It would take time. Michael would need nurturing and she had never been good at that. But she would learn. Eventually, all would be well.

That night, the storm broke. Rain hammering the roof and the windows.

Michael remained at home, working in his study in the morning. When the rain ceased, he said he would spend the afternoon in the garden. The ground would be softer, and dry weather was forecast for the remainder of the day. When Kate agreed to join him, he looked surprised and pleased. While he built wigwams for runner beans and cleared spaces for planting, she attacked the weeds in the flowerbeds. Jen's advice drifted in her mind. *You don't have to believe it. Just act it.* She acted the good wife, and a quiet contentment stole through the slow rhythms of their joint project.

It was late afternoon, and she was preoccupied with untangling bindweed from an ancient rose when she heard the squeal of brakes and scrunch of tyres. She carried on working. Visitors usually walked round to the back if there was no reply at the front door. But no one came, and seconds later she heard a car roaring away. Thinking it must have been a delivery, she went through the side gate to the front. Nothing had been left in the porch.

'Who was it?' asked Michael.

'No one. At least no one who wanted us. Someone must have made a mistake.'

'I'll clear the sign at the top of the drive. It's covered in ivy. And the satnav's not much use down here.'

A chill of fear ran through her. It was ten minutes past five. The butcher's shop closed at five. Ten minutes was just long enough to drive from the town. Had the driver turned away at the sight of Michael's Audi?

She needed to get out and told Michael she would take Timba for a run. He nodded and she set off across the fields, pushing past her limitations in an effort to kill the thoughts that were crowding her mind. Weary and sweaty she returned home and jumped in the shower, drank a pint of water, and started to prepare the supper. She would handle this moment by moment. Day by day. But she could not escape him forever.

At the same time on the following day, she heard the car again. She stared out through the window of her studio as it stopped, made a three-point turn and drove away. This time she was able to study the vehicle, a four-by-four, even take the number plate. It was impossible to see the driver clearly, but she knew that head too well to mistake who it was. She said nothing to Michael about another lost driver.

On the third day, Michael left the house early. He had a difficult conference for which he needed to prepare. Then a meeting of the management committee. Decisions would be made about the future of his chambers. She shouldn't expect him back till about eight.

'Drive carefully,' she said as she kissed him goodbye, rain lashing her face as she stood in the open doorway.

'Go inside. You'll get soaked. And don't worry about me. I'm always careful.'

His car disappeared up the drive. She waited until the sound of the engine had faded, then went back inside, locking the door behind her, wondering at the change the last few days had brought about. Michael had often driven off early and left her alone. Till now she had welcomed the solitude, the chance to get on with her own work. But today, the first time for months, she hadn't wanted him to leave. She would miss him.

She sat at the table after breakfast, unsure what to do next. Gardening didn't appeal any more than house-work and there was always plenty of both. Michael's dig about her slovenly habits had been painful but there was some truth in the accusation. They employed a cleaner because they could afford to. And because if there were no cleaner, the house would be an unrelieved tip. But there was another way of looking at it. She was living off her husband and relying on another woman to clear up her mess.

Such thoughts turned in her head as she pushed the vacuum around the bedrooms. She had locked the door. Steve would come again one day she was sure of that. He would keep on coming until this was resolved. Would it be wiser to let him in, listen to him, give him the space he needed? Then tell him, as gently as she could, why they could not continue?

Yet each time a car or van drew up she tensed. The postman. The milkman. A delivery. No, the parcel had come to the wrong house. She explained how the satnav foundered in these winding country lanes, directing the confused driver back to the main road towards the village.

—

Later that day, she decided to finish the reclining nude. No one would recognise Immy. The face was deliberately vague. It was the shape and gesture of the limbs that Kate needed. She worked from photographs; she was perfecting the bend of the knee, the swell and curve of the thigh. It was still raining, and she worked to the soundtrack of weather as it battered on the tiled roof, peppering the skylight like shrapnel, lashing against the windows when the wind came up.

She didn't hear the car stop outside. But Timba heard, and when Kate turned to the window to see why he was barking, she saw the same four-by-four that had turned up and driven away yesterday. Her heart lurched when Steve stepped out and slammed the door behind him. It was the old electricity, only this time laced with something sharp and painful. She had not locked the door and within seconds he was inside. Timba was still barking as Steve fell on his knees and threw his arms around the dog.

'Hey old boy. Easy does it. Good to see you, mate.'

The dog quietened, lay on the floor, and let himself be stroked. Then Steve raised his head and his eyes met hers.

'Hi there.'

She said nothing, only stared as he stood up. She had forgotten his slow grace, had underestimated how his presence would affect her. She looked at the floor and said, 'Hello.'

She didn't wish to be cruel. But she needed him to go. When she let her eyes drift back to his, she felt crushed by the weight of his glare. The rain had stopped. Everything was still and quiet.

'So, you're dumping me.' The accusation was a thump across the stomach.

'That's not how it is.'

'You're not answering my texts.'

'It's been difficult.'

'We're on, then?' He threw out the laughing smile that had once so entranced her but now felt crude, thoughtless.

'How can we be?' But she hadn't meant to ask a question and immediately she said, 'Please go.'

He didn't leave. Instead his eyes narrowed, and he took a step towards her.

'Husband not at home?'

Apart from Steve's car, the only car in the drive was hers. She could lie, tell him Michael was inside. She had told so many lies, one more would make no difference. But it was easier to lie to Michael than it was to lie to Steve. He had known her for less than two months, but it was as if he knew her better than her husband did. She chose a half-truth.

'He's at work. In Bristol. But he'll be back any moment.'

'What about the stepdaughter?'

'She moved out a couple of weeks ago.'

'Pity I never met her.'

'You may have done. She works in the Gallery Cafe in town.'

The smile broadened.

'The new girl? The sexy one?'

'I guess.'

Back to the old flirty ways. It was a good sign. Maybe he wasn't obsessed with Kate. Maybe this visit was just a symptom of hurt pride. But all the time he was moving closer to her. And now he was only a few feet away. She could smell beer on his breath, his clothing. The reek of it burnt her nostrils, made her nauseous.

'Nice house you got,' he said.

'You've seen it before.' A voice in her head was telling her not to engage with him. But she had already started.

'How much did it cost then?'

'Please, Steve. It doesn't matter.'

'What would it be? Five bedrooms? Six? Big place for two. Worth a few bob, I reckon.'

'You should go.'

'Not yet. Unfinished business.'

He was only a couple of inches taller than her, but he was young and strong and smarting from her rejection. She had upset men before, men who had stormed off, slunk off, waited in vain hope, looked miserable. But there was something in his taunting, disrespectful manner that told her he would not leave until he had won something back from her. And she was alone, half a mile from the nearest house. No one would hear if she screamed. *Get a grip*. Why should she scream? He hadn't touched her. Wouldn't touch her. Not if she said, 'No.'

'Forgive me, Steve. It's my fault. I should never have invited you back. But we both know this can't go anywhere.'

'Doesn't have to go anywhere.'

He was standing less than two steps away from her, on one side of the worktable where she'd been sculpting. She had her back to the shelves which lined the wall. She held his gaze, willing him not to focus on her arm as it crept behind her.

'You been messing with me,' he said in a low voice laced with threat. Timba must have picked up the shift in atmosphere. From his bed in the corner, he let out a low, slow growl.

'No,' she said, immediately realising 'No' would not be enough.

'Anyone ever tell you you're callous?' It was more statement than question. 'You use people. Take what you want, then chuck them. I'll bet you've done it before.' The words stung. She thought of the days before Michael. Was that why she'd turned to Michael, stayed with Michael?

He had taken a step closer, and now he was walking around the reclining figure, inspecting it from each side, running his fingertips over the damp clay, lingering on Immy's small breasts and prominent nipples. This was her chance. She stretched her arm along the shelf behind her.

'So, who's this?' he asked, straightening. The smell of alcohol was strong. So strong she wondered if he had chased the beer with whisky. She noticed he was swaying slightly.

'My stepdaughter.'

'Yeah, thought I recognised her.'

'Get out, Steve.'

He stepped around the table and now stood less than a couple of feet away from her.

'I never hit a woman.'

'That's good to know.'

Using tiny movements with her first finger she was drawing a metal-tipped tool towards her.

'Even when they deserved it.'

And now it was close enough for her to grasp the handle.

'I love women too much. That's my problem. Love them too bloody much.'

His eyes were burning and she flinched. At that moment he lurched forward and grabbed her shoulders, pulling her towards him and pressing his mouth on hers. Then his tongue was in her mouth and one hand was inside the waistband of her trousers. She struggled to get away. Now both hands were on her bare flesh, squeezing so tight that she heard herself cry out in pain. The cry seemed to excite him, and he slid one hand to her crutch, forcing his fingers inside her. Blind with fury she swung out her right arm. He let out a howl and fell away, clutching his bleeding face. The metal tool had pierced his cheek. Timba ran over, barking hysterically.

Blood was splashed across Steve's white T-shirt, puddling on the wooden floor. He was doubled over, moaning, holding the wound. She spun quickly round to the shelf where the bigger tools were laid out: mallets, wire cutters, a pair of long, sharp scissors which she used to slice open the heavy bags of clay. Snatching up the scissors, she swivelled round to face him, waiting for him to straighten up. She had a brief urge to stab the scissors hard into the flesh she had once so ached for, to watch while his blood spilled out across the dusty floor. She had the power to do anything to him. But when he uncurled, she merely held out the scissors in front of her.

'Get out.'

Timba was snarling now, haunches low, eyes burning. Steve had been his friend, but the dog looked ready to spring. What had she done to him? His face was a mess. He didn't move as she continued to hold the scissors level with his chest, pointing at his heart. Timba held back; his snarl lowered to a rough growl.

'I said get out.'

The pain and rage in his eyes was scalding. She was less than an arm's length away from him, bracing herself, fearing he might stretch forwards and grab the scissors. And now he was leaning towards her, but he faltered, stumbling against the edge of the table, raising a hand to his bleeding cheek.

'Insane bitch.' The words came out hoarse, weak, as if the metal blade had caught his throat not his cheek. With blood still dripping from his cheek, Timba's snarl now an insistent bark, he turned to the door, stepped down the steps and onto the drive.

At the car he hesitated. She waited with the scissors. Was he planning to come back? He would have a jack and tools in the boot, any of which could serve as a weapon. She ran to the door and slid the bolt. It was flimsy. She would need to get a better one. She looked out of the window. He was still leaning against the car door. How badly had she hurt him? There'd been a lot of blood. Then he turned back to face her. She grabbed hold of a wooden chair and wedged it against the door.

When she looked out again he was already in his car. Within seconds she was listening to the engine roaring into life, watching him disappear out of the drive and up the lane to the main road.

She collapsed on a chair, breathing heavily, numb with exhaustion. It took a few minutes for her to remember where she was, what had happened. As it flooded back all she could feel was relief at her escape, horror at her own violence. Timba had stopped barking. He lolloped over and stood by her as she calmed him and stroked his back. Stroking him calmed her in turn and she was able to think again. If Steve tried to report what she had done she would tell the truth. He had assaulted her. There would be bruises on her buttocks where he had squeezed her.

She twisted her head, pulled down the top of her trousers and inspected the area. Red marks. Her pale skin bruised easily. The red would darken and spread. By tomorrow they would have become large purple patches. She would need to hide them from Michael. She would take photos of herself, just in case. She picked up her phone and stretched her arm behind her to take photos. It was hard to reach and press the shutter at the same time, so she hit the video button and passed the phone twice across the exposed top of her buttocks.

Still shaking, she walked to the storeroom to pour herself a glass of water. Timba was standing behind her, trembling. She stroked his back and took him to his bed. There was blood on the floor. And a line of drops on the steps and across the gravel.

She put on her rubber gloves, filled a bowl with soapy water and began scrubbing the floorboards. There might be some staining, but no one would notice in a studio where all sorts of spillages were common. When she had finished inside, she un-looped the hosepipe attached to the outside tap and sprayed the gravel. The whole task took her more than an hour. She surveyed the area. It was a beautiful evening with a sky of purest blue. Everything smelt fresh after the rain. The song of a blackbird was loud and piercing, wood pigeons cooed. It was as if nothing had happened to ruffle the peace of this special place.

Inside the studio she wiped the metal tool and returned it to the shelf. She put the scissors in a drawer and covered the reclining figure in plastic. Then she called Timba and stepped out onto the drive. He leapt down the steps and ran into the house and she locked the door behind them.

Back in the kitchen, she sat and poured herself a large glass of brandy and felt her breathing grow calmer as she looked ahead. She would take it hour by hour, minute by minute. She would bring up wine from the cellar, cook something spicy for dinner. It was the kind of food Michael liked and she could drown her own helping in yogurt. She suspected she wouldn't be able to eat much anyway.

The bruises would fade. Visible and invisible. She would start again, try harder with Michael. He must never know. And with the thought came the stinging realisation that there was no one she could talk to. Jen would be horrified as much by Kate's actions as by Steve's. She thought of Immy. So open, so trusting, so generous. Something deep in her heart told her that Immy would understand. But how could she burden this fragile girl with her terrible secret? She had brought this on herself. She could only pray that Steve would disappear, that time would heal, and she could put all this behind her.

Chapter 22

They sat with their drinks in the clear summer evening. The last rays of sun lit up the terrace and long shadows of trees spilled across the lawn. The men were in shirtsleeves, the women in cotton dresses, all except Kate who wore her usual loose trousers and a silk vest. She smiled as she considered the scene. It was as if in organising this little mid-week gathering she had created a miniature work of art.

It was two weeks since her encounter with Steve and she had seen and heard nothing from him. Had he let go of his resentment? Perhaps he had found some other way of venting his anger. She didn't need to know. Best to blot out all memory. The only thing that remained of him was his sculpted head. It had been fired and left to stand on a shelf in her storeroom. One day she might sell it.

She sipped her wine and her eyes swept the garden. It looked stunning. They had summoned a gardener to rescue it from neglect and now the flower beds were cleared of weeds, organised and flourishing, the roses in full bloom. A fitting background to their recovering marriage. Michael looked distinguished in a blue, linen shirt that drew out the colour of his eyes. Something had shifted in him since she'd agreed to host the dinner party, since she'd tried to be kinder, gentler. She stopped referring to his long silences at meals, his rants about politics, and, with each day, he seemed calmer. The Immy suspicion appeared to have faded and their lovemaking had grown more affectionate. Tonight, he appeared brighter than he had for years.

Until the last minute, Kate had been unsure whether Immy would come. She hadn't seen her for three weeks and she missed her. A couple of times Kate had rung to suggest a meeting in town, but Immy had said she wasn't feeling well. When she dropped into the cafe, Jen said she was taking a few days off. And when Kate rang Immy's mobile a third time, Jo answered.

'She's going through a bad patch. But she'll be fine. She just needs rest.'

Kate barely knew Jo and didn't push. She had warmed to Jo on their first meeting, but she was beginning to question the way the woman had taken control so quickly. Everything was racing ahead for Immy. Leaving London, the sexual approach to Kate, the cafe job, the bizarre declaration of love, then Jo. It was as if having survived her attempt to kill herself, she was grabbing at life in case it let her down again. Kate had prayed it wouldn't. And today she was relieved when Immy answered that morning's call herself and agreed to come. Jo would stay at home. It was easier that way.

Immy had arrived early, walking down from the bus stop.

'No bike?' asked Kate.

'I've given it up. Too scary. Dad can pay for a taxi back.'

'We'll get you a lift. Come and meet everyone.'

And now she was sitting quietly with her fruit juice, listening to everyone talk. Unlike many of Kate's contemporaries and most of Michael's, Immy appeared to have no need to lob her pennyworth into every conversation. She looked very pale, more beautiful than ever, subdued, but not unhappy. Kate felt a rush of affection. It was so good to have her back.

Kate had invited Susie, the older woman who had so taken to Immy at the sculpture class. Jen was there, of course, at this moment laughing at a witticism from Michael, while her partner Azeem looked on in discreet understanding. Their daughter, Lina, a mature eight-year-old was upstairs watching cartoons on her laptop.

'We love it here,' Susie was saying. 'Mind you, we were worried about flood risk at first. That's why we chose to live on the hill.'

The conversation turned to local matters, the work of the Environment Agency, the danger of new builds too close to the flood plain. Kate didn't attempt to follow what was being said, preferring to watch the shift of expressions on the faces of her guests as they enjoyed the soft still evening, the distant birdsong, the good wine.

As she gazed out towards the moor, she thought of the moment she had first seen Steve, leaning on the gate. Other images and sensations flashed through her mind, his dark hair against her white skin, those long eyelashes, the way he held her face between both hands before he kissed her. The sound, smell and feel of him. Their mutual longing. Then the other Steve, angry, desperate, blood pouring from his injured cheek.

She took a gulp of wine, reminding herself he would have nothing to gain by reporting her actions. If he did, he would be asked what he was doing in her studio. He would get little sympathy from a jury. A jury? Why was she even thinking about a jury? It would never get that far. She wondered what he had said to his wife. He would have thought of something. A butcher. Working all day with knives. Accidents happened.

She swallowed another mouthful, stood up and went into the kitchen to set out the food.

It was impossible to follow the substance of the chat from inside, but she picked up the sound of friendly banter between Jen and Michael. It was great that he was enjoying himself. For months he'd been so down. Tonight it was as if he had been let out of a cage. This was the Michael she had met all those years ago, charming, funny, flirtatious.

She set out six plates of crab salad, then something she had concocted from smoked tofu, cashew nuts and rocket for Immy. The voices outside were rising in pitch. Michael must have topped up the glasses. From the door she could see Immy standing close to Susie. As usual Susie was doing the talking. Azeem and Andrew were strolling in the direction of the vegetable garden, Jen stood close to Michael. And now he had his hand on her arm. Kate felt a twinge. Of what? Irritation? Not jealousy, surely. But what if it was? She smiled inwardly. Her reaction was a welcome reminder of her deep connection with the man she had married; that, in spite of everything, he belonged to her.

In quiet satisfaction she carried on preparing the table, adjusting the flowers in the central vase, straightening the plates and napkins. The spread was impressive, like something from a magazine. Michael would be pleased.

As she stepped out to call in her guests she heard her mobile. Probably a wrong number. Unless it was her father. It would be typical of him to call at an inappropriate time. The thought that it might be Steve flashed through her mind. But she quickly rejected it. It would be out of character for him to ring. He was too proud. He was more likely to turn up unannounced. Fearing this she had arranged for a locksmith to put stronger locks and new bolts on all the outer doors.

'Why this sudden security obsession?' Michael had asked.

'You're away a lot. Sometimes I get scared.'

'OK. If it makes you feel better.'

She stood by the kitchen door looking out to the terrace and the sunset beyond, enjoying the cooler air on her bare arms. In the ten minutes she had been inside, the sky in the west had been transformed from blue tinged with gold to an orange glow, streaked with dark cloud in alternating bands of smoke and fire. The phone had stopped ringing.

Michael called across the terrace.

'Do you want us in?'

'Yes,' she said. 'Everything's ready.' Her voice sounded light and welcoming. The guests began strolling towards the house.

The phone was on the counter, less than an arm's length away. It would be easy enough to check the number. Not now. Later. When she was alone.

They moved to the table and she suggested where they might sit, conscious that Immy may feel awkward as the only single person, the only vegetarian.

There were the usual murmurs of appreciation as her guests tucked into the crab salad. Then Susie said, 'I'd love to see your latest work. Immy tells me you're preparing for an art fair.'

'It's nothing much,' replied Kate. 'Just a stall in the craft centre at Somers St Nicholas. Modest stuff. Small animal sculpture. That sort of thing.'

'Don't undersell your work, darling.'

She smiled to herself. It was a long time since Michael had called her 'darling'. He was clearly enjoying playing the host. He circled the room, topping up glasses, stopping behind her and pressing a hand on her shoulder. Turning to the group, speaking as if she were not present, he announced, 'Her latest piece is amazing.' She swallowed her wine and stared at the table.

'Are you casting your own work now?' asked Susie.

'Not yet,' replied Kate. 'I don't have the space. But we're planning an extension to the studio.'

'Plenty of room to build out,' commented Andrew. 'What exactly is your acreage?'

'Not much. Just under five, with the wood,' said Michael before Kate could answer. 'A bit more than a garden, but you could hardly call it land.'

'You own a wood? How marvellous!' said Susie.

'That was the idea when we bought the place,' said Michael, still circulating with the wine. 'Room for the studio, easy access to the town but sufficiently cut off. You can stay here for days and not see a soul. That's how Kate prefers it.'

'The extension will be great. I'm meeting the architect soon.'

Michael grinned. 'Provided the work keeps rolling in.'

'Hard times at the Civil Bar? Surely not,' laughed Azeem, who ran his own practice as an accountant.

'Not all barristers are fat cats.'

No one spoke. Kate threw Michael a look. He had broken one of his own rules. Never talk about money in company. Particularly your own money. She hated even thinking about it, left all that to Michael; hadn't expected him to bring up the subject over dinner. He'd already told her there was a problem. Then she remembered. She had never asked about the important chambers' meeting two weeks ago. She'd been too busy mopping up Steve's blood and slapping make-up on her bruises.

Michael began clearing the plates, and she was setting the large casserole down on the table when she heard the piping of a child's voice behind her.

'Mummy!'

She spun round. Jen and Azeem's daughter, Lina, was standing in the doorway, a slip of a girl in pink pyjamas with long, straggly dark hair. Her pretty face was a miniature version of her mother's, if it were not for the round anxious eyes inherited from her father. And as she studied the child's lovely face she noticed a reddish-purple bump above her right eyebrow.

Jen pulled out her chair and opened her arms. 'I thought you were asleep.'

'I can't sleep, Mummy. My head hurts.' The little girl padded across the room. Jen enfolded her in a hug, then backed off to inspect her daughter's face.

'Let me look, sweetie. Oh yes, I see a bruise coming up.' She stroked the bump. 'But remember, that nice doctor said it would be fine.'

'Goodness that looks bad,' said Susie, abandoning her chair and standing up to get a better look. 'What happened, honey, did you fall over?'

'A boy hit me.'

'Dear God, we brutes start young,' muttered Andrew.

'This one was four years old,' announced Azeem, walking over and clasping his daughter's hand. 'Come on, little one. I'll take you up.'

'Don't call me little one,' said the child. 'My name's Lina.'

'OK, Miss Lina,' said Azeem, lifting her to his chest so that her grinning face could peek over his shoulder, her big eyes fixed on her mother.

'Kiss!' she commanded. Jen stood, walked over, and kissed the proffered cheek. As father and daughter headed for the stairs, Jen turned back to the table to explain.

'I was looking after two little boys. One of them got a bit enthusiastic with a plastic sword.' She paused as everyone waited for more. 'Poor kid lost his father a couple of weeks ago. You knew Steve, didn't you Immy? He came in the cafe with his family when you were there. Remember the little kid running under the tables? That's the one.'

Steve. The name echoed around Kate's head. She had one hand under the table and was digging her fingernails into her thigh. The other hand clutched her wine glass so tightly she feared it might break. Her breath stuck in her throat. Her heart was banging in her chest.

'That was the last time I saw the man,' Jen continued. 'He was looking a bit distracted. Tamsin was giving him a hard time. Terrible accident. Mown down by one of the abattoir's lorries. The police are looking into it.'

And now Kate was breathing too much, too fast. Something was fighting to come out of her. She slid her hand down the glass, pressing it hard against the table, gulping down the urge to scream.

People were talking but she couldn't hear what was being said, though she could hear Immy's voice. She sounded agitated, but Kate was too stunned to make out the words, and when she looked up Immy's face was even whiter than before. Now Michael was speaking, loud, authoritative, back in barrister mode, explaining the law to anyone who cared to listen. And as the voices floated past her, memories bubbled up. But this time there was no satisfaction at dispelling the pain, no trusting it would drift and fade. Now there was only disbelief as she revisited the past. Steve, smiling by the gate after her escape from the cattle. Brushing past her in the vestry, shafts of sunlight streaking through the stained glass. Warm, alive. And now his body was pressed against hers. She could feel the weight of it, smell his sweat. The horror had gone and there was only the desire. And then a new horror. She stared at the meat on her plate, willing the pictures to disappear, willing the sensations to stop, but they reeled in a relentless loop, growing more intense until it seemed his soft breath was skimming the pores of her bare skin.

Michael was close to Susie, poised to fill her glass. He stopped and put down the bottle, moving towards Kate. She prayed he wouldn't touch her, wished she could disappear. As a child she had willed herself invisible. But there was nothing she could do now. This moment was real. She was hosting a dinner party in her expensive kitchen while hearing about the death of her lover. And Michael had a hand on her shoulder just as before. She flinched. Did he notice? She wanted to hurl him away. Hurl them all away.

Andrew was speaking. 'Let's have a blow by blow, we're a bit out of touch up the hill.'

'I thought everyone knew,' said Jen. 'There was a sign in the butcher's window. The place was closed for a week. You must have seen it, Kate?'

Eyes swivelled towards her. 'I don't go there much. We prefer to buy organic stuff from the farm shop. And there's a good meat counter at Waitrose.' She was babbling. Over explaining. Jen would see through her lies. She had always felt transparent with Jen. She reached for Michael's hand, squeezing it, removing it from her shoulder as she stood up. 'Sorry. It's a shock. I mean even if you don't know someone.'

'Where was this accident?' asked Michael. His voice sounded strangely flat.

'Just at the end of your lane. I'm surprised you weren't aware of it. It took ages to move the lorry. They had to shut the road overnight.'

'Oh that. Remember, Kate? That night I was late back? I had to drive the long way round. I told you there'd been an accident.'

'Vaguely. Yeah, I guess so.' She didn't remember. Only that Steve had driven away fast, that she had washed away his blood, that she had bruises on her buttocks. The rest of the evening had been a blur. She was still hiding the vestige of those bruises from Michael. She looked for Immy. She had disappeared.

'Some of us have been campaigning for years for a sensible speed limit on that bend,' Jen continued. 'I warned you when you bought the house.'

Kate said, 'We're always careful.'

'I'm sorry. I've upset your dinner party.'

'Don't be ridiculous. Terrible things happen. We can't go around pretending everything's comfortable all the time. I'm glad you told us.' She was amazed at her ability to speak.

'It's fine. She's settled now,' said Azeem, coming back into the room.

'Was he alone?' asked Susie.

'Yes, thank God. The kids were with their mother,' said Jen.

It was just after six when he'd stormed out of the studio. Kate remembered the position of the hands on the wall clock moments before his car roared off towards the main road. When she'd driven out the following morning, the road was open as if nothing had happened. Later she'd noticed bunches of withered flowers lying under the hedgerow. Still, she had never considered that they might be for him. And what about Maxie? He went everywhere with Steve. Had the little dog also been in the car? If so, had he survived?

'Is Immy all right?' said Susie.

Immy had still not returned to the table.

'She's probably upset,' said Jen. 'She's a sensitive soul.'

'What was he driving?' asked Andrew. 'I only ask because I know they've had a recall on some of the new Fiats.'

'It was a Toyota,' said Jen. 'And no, there was nothing wrong with the car. Not according to Tamsin.'

'You seem to know a lot about it,' said Michael.

'Tamsin's sister's a friend of ours. Her daughter Sophie's at school with Lina,' said Jen.

'Vicky. Her husband's a client. Nice chap,' added Azeem.

A sister. Tamsin, the invisible wife of the man she had so casually picked up had a sister. A sister who was friendly with Jen and Azeem.

'Those bloody abattoir lorries. There was bound to be an accident some time,' exploded Susie.

'Of course, we don't know who was at fault. Best not to take a view until you've heard all the facts,' urged Andrew, and Susie gave him a look.

'You must all take extra care as you leave,' said Michael picking up the bottle and moving on round the table.

'Let's not talk of leaving,' said Kate brightly. Her voice sounded high-pitched, as if it belonged to a different woman, coming from outside herself, while the real Kate watched from the other side of the room. 'We haven't even finished our main course.'

But the happy mood was tainted. Michael went for another bottle. Kate wondered if she ought to go and find Immy.

'So, how's the poor widow getting on?' asked Susie between mouthfuls.

'Struggling. Apparently it'll take months, maybe even years to sort out compensation. But you'll know about that, Michael,' said Jen.

'It depends on fault.' Michael had adopted his professional tone, the dispassionate authority that seeped into his voice whenever he spoke of legal matters. 'Might be difficult to prove and the compensation for fatal accidents is only £10,000.'

'That would be a lot for Tamsin.'

'What if it's no one's fault? What if it's just an accident?' asked Kate.

'It's always someone's fault in a road accident. Unless it's an act of God, which is unlikely. That doesn't mean it's always worth pursuing. If you've less than a 50 per cent chance, it's not worth it.'

Voices were rising again, the wine disappearing fast. Immy had come back in as Michael was speaking. Kate heard her apologise, saying she'd been feeling a little unwell, she thought it might be a bug coming on.

'So, how come you had the boys?' asked Susie.

'Tamsin had to get the bus to the Job Centre in Yeovil. Sorting out Universal Credit. I understand Steve left them pretty skint. I offered to look after the kids for her. It's tragic. She's only twenty-two.'

The same age as Immy. A widow with two children. Kate's attention drifted in and out of the conversation. She struggled with the lamb tagine, chewing slowly, swallowing with difficulty. She was there and not there, mostly not there, under the railway bridge, water dripping down her back, Steve's hand below her dress, pushing himself inside her with primitive urgency.

'They were planning to go to New Zealand,' said Jen.

'So, she must have some savings,' ventured Kate, fingers tightly crossed under the table.

'Apparently not. According to Vicky, the stupid man lost most of it in online gambling. All in the week before he was killed. It's like he was on some self-destructive spiral. Poor girl. Vicky says it's destroying her.'

Kate stood up to clear the plates, her thoughts racing. It was too much to take in. Talk swirled around her. Sudden death. The iniquities of the gambling industry. Michael's work on fatal accidents. Azeem, an accountant, was interested in the latest case law. Susie steered them off towards the plight of the single mother.

Kate brought out the pudding. A home-made strawberry mousse with crème fraiche. She was exhausted before, but now she could barely lift the dish. She handed round the mousse.

The talk had moved on to politics. And despite her horror at what had happened to Steve, she felt a stab of irritation at the arrogance in her husband's tone. Not so much his views, but the way he managed to express them as if his opinion were the only truth. Or had he always done that?

The rest of the dinner passed in a blur. Immy remained quiet. Susie and Andrew offered to drive her home. It was not until after midnight that she and Michael were alone.

'Nice evening,' he said.

'Yes.'

'You don't agree.'

She could hear the disappointment in his voice. 'I'm not as sociable as you. Maybe I drank too much. Then the stuff about the accident.'

'Sounds like it was his own stupid fault.'

She couldn't speak. He took a step towards her. And now his hands were on her waist, eyes on hers. Blue-grey eyes. Slightly bloodshot. The wrong eyes.

'You were wonderful. The food was wonderful. You look beautiful.'

Three hours ago, she would have responded, forgiven him his mild intoxication, stroked his thinning hair. But now Steve's ghost hovered over them, a dark shadow. She needed time alone.

'Michael, would you mind very much if I pop over to the studio? I need to check I've covered everything properly. I don't want the work to dry out.'

He raised an eyebrow and gestured to the debris of dinner strewn around the kitchen.

'We'll do it in the morning. Go to bed. I'll join you in a minute.'

'Don't be long... I'll be waiting.'

He had been eager for talk and now was eager for sex. But she doubted he would stay awake long enough. He would be asleep, snoring when she returned in ten minutes. She picked up her phone and walked into the night.

The cool air brushed her skin, and she tilted her face towards the canopy of stars. Bats were flitting across the drive. Steve would have named the species. She remembered how he once pointed out damsel flies by the river, telling her where to go to see glow worms at night. He may have spent his days cutting up dead meat, but he had a connection with the land she could never share. Did he die in an instant? Did he suffer? What was he thinking in those last moments? Of his children? Tamsin? Of her? She thought about his angry words, the way he had grabbed her. Then the good bits drifted back. The first time. The smell and sight and touch of his body.

She looked back across the drive to the kitchen. Michael was still there, moving around, clearing up, waiting for her. Back in the studio her gaze travelled over the animal sculptures, the reclining figure, the few older heads she would be packing up for the art fair next week. And then close to her feet, the dark stain where Steve's blood had dripped on her floor. Images tumbled through her head, her flesh stirred, and she heard again the laugh that had once so entranced her, later appalled her. She sat down, closed her eyes, tried to breathe steadily until something like peace returned. It was over. He could no longer touch her.

Then she remembered the phone call earlier that evening. She hadn't answered for fear it might be him. At least now she could be sure it wasn't. She opened her phone and tapped, Recent. The number looked familiar. And then it hit her, and her stomach surged up through her heart to her throat and she thought she would choke. She leant forward, elbows on her knees, head in her hands. When she felt steadier, she sat up and looked through the window for Michael in the crazy notion that he could rescue her. But either he was out of sight on the other side of the kitchen or he had gone to bed. The kitchen light was still blazing.

She checked her voicemail. There was one new message.

'To listen to your message, press three.'

She pressed three.

The voice was young and female, the accent broad Somerset, the message stark.

'Murdering bitch.'

Chapter 23

For two weeks, she watched her phone as if it might leap up and bite her. There were few calls. A student. The bank. Mobile reception wasn't good in the house and most people who knew her texted or used the landline. Every night she checked her voicemail. Nothing. By the time of the art fair she was feeling calmer. She hadn't forgotten the furious voice at the end of the line, could only pray she would hear nothing more.

Tamsin must have found Kate's number on her dead husband's phone. With luck he would have deleted the texts. Just as he would have deleted the photographs. Kate was an ordinary name, not one to arouse suspicion. An unknown Kate in his contact list might be a distant cousin, the wife of a friend, a colleague. There must be a few female butchers.

She had deleted her own messages and couldn't remember exactly what she had said. But she'd been careful. They'd all been pretty neutral. No endearments. Nothing affectionate or sexy. Just brief arrangements. Then his increasing demands. She hoped she would never have to explain herself but if she did, she would present it as a clear case of stalking. At worst she would have to own up to using him as a model. That had been unwise. But it hardly made her a murdering bitch. She would have some explaining to do to Michael. It wouldn't be the first time. There'd been a couple of occasions in Bristol.

'I can't help men falling in love with me.'

'Are you sure about that?'

'I'm just being friendly. Anyway, you're the flirty one. One rule for men.'

'Probably true,' he had conceded.

That was then. She'd been working in the Bristol gallery. Looking good and charming wealthy men had been part of the job. This was now. Everything had changed. They were married.

On the day of the art fair she drove to pick up Jen.

'Hi Kate. Got room for Lina?' Jen asked, indicating her daughter, who was clutching at Jen's skirt.

'Sure. I managed to squeeze the sculpture in the boot. There's not that much and it's all quite small.'

'Great.'

Kate was fond of Lina, but she would find it more difficult to chat in her presence. She wanted to find out more about Tamsin. How the woman was managing. What her plans were. But just as she was about to speak, Lina asked, 'Will the naughty boy be there?'

'Quite likely, sweetheart, but don't worry. He won't hit you again. His mum will keep an eye on him.'

'You didn't keep an eye on him.'

'You're right. I should have done. I didn't expect him to be naughty like that. I should have been more careful. I knew he was upset. People who are upset often hurt other people.'

'Why was he upset?'

'Because his daddy died.'

Lina then asked if her daddy was going to die and Jen, who was always honest with her daughter, began a long explanation about death, which seemed to satisfy her. After Jen had finished, Lina said firmly, 'If he hits me, I'll hit him.'

Jen sighed. Kate sensed she was about to embark on a mini lecture about turning the other cheek when she heard herself asking, 'How is Tamsin? Have you seen anything of her?'

'I've not seen her myself since we looked after the twins. Her sister Vicky keeps me updated. Tamsin's tough. She's still hoping to go to New Zealand but God knows how she'll get there. She's looking to get compensation. Maybe she could chat with Michael if he turns up.'

Kate clutched the wheel. Michael had said he might come over with Azeem later. The thought of him giving Tamsin legal advice made her feel queasy. She must have missed a warning sign because they were suddenly bouncing over a hump-backed bridge.

'Steady,' yelled Jen.

'Can we do that again?' shrieked Lina.

'Sorry. Oh, Michael. Yes. Though fatal road accidents are not really his thing. He's more about doctors making mistakes.'

'Still – it's all compensation, isn't it? He'll know more than we do.'

'I guess.'

'Great. Would you talk to him? If I see Tamsin, I'll introduce you. I think you'll like her. She's a tough cookie. You told me you wanted to make more local friends.'

Kate drove on, gripping the wheel, eyes fixed on the road ahead as Jen related how the twins were playing up at nursery, leading to a visit from social services. Vicky was trying to help but there was only so much she could do. And Kate wanted to shout: Stop! Stop! Don't you see I don't need to hear any of this? But it was she who had asked. She who had wanted Jen to say Tamsin was doing fine. But people don't say what you want them to say. Twenty minutes later, still feeling queasy, she drove into Somer St Nicholas and followed the signs to the art fair.

The car bounced across a playing field and they parked at the back of the village hall to unload the sculpture. Jen and Lina carried some of the smaller animals inside, and Kate waited by the car for a few seconds, breathing steadily in an attempt to gather her strength and refocus. The sky was a pure blue, dotted with puffy white clouds like a story book and she could feel the warmth of the sun on her neck. She looked about her. This was more than just an art fair. There was an area set aside for 'bygones', rusting agricultural machinery which interested the older visitors. For the children there was a bouncy castle as well as rides, stalls and an area lined with flags where Jen had told her they would be organising games and races. Standing in the fresh air, the sick feeling began to fade. She took several deeper breaths. Brightly clad men and women drifted across the grass. A voice came through the tannoy announcing the first race. Egg and spoon for under eights. Families were making their way to the start line. This was a public place. The mood was cheerful. Nothing bad could happen here. She picked up the reclining figure and carried it into the hall.

Trestle tables were ranged around the walls; artists and craftspeople setting out their wares – watercolours, stone carving, knitted dolls, silkscreen, quilting, pottery. A banner hanging from the ceiling read, Arts and Crafts of Somerset. Kate had been allocated a table at the far end in front of the short wall. She laid out her trusty grey blanket, and Jen and Lina helped her arrange the pieces. Small animals at the front, rising to the heads and the reclining figure on a wooden plinth at the back.

'You need to put out those leaflets,' said Jen, stepping back to admire the display.

'I'm not sure. It looks a bit pushy. If someone's interested I can hand one over,' replied Kate. If Tamsin appeared she didn't want to advertise her name and phone number.

'Don't be silly you need people to know who you are. You've got a career to build.'

Did she? It seemed suddenly irrelevant.

'OK.' At least the address and phone number were on the back page.

She reached into her bag and handed Jen the leaflets. 'Here, you do something with them.'

Jen fanned them across the table at the front of the display. The name was prominent, vibrant yellow on blue, designed to stand out – Kate Leonard, Sculpting. It was a three-page fold-out with photos of her best pieces; students at work in the studio; Kate herself, hair like a medieval halo, lifting one of her heads out of the kiln. Immy had taken that one. She had a flair for photography. Kate had spent almost a week designing and putting the leaflet together. As she saw her face and name spread out for all to view, she felt suddenly cold and realised she was trembling slightly. But there was no reason for Tamsin to connect the name with the number on Steve's phone. The world was full of Kates. Plus, Tamsin had two little children. They'd be interested in the activities, not the art. Kate could only hope that Jen would forget about the proposed introduction.

'Mum,' said Lina, tugging Jen's arm. 'Bouncy castle. You promised.'

Jen made an apologetic face.

'Go,' said Kate. 'I'm hardly overwhelmed with punters.' It was true. The fair had started at ten a.m. It was now ten thirty and the hall was empty but for a couple of elderly women making slow progress around the exhibits. 'I'll call if I need help.'

Jen and Lina disappeared, and Kate sat on the hard chair provided, pulled out her phone and scrolled through her games. Desultory chat drifted past her, interspersed with sounds from outside, the ringing voices of children, old steam tractors rumbling across the field. The sensation of cold had passed, the effect was soporific, and she felt herself dozing over her third game of solitaire, when she sensed a presence beside her and looked up.

A man was standing at her table, scanning the display with interest. He was a little older than her with cropped blond hair, shining skin and small bright eyes. He wore a neat collarless shirt which was too tight for his rounded torso; a satchel was slung over one arm. He picked up a leaflet and flashed a quick smile while extending a hand. She took it. 'We've already been in touch. Jason Gill. Horizon Art, Bath.'

'Oh, lovely, I was hoping you would come.'

'They're good. Is this a representative selection?'

'There's more in my studio, but yes, I'd say it was representative.'

'The only thing is, they're a bit traditional for my market.'

She felt a flash of irritation. One minute they were good, the next minute they were too traditional. If he didn't like them, why talk to her? She was wondering how to respond without being rude. He seemed to read her mind because he started to speak again.

'Listen, I'm not an artist. Not even a critic. I'm just a salesman and I can tell you what sells. The technique's exceptional. Lots of punters will love it. But what most buyers are looking for is something with a twist.' He was studying her face and it was obvious he could read her. 'Now I've upset you. You asked me to come so I assumed you wanted my opinion.'

'It's fine. I'd love your opinion.'

'My clients would be more interested in something like this.'

And he picked up her most recent sculpture of Timba. Inspired by a memory of him leaping through a cornfield she had elongated the ears and tail. Of all her work on display, it was the least realistic. He was balanced on a delicate metal stand and looked as if he were flying, his legs two pairs of horizontal wings. It was not the first time it had attracted attention. Immy had noticed it too.

'So, if you have more like this.'

She did. There was a flying horse. And she'd been playing around in a new elongated style, inspired by the photos she'd taken of Immy. Flying dancers. They were experiments and she hadn't thought to bring any of them. But perhaps experiments would prove popular. He handed her his card.

'In case you mislay my number. Give me a call. I'd love to see something more dynamic.' He was at once childlike and appealing in his enthusiasm. 'The art world's a crazy place. But I have a bit of influence in the south-west and I'm always happy to look at stuff. I sometimes buy individual pieces. If something really appeals.'

He moved on, passing quickly by some watercolours to a local wood and stone carver. Kate knew the man's work.

If she was traditional, he was antique. But Jason seemed interested in his primitive chess pieces.

More visitors came to look, glancing, assessing, walking on. It was dispiriting. She had been excited about coming, but now she felt vulnerable, exposed. Every piece had taken hours. If she thought about the time spent making and the prices she charged, her profit amounted to about £1 per hour. Ridiculous. She'd thought a traditional style would appeal to the country audience. But she'd underestimated them. They seemed more interested in the brightly coloured abstracts and lumpy carving. Still, Jason's enthusiasm was encouraging, a seed of interest that might lead somewhere. She'd been missing external endorsement. Michael was happy to pay the bills and leave her alone to get on with her work. But she'd often wished he would show a bit more interest.

She was still thinking about Jason when she spotted a small boy drifting aimlessly across the room, one little hand clutching a stuffed toy monkey. The monkey's arms and legs were so long, and the boy so small, that the toy's feet were being dragged along the ground as he walked. And as he walked he seemed to be chatting to some invisible being. His hair was a curly brown mop and as he drew close, she realised he had the longest lashes she had ever seen on a child. When he reached her table, he began running his finger up and down the edge which was about his eye level, gazing at the models on the front row. Then, without looking up at her, he curled his fingers around a small dog and sat on the floor. The dog began to talk to the monkey. Kate moved round the table and crouched down.

'Hello,' she said. 'Is someone looking after you?'

'My mum lost me.'

'Then we better go and find her.'

'I like this dog,' he said. 'It looks like my dog.'

And he jumped up with the tiny model and tore off across the room. Kate asked her neighbour if she could keep an eye on her stall and ran after him. It had started to rain. The hall was quickly filling up with visitors sporting wet hair and dripping umbrellas. Briefly she lost sight of the little boy. When he was back in view he was being squeezed very hard by a stocky young woman with straggly blonde hair. The woman lent down and said something, and Kate saw him hand over the model dog. The woman put it in her bag and the pair moved slowly back towards her display table, the boy still trailing his monkey in one hand. Kate followed and soon she was close enough to hear the woman's light Somerset burr.

'Now Logie, you don't do that. You don't wander off.'

'You lost me, Mum.'

Kate stood by them transfixed. Logie.

'Don't give me that cheek,' grumbled the woman, removing the model from her bag and handing it to the boy. 'Now, put it back.'

'He can keep it,' said Kate, drawing near.

'Oh no. I couldn't allow that. No more could his brother. He'd only…'

As she spoke, the words trailed off and the woman was staring at Kate, then at the brochures spread across the table, then back to Kate as if she couldn't believe what she saw. Kate didn't turn away. Out of the corner of her vision she spotted Jen, running over with Lina and two other children.

'Hi, Tamsin. What a relief. I told you she'd be here. Tamsin, this is Kate. Her husband's the lawyer I was telling you about.'

'Kate,' repeated Tamsin in a low, flat voice.

'Yes,' said Kate, still holding the other woman's hostile stare. 'Kate Leonard.' She wouldn't, couldn't, pretend to be anyone else. She'd been a fool, handing Steve her card on that first meeting when she was still kidding herself she only wanted to sculpt his head. The brochures fanned out across the table screamed her identity. Unless Tamsin recognised her from the photos. But no, it couldn't possibly be the photos. He'd promised to delete them. She'd seen the gallery on his phone. Nothing but lumps of meat.

Tamsin's stare hardened. It was as if someone had pulled down a blind and shut out the light. She thrust the dog towards Kate.

'Take it back.'

'No, please. I'd like him to have it. I've got another small one for his brother. If you'll wait a moment.'

'I said take it, didn't I?' She scowled and barked at the children. 'Come on kids.' And she grabbed the little boys by the hand and dragged them out, the monkey with the long arms and legs trailing behind them.

The girl, Lina's age, stood staring.

'Go with your auntie, Sophie,' said Jen. When the girl had disappeared, she asked, 'What was that about?'

'I've no idea.' said Kate. She looked Jen straight in the eye as she spoke and thought she detected a glimmer of uncertainty in her friend's expression. How much longer before news of her affair became public know-ledge? When the story of Steve's accident came out at the dinner, she had avoided saying much. But what if they had been seen together with their dogs? Word might have got around. In front of Michael and their friends, silence had felt like the only option. But this was the first time she had lied to Jen and it hurt. Jen went off to join Tamsin and the children. She would ask Tamsin the same question and soon she would know that her best friend, Kate, was a cheat. Would Tamsin say anything to Michael? Would Jen? Kate knew Jen wouldn't stay silent for long. And, very quickly, Kate needed to work out what she would say.

Chapter 24

Michael was late. When she rang, he explained he'd missed his lift with Azeem.

'Got stuck on a work call. Sorry, Kate. We'll talk when I get back. Can you manage?'

'Sure. Jen can help me with the sculptures.'

But Jen hadn't returned to the stall after the Tamsin incident, and Kate had to ask the guy with the carving to watch her stuff while she carted pieces out to the car.

Back home Michael was seated at the kitchen island staring at a newspaper. He glanced up when she came in.

'Hi. How did it go? Sold anything?'

'A couple of things.'

But there was little interest in his expression. For one crazy moment she wondered if he'd been on the phone to Jen. Was this grim indifference a mask? Would he suddenly explode in rage? He'd thrown a plate once. He could do it again. And as she stood there waiting for him to respond, an imaginary conversation whizzed through her head.

'Hey, Michael, I just rang to tell you Kate was shagging that dead bloke. Thought you should know.'

'Thanks, Jen. That's kind of you.'

No. Impossible. Jen was principled, she was fond of Michael, but fundamentally she was Kate's friend. She would never be disloyal. If she were going to say anything, she would say it to Kate.

'Any sign of Immy?' he asked.

'No. Jo works at weekends.'

'Since when were they joined at the hip?'

'Don't be absurd. You know she's dependent on Jo for transport.' And when he said nothing she added, 'Maybe you should buy her a car.'

He scoffed and turned back to his paper. 'You're joking.'

But Kate knew it wasn't just the transport. Immy had made it to the dinner party by bus. She'd even mentioned she was applying for a UK driving licence now she wasn't cycling. But she'd behaved strangely that night and since then, nothing. Kate resolved to call her again, invite her for supper. Just the three of them. With Jo if that was what she wanted. The main thing was to let her know they were there for her. Immy was fragile. What if she was descending into another depression?

Kate cast a quick look at Michael as she made her way over to the sink. He was staring blankly at the news-paper. He wasn't reading it, that was certain. And if he hadn't heard anything terrible from Jen, why was he so unwelcoming? She'd been out all day attempting to sell her work. He might at least have offered to make her a cup of tea. She walked over to the kettle, picked it up and took it to the sink.

'So, this gallery owner. Is he going to make you rich?' he asked.

'Hardly. Though he liked my flying dog. And he gave me a few ideas about what might sell. I'm going to try a different approach, more dynamic, expressionist...'

Her words petered out. Michael's unaltered expression suggested he wasn't interested in the detail of her developing style. He said, 'Only it looks like you might have to support me soon.'

She turned from the sink and for the first time since arriving home she studied his face. The muscles in his jaw were working hard, and she found herself thinking, Stop grinding. Your teeth will fall out. The bags under his eyes looked more pronounced than usual and as she continued to look at him they widened, darkened. And for a moment it was as if she were gazing into a different pair of eyes, the intense, brown eyes of her dead lover. She took a step towards him, sat down on the stool next to his and in a gentle voice she asked, 'What is it, Michael?'

'I told you what was happening in chambers.'

He had spoken of a crisis on the management committee, but she had become lost in the detail: new entities; a fused profession; changes in regulation. It all sounded so technical. She trusted him to sort it. He always had done. He didn't talk much about work.

'You sounded so much better at the dinner party. I thought everything was sorted.'

'You know what it's like. Something bad is about to happen only you're not 100 per cent sure. And until you are sure, you refuse to believe it.' She knew. Only too well she knew. 'After you left this morning I had a phone call from Matthew.'

Matthew? Then she remembered. The guy from chambers. Some kind of big shot. Was he the boss? No, of course, she reminded herself, barristers didn't have bosses. They were all equal, though, in the usual way, some were more equal than others.

'And?'

'We're splitting.' What was he talking about? He read her mind and threw out a wry smile. 'Not you and me! Chambers.'

She was still unsure what he meant. 'Is that a bad thing?'

'Depends which side you are on.'

'And which side are you on?'

The wry smile collapsed.

'It's not great. Matthew's setting up a partnership with some of our main solicitors and a few of the new tenants. Young bloods. You know the sort of thing.'

She did. He had complained of it before. Ever since he hit forty, that magical age when life either took off to greater heights or wound down to failure. She hadn't reached it and didn't look forward to it. But even she understood the sense that others were creeping up behind you, that life was passing you by. Was that the reason he had wanted a child? Was it her reason too? Was that all it was about? And did he still want a child? She dared not ask.

'It could be good. I could still be invited to join them. But it's unlikely. And if I'm not, it would be less than good.'

'Don't you know? I thought you were on all the committees.'

'Nothing's final.'

He had picked up a pen off the counter and was gripping it in his long, thin fingers. A writer's hand, a thinker's hand. There was a scratch where he had nicked himself with the loppers while pruning the cherry tree. But it was not a worker's hand. It had never handled livestock, never wielded knives to chop carcases. She reached towards it, but something stopped her touching him.

'There may be tough times,' he continued.

'That's OK, I can do without holidays,' she responded brightly. 'I've been looking at brochures but, to be honest, I haven't got very far.'

She hadn't felt able to contemplate a holiday. In going away, you took what you left behind. She didn't want to take the memory of a dead man and his grieving widow. She needed time to process it all. Above all, and for the first time she acknowledged it to herself, she needed someone to talk to. To confess everything. The burden was too heavy to carry alone. There had always been Jen. It was Jen who had seen her through anguished break ups, men who turned out to be the opposite of what they promised to be. And Jen had understood, supported her. But now? Michael was silent, apparently waiting for her to speak.

She said, 'I've got enough clothes. We'll manage with one car.'

He shut his eyes as if banishing the thought, but what he said was, 'It could be worse than that.'

'How much worse?'

'Hard to say. There's a lot up in the air. I just thought you should know. It may not be so easy. In case you had hopes, expectations.'

Who didn't have hopes? She was less sure about expectations. But from the look he gave her, she knew not to press him further. There was already enough to take in.

Kate's mind flitted back to Steve. Would Jen say anything? Perhaps not. But at some point she would ask Kate. What if Kate called her first to talk to her? She could pre-empt Jen's suspicions, give her an airbrushed version – explain how she had behaved foolishly, grown over friendly, how Steve had got the wrong idea. Yes, that might work.

'I've still got a handful of cases,' he continued. 'You always wanted me to act for patients. It's risky of course. No win, no fee.'

She was no longer sure it mattered for whom he acted as long as he was paid. And there were more important things than money. She said the first thing that came into her mind.

'You won't take on a loser?'

He winced and she realised she had hit a nerve and something in him hardened.

'Don't push me, Kate. All I'm saying is... Maybe we can't rely on things as we used to. Two homes are expensive to run.'

So, sell Bristol, she thought. But something told her it was time to stop giving him advice. He pulled back his chair.

'I'll take Timba out.'

The dog must have heard his name because he stood up in his bed. The muscles in his shoulders rippled as he straightened his front legs. Timba was so beautiful. Sometimes it felt as if he was the only creature she had ever truly loved.

'Look after him,' she said, remembering the time Michael had let him off the lead and they'd waited all night for him to come home.

'Of course, I will. Anyway, he doesn't run off any more.'

–

She went to her studio to prepare for tomorrow's class. The tables and armatures were set out but there were materials she needed from the store-room. As she walked through the narrow doorway, she immediately encountered the shrouded head of Steve. She pulled off the black plastic. His wild eyes met hers. After firing, only the white of the silicates and the red of the iron oxide remained, leaving a rose-pink hue. It looked wrong. Steve needed a glaze. Matt bronze or silver and charcoal would be awesome. She twisted him round to see the face. But even as she visualised the finished piece, a voice was nagging in her brain. Why was she even contemplating a glaze? She wasn't going to keep him. Next time she went to the dump she would take him with her and chuck him in a skip. She stared again at his powerful features. Not yet. She was not ready to let him go.

In a moment of madness, when everything became too much to bear, she had thought about giving him to Tamsin. A peace offering. More like an act of lunacy. Since that terrible moment when she'd heard of Steve's death her emotions had been so turbulent and unpredictable that she had sometimes wondered if she was going mad.

Tamsin knew who Kate was and, even if she hadn't picked up a brochure, it wouldn't be difficult for her to discover where she lived. At the art fair she had rushed away from Kate as if all she wanted was to place a distance between them. Perhaps she did. Perhaps the anger down the phone had been enough. Kate thought of Michael's words, 'Something bad is about to happen only you're not 100 per cent sure. And until you are sure, you refuse to believe it.'

As she walked away from Steve's shrouded head, his widow's furious stare hung in her mind like a thunder cloud in a darkening sky.

Chapter 25

The summer floods were too high for a run on the moor, so Kate set off in the other direction, up the drive onto the lane and the main road at the spot where Steve had died. The withered flowers were still there. More bunches lay under the hedgerow. Someone must have been leaving them regularly. She didn't stop to read the sodden messages, darting across as soon as the way was clear.

At the bottom of the narrow footpath through the woods, she let Timba off the lead, and he raced ahead up the steep climb, Kate following at half his pace. When they reached the ridge at the top, the path across the field was flat and easy. Timba leapt from scent to scent while Kate bounded along, twisting her head to take in the view across the plain towards the Quantocks, waterlogged fields glistening like mirrors in the afternoon sunlight.

Her knotted thoughts unravelled; the things she couldn't change, the things she could change. She had shown sympathy for Michael's work problem. It was the best she could do, and she trusted him to come through it. There had been lean times in the past, but he'd always bounced back. He had another big meeting tonight and had no idea how long it would go on.

'That's a shame,' said Kate, 'I invited Immy for supper.'

'You didn't tell me.'

'I wasn't sure if she was coming. You know what she's like about answering invitations. Anyway, I'm telling you now.'

'I should be back around eight. If not just go ahead without me. I'll text you when the meeting finishes.'

She hoped he wouldn't be late. More than ever she wanted to heal that wound. She might never have a child. But, with Immy in the fold, they could be a sort of family.

Feeling better the further and faster she went, her head began to clear till there was nothing but the wind and sun on her face, the air in her lungs, the power in her limbs. The rain started up again as soon as she reached the front door an hour later. Good timing.

She showered and changed into loose work clothes. The run had unleashed her creativity and she was eager to start. Immy was coming over on the last bus and Kate would drop her home later.

In the studio, she took out the photos she had taken of Immy dancing. A moment of perfect balance. Kate's three earlier attempts to capture it had ended in the recycling bin. But it was worth pursuing. A flying dancer would appeal to Jason. There were plenty of cheap ones on the internet, but she could do better than that.

You couldn't hear the road from the studio. The only sounds were the wind in the trees and the battering of rain on the tiled roof. The conditions were perfect. Wild weather swirling beyond the security of her indoor space always energised Kate. She had produced some of her best work during violent storms. She cleared the counter and one of her mobile worktables, shut her eyes as she contemplated the structure of her imagined piece.

This was the best time. When an idea was taking shape, when everything, anything, was possible, and hours of undisturbed work stretched out before her. Then, just as she was about to start, she heard a plop and noticed a splash on her sleeve. Glancing up she saw water seeping through a crack in the ceiling plaster. She heard herself sigh. Another job to organise. The roof would need repairing and she couldn't trust Michael up a ladder. As soon as she finished work she would call the roofer.

Irritated, she wheeled away the table, found a bucket and stuck it under the leak. It was hard to ignore the persistent drip-drop. The only answer was loud music. There were wireless speakers attached to the wall. Kate was scrolling through her playlist for something with a strong beat when a cold draught grazed the back of her neck. She spun around.

Tamsin was standing in the open doorway. Her dark blonde hair was flattened by the rain, lying in streaks across her wide forehead. Water dripped down her square face and onto her broad shoulders.

She wore a blue waterproof jacket, jeans tight on heavy thighs, impractical sandals. Wind and rain were swirling through the open door behind her and, without taking her eyes off Kate, she took a step forward and swung it shut. Then she straightened. She was a small woman, but she looked solid as a wall. Her arrival had roused Timba who had leapt off his bed and was now crouched a few metres away, greeting the unexpected visitor with an ear-splitting bark.

'Can't you keep that dog under control?' shouted Tamsin in a voice edged with panic.

'He's only doing his job,' responded Kate. She reached for Timba, hauling him back to his bed. 'Stay,' she commanded. And the dog lay down, trembling, his bark resolving into a muffled growl. 'It's usual to knock,' she said.

'I did,' said Tamsin, keeping her eye on Timba. 'You didn't answer. You should tie him up.'

'He won't hurt you.'

Tamsin looked unconvinced. But then the hard face returned, and she glared at Kate. What did she want? Her husband was dead. Visiting his other woman wasn't going to bring him back. Kate thought about the texts. Steve had promised to delete them. And the photos had gone. Hadn't they?

All this tore through her mind as Tamsin's eyes drilled into her soul. It was as if the woman could see everything Kate had ever done or even thought. What if they were stored somewhere else? What if everything he'd deleted was backed-up?

Then, in a voice, thick with pain and anger, Tamsin said, 'You were sleeping with my husband.'

'He came here to sit for me. A couple of times.'

'That's a good one,' sneered Tamsin. And Kate real-ised she had made a mistake. She should have admitted nothing. Ordered the woman out. Instead she had offered her a way in, and now Tamsin was circling the studio, picking up small clay sculptures, feeling their weight, tracing their form with stubby fingertips that ended in ugly, purple-painted nails. Kate leant down to Timba. He was shaking, the growl was getting louder.

'Can't you stick that dog outside?'

'It's raining.'

'So?'

Instinctively Kate placed a hand on Timba's head. She sensed her dog's anxiety and didn't want him upset. Timba was used to students coming in and out. After the initial bark of greeting, he was usually quiet. But something about Tamsin troubled him. Steve had told Kate that his wife didn't like dogs, had put up with Maxie as a condition of having Steve. Dogs picked up that kind of thing. Kate stroked Timba behind the ears to calm him. Normally he would have settled by now, but he remained alert, watchful, as Tamsin sauntered among the tables, inspecting Kate's tools and the half-finished sculptures wrapped in plastic. Then she stopped, turned to face Kate, and spat out her question.

'So, where did you do it?'

Kate said nothing. Her pulse was racing but she tried to stay calm. She only had to wait. Tamsin would leave eventually. And aside from hurling her out bodily, what could she do? She had done her best to keep the temperature low. A scuffle would be unpleasant. Tamsin was small but much younger, and Kate sensed a power in her she would rather not confront.

The young woman continued circling the room. In some perverse way she seemed to be enjoying herself. Was she revelling in the thrill of imagining her husband with another woman, a woman so different from herself? When Tamsin turned back towards her, Kate felt a pair of sharp eyes inspecting her, scanning her body, as if looking for clues as to what had drawn her young husband to this much older specimen.

'Bit public here with all these windows. What about back here?' Without waiting for an answer, Tamsin opened the storeroom door and walked in.

Timba's growl was muted but it was increasingly audible as the rain eased and the wind dropped. By now Tamsin must have seen the head. Kate was not afraid, but neither was she foolhardy. Immy had witnessed Tamsin hitting one of her own kids. If you could be violent to the child you loved, you could surely be violent to a woman you hated. With that thought she stretched out an arm for the metal-tipped tool on the counter beside her. As she did so, an image flashed behind her eyes, Tamsin's husband staggering out of the studio, head in his hands, blood dripping from the wound Kate had inflicted.

Beside her Timba was still growling, his body aquiver with anxiety. Abandoning the metal tool, Kate leant down to stroke him and, as she did so, she heard a loud crash. Hanging onto Timba's collar, she looked up to see a cloud of dust billowing out through the storeroom door. Timba leapt up and strained against his collar. Kate held onto him. Silica dust was lethal to humans and equally dangerous for dogs. Then she heard coughing and out of the cloud stepped Tamsin, holding up the smashed remains of Steve's sculpted head. Forehead, eye, nose, cheek and ear were intact. The rest was a mess of dust and fragments on the storeroom floor.

Timba was still straining and, before Kate could stop him, he had lurched from her grip towards Tamsin, barking and snarling.

'Get him away from me,' screamed Tamsin.

'Just walk out,' shouted Kate. 'And for God's sake put down the head. Timba won't hurt you if you put it down.'

But Tamsin didn't walk out, didn't lower the head. She just backed into the storeroom, holding the broken head like a shield, shouting, 'Get him away, get him away.'

But before Kate could reach Timba's collar the dog rushed forward like a police dog pulling down a suspect. The cloud of dust made it hard to see exactly what was happening. For a moment he seemed to be tugging at Tamsin's jacket. Then Kate heard one final ear-splitting bark followed by a thud, and in the settling dust she saw Timba at the entrance to the storeroom, down on his four legs, shuddering, looking as if he were about to topple to the ground. Kate raced towards him, but he turned and slunk past her, heading unsteadily for his bed.

'Look what he did to me,' said Tamsin.

She held out her arm and Kate could see the unmistakable signs of a bite mark on her hand. 'You shouldn't keep a dog like that. It's against the law.'

Kate turned back to Timba who was stretched out on his bed. She fell to the ground beside him, stroked him. Her hand felt wet. She looked down and saw blood. Tamsin was still standing in the doorway to the storeroom, still holding the broken sculpture. Something flicked in Kate and she leapt up and rushed at Tamsin, grabbing her around the neck, and causing her to drop the sculpture and stagger back.

Kate's hands were large and strong. All her life she had used them to fashion clay, carve wood, bend metal. She had studied anatomy and knew where to press. Tamsin let out a cry which turned to a squeak as her face darkened, her eyes swelled. Kate squeezed. Nothing would stop her. Tamsin was struggling, but her struggle was weakening.

Then everything stopped. Pain stung Kate's arm and it dropped away from Tamsin's neck. She fell backwards. Something had sliced into her skin. With the other arm, she reached for a chair to steady herself.

When the room returned to focus, Tamsin was standing a few feet away, pointing a long, thin tool at Kate's heart. It was the dental probe, the delicate point of which Kate had been planning to use to pick out the fine detail on her flying dancer. Where she had squeezed

Tamsin's neck, she could make out her own handprints, stamped in Timba's blood.

'Get out,' Kate grunted, her voice sounding hoarse, distant, as if coming from some other place.

She fell to her knees, stripped off her shirt with her good arm and held it against Timba's wound to stem the bleeding. But it was too late. The movement of his chest had grown slow, the whining sound was fading, his enormous brown eyes were turning cloudy and unseeing.

When she looked up, Tamsin had gone.

Chapter 26

In the fading light she sat on the wooden floor, leaning against the wall of the studio, rocking her dog's head. A great ache filled her body. She had no idea how much time had passed. Everything about her felt clogged, stuck. Everything except this slow, steady rocking.

'I'm sorry Timba,' she whispered. 'I should have protected you.'

His breath was fast, shallow, desperate.

She heard the squeak of the door and turned. Immy stood in the threshold, her eyes wide. Kate glanced down at her blood-streaked arms and hands. How long had she been sitting here?

She waited for Immy to speak, but Immy said nothing, only walked over, sat on the floor next to Kate and buried her head in Timba's furry coat. In her short time with them, Immy had come to love him too. Then she raised her head towards Kate, her lovely young face crumpled in sadness and incomprehension.

'Tamsin was here,' said Kate. 'She...' But words wouldn't come.

'Why?'

'I'll tell you... only... not now...'

They sat in silence for a few seconds then Immy said, 'What happened to your arm?'

'It's nothing. Just a scratch.'

'Hang on.' The girl was suddenly efficient, standing up and crossing the studio to the sink, returning with a damp towel. 'Let me wash it.' Kate winced as Immy wiped away the blood exposing a small cut on her lower forearm.

'Here, hold this on it.' She handed her a tissue. 'I'll get you a plaster. Poor Timba. We should call the vet.'

'No. It's too late.' His breathing had ceased. His suffering had ceased. Kate's tears fell on the body of her poor dead dog. Through her anguish she heard Immy's voice.

'I'll ring the police.'

'No.'

The touch of his fur was so soft. She had loved him so much. She heard Immy's voice again.

'They should know. You've been hurt too.' And when Kate looked up she saw pain in Immy's eyes. 'What happened, Kate?'

She would have to tell her. She would need help and the only person who could help her now was Immy. But she didn't know where to start.

'Where's Dad?'

'Work. He said he'd be back late.'

Immy was staring at her hard. But there was warmth in her voice as she reached for Kate's hand and said, 'Tell me.'

'She saw the head. The one of her husband.'

Immy nodded, listening intently.

'It's complicated. There was other stuff.' Kate stopped. How could she dump her guilt on this innocent girl?

'Other stuff,' repeated Immy. Kate sensed the possibilities that must be whirling through Immy's mind. How much should she reveal? But before she could say more, Immy asked, 'Does Dad know?'

'He doesn't even know Steve came here. If I told him he would never believe Steve was only a model.' She couldn't go on. Immy must have guessed. Kate found herself scanning Immy's face, searching for signs of revulsion, anger, disapproval. Would the girl she had grown so fond of start to hate her? And why couldn't she say it: Steve and I were lovers. Why this skirting around the truth of what had happened?

No one spoke. Immy turned her face away towards Timba, stroking his neck, staring at the floor before raising her head and looking at Kate. Her blue-grey eyes glimmering in the evening light.

'I'm not judging, Kate. But I think we should be careful now. Dad can be… well… Has he ever hurt you?'

Kate thought about the plate. The fury in Michael's eyes. But no, not directly.

'No.'

'Tamsin might say something.'

'I've no idea what she'll do.' It was true. And yet if Tamsin wanted to destroy Kate she had everything she needed: the texts, the fingermarks on her neck, the dog bite on her hand. Photos? Tamsin had said nothing about photos. Steve must have deleted them.

'What will you tell him?'

'I don't know. It was an accident. In a way. I mean Tamsin didn't mean to…' She couldn't say the words. 'But I'd have to lie. About why she was here. Why she was so angry… I've already… lied so much…' And she felt the tears welling up again, for Timba, for herself, for Steve, for Michael, who had his own problems and knew nothing of all this.

Immy was silent, stroking Timba's furry coat. Then she sat up and in a determined voice said, 'We'll take him out. Bury him.'

This slip of a girl. Two months ago, she'd walked into their lives, awkward, shy, moody; with the manners and behaviour of an adolescent. Now she was taking control.

'Where?'

'We could drive up to the wood. I've been walking there with Jo. You can park at the end of the footpath near the firing range. It's pretty overgrown. Not many people go there. There'll be no one there at this hour.'

Kate knew it well. The wood belonged to the Wildlife Trust. There was an abandoned farm at one end. Steel troughs. Broken-down sheds. Sheets of corrugated iron swathed in ivy. You could hide a body there. But the ground would be thick with roots. It would be impossible to dig deep. 'We're not just dumping him. He needs a proper grave.'

'Where then?'

'I'm thinking. We'll find somewhere.'

'What about Dad?'

'I'll tell him Timba ran off. He does that sometimes.' But he had always come back.

'Wouldn't someone find him? He'd have been wearing a collar. And doesn't he have one of those chip things?'

'The vet couldn't find it when I took him. I meant to get a new one implanted, but I never got round to it.'

'Wait here,' said Immy, disappearing out of the studio door.

Kate's legs were numb from Timba's weight and she slid out from beneath him, an ache in her heart at this first step towards separation. Where would they take him? He deserved dignity in death. She studied his dear face.

His eyes were milky, his mouth had dropped open on one side. He should have solemnities, rituals, incense, candles, precious words.

Immy returned with rubber gloves, floor cleaner, disinfectant, cloths, a plastic bowl, heavy-duty garden bags. She had found a packet of Elastoplast and she peeled one open and stuck it over the cut on Kate's arm. The laceration was small. Little more than a nick. Michael wouldn't even notice.

Half an hour later, the floor had been scrubbed and sanitised. There was nothing but a dark stain to indicate what had taken place. If Michael mentioned it, which was unlikely, she would tell him she had spilt a pot of coffee. If it started to smell, she would replace the boards. The storeroom was swept and cleared. The fragments of clay binned; the remnant of the broken head returned to the shelf.

Immy put down the bin bag and started to lift Timba.
'No. Wait.'

Kate went into the storeroom, opened the cupboard door and lifted out the old blanket. She had made love on this blanket. Immy had modelled on it. She had displayed her work on it at the art fair. Now it would act as Timba's shroud. She leant over him and unfastened the collar and tag. Then she kissed them and took them back to the storeroom where she put them in one of the lower drawers. Small keepsakes. Not that she would ever forget Timba.

By now she was feeling faint. She hadn't eaten since lunch. But Immy had thought of everything. While in the house to pick up their equipment, she had prepared cheese sandwiches and the women sat on the studio steps under the light of the door to eat them. Kate could only manage small bites. They both froze as they heard a car passing the top of the lane.

'Shit. It's Dad.'

Kate's mind was racing. If it were him, she would tell him everything. They would mourn Timba together. Then she recalled his rage about the earring. His burning eyes, his concerns about work, money. He had never raised a hand against her. But she was terrified of what this would do to him. But as the sound grew louder, her body relaxed. It was not the soft purr of Michael's two-year-old Audi, but the rumble of a much older car. And now it had turned off down the fork in the lane that led to the other side of Kilver.

'It's OK,' she said.

'What if he comes back when we're gone?' asked Immy.

'We'll tell him we were out looking for Timba.'

They lowered the back seats of her little hatchback and heaved the dog into the space. Kate ran to the garden shed and brought back two spades. His and hers, dating from those enthusiastic days when she and Michael had just bought the house and imagined shared Sundays digging in the garden. It hadn't happened. His showed the marks of use. Hers had barely been touched. Then she ran to the boot room and pulled out two pairs of Wellington boots which she threw in the back with the bin bag and the spades. Her arm stung a bit, but she would manage. She turned off the lights in the studio.

Chapter 27

The wind had dropped, the rain had ceased, there was a sliver of moon and the cloudless black sky was peppered with stars. Its beauty brought a lump to Kate's throat. As if Timba had ever cared about stars. Yet it seemed right they should bury him on such a night. Immy was waiting ·in the passenger seat.

They set off towards town and beyond, onto the area known as Lower Moor. A few minutes' drive brought them to one of the more remote drove roads. An old car was parked in the space by the gate at the end. In the glare of the headlights, it looked abandoned. Kate jumped out and shone the light of her phone on the interior. A sleeping man was curled up under a blanket on the back seat.

'We'll try the next one,' said Kate.

They continued in silence, the ghostly white of a barn owl swooping low across the windscreen. Another drove, another turning space, another gate.

Kate turned off the lights, waited for her vision to adjust. Then she stepped round to the back of the car. The boot light glimmered as she opened the hatchback, lifted out her spade and changed into Wellington boots. Her eyes alighted on the lump in the blanket lying on the lowered seats and she swallowed hard.

'Wait here,' she said, clambering over the gate and stepping carefully across the partly flooded field towards a narrow footbridge over a drainage canal. Here there was a strip of clear ground where the dredgers had dumped the silt from the river. It was exposed, but the freshly dug clay would be perfect. Back at the car, Immy was standing ready in her father's boots. They took out their spades. Leaving Timba's body resting in the car, they climbed back over the gate and stomped across the wet field.

Immy's voice whispered through the darkness.

'Isn't it a bit open? I mean, the woods might...'

'I told you, we're not dumping him. Have you ever tried digging a three-foot hole in the middle of a wood?'

'No,' murmured Immy.

There were few sounds. The occasional scuffle and rustle of something in the riverbank, the low soughing of the wind through the line of willows along the drainage channel, the hoot and squeals of owls. They started to dig through the fresh mud and clay.

'Is your arm all right?' asked Immy.

'It's fine. I can barely feel it.'

It was a lie. The stinging had turned to burning, but the rhythmic effort of digging seemed to dilute the pain so that after a while it turned to a dull throb. Every few minutes they stopped and leant on their spades. Progress slowed as the hole deepened and the ground became more compacted.

'What if someone finds him?' asked Immy in a whisper. 'It'll be obvious we've been digging.'

Kate reassured her. 'They're dredging all the time here. I'm always walking past new patches. And the guys in the excavators never get out to see the mess they're making. It changes from day to day.' She wasn't sure if what she said was accurate.

When the hole was deep enough they returned to the car for the body, tried and failed to heave it over the gate. Kate felt for the bolt and metal clasp and managed to swing it open. It made a loud squeak. Back at the spot where they'd been digging, they unwrapped him and Kate fell onto her knees on the cold ground.

'I need to say goodbye.'

He was already stiffening. She leant forward and kissed the face between the eyes, just below the point where the skull had been battered. Then she pulled off her jacket and T-shirt, and dug her teeth into the thinly woven cotton, ripped off part of a sleeve and placed it by his head.

Together they tugged the blanket closer to the hole. Then, each holding a corner, they lowered him gradually down.

'Let him go,' said Kate. And they pulled the blanket away. His stiffening body tumbled into the makeshift grave. Immy aimed her torch into the hole. Kate couldn't bear to look. Instead, she began shovelling back the silt and clay, tamping it down. Then she flashed her own phone torch over the plot. It looked so newly dug, so obviously different. She knelt again and placed her hand on the cold clay as a sudden gust of wind rushed through the willows. Spots of rain followed.

'We should go,' she said.

In the darkness, Kate could just make out Immy removing something from her pocket and dropping to her knees. She laid her hand on the newly turned ground.

'What are you doing?'

'It's a piece of quartz,' replied Immy, straightening. 'I carry it with me. For luck. You never know when you might need it.'

—

Back in the car, Kate said, 'I don't know what I would have done without you.' Immy said nothing and she added, 'You're a good person, Immy.'

'Not that good.'

'You've always been good to me.'

'Have I?' Her voice sounded as if it was coming from far away, as if she were trying to work something out.

'Come on, I'll drop you back.'

They drove in silence down the empty drove road and through the quiet town. It was past ten and everyone seemed to be safely in their houses. She pulled up outside the front door of Jo's flat, turned off the engine and waited, expecting Immy to open the passenger door and get out. But she made no move, and only said, 'Can I ask you something?'

'Ask away.'

'It might sound a bit weird.'

'For God's sake. It's not like we're hiding anything from each other after all this.'

'When you heard about Steve, how did you feel?'

It was a strange question, but she could only answer with the truth. 'Devastated. Everyone was. He was so young. Two kids. A wife.'

'Not a bit relieved?'

'God, no. He might have caused me problems. But no, of course not. That would be a terrible thing to feel. I know I've done bad things, but I'm not that bad.'

'Only people have mixed feelings.' Immy was right. But how could Kate admit such a thing. Even to herself. 'Did you ever find out more about what happened?'

'He was in the wrong place at the wrong time. It was a terrible accident. Why, have you heard anything?'

Immy was in the cafe all day. She might have picked up rumours.

'No. It's just that, like Dad said, it's always someone's fault. Unless it's an act of God.'

Immy was staring through the windscreen into the darkness. Then she leant towards Kate who opened her arms. They held each other tight. Immy was trembling and Kate thought she heard a sob. Then Immy pulled away, wiped her face and opened the passenger door.

She said, 'Good luck with Dad. Let me know how it goes.'

And she walked across the garden, unlocked the front door and disappeared into the house.

Part Two

Chapter 28

The email was brief, peremptory:

> Meeting today. 5.30pm. All tenants expected
> to attend.

It was three years since the last full chambers' meeting, and then they'd hired an outside hall. This afternoon they fitted easily into the large conference room. He counted. Twenty-seven. It was not enough. An equal number had already left. Some to the new Legal Practice Partnership that had offered Gillian a place. Others to larger sets in London. From an original team of ten, only two clinical negligence specialists remained. Himself and Patrick, a bachelor in late middle age who was rarely seen either in court or around chambers, and whose entries in the chambers' diary were even more sparse than Michael's own. It would be absurd to rely on Patrick.

There was only one issue for discussion. How would chambers survive with so few members? The central Bristol premises were too large, too expensive.

Michael looked about him. There was a rough and ready arrogance to the criminal lawyers in their sweaty waistcoats and open-necked, collarless shirts. The women wore tight blouses and either too much make-up or not enough. One had long, black-painted nails which she waved like claws as she spoke. He thought wistfully of his former colleagues. Civil lawyers had an elegance you didn't find in the criminal bunch. Men and women in well-cut suits with a poise in demeanour, detachment in their speech. They'd all buggered off. Leaving Michael with the dregs.

How could he contemplate taking on criminal cases? All those new rules and statutes. He'd have to start at the bottom. Road traffic, minor pub brawls. There was something painful about a middle-aged man defending pub brawlers and boy racers. It was a young man's game. No, a young woman's game. The women were raking in the criminal work these days, snapping up the sex abuse cases.

As for family law, domestic violence, divorce, child abuse – how could you maintain objectivity in the heat of all that emotion? He'd always felt more comfortable with professional clients.

Words swirled about him. Someone was talking about the importance of recruiting more members. More noisy family and criminal lawyers.

And now Patrick was speaking.

'Difficult as this may be for my fellow tenants, it comes at an appropriate time for me. I propose to take early retirement.'

There was a shocked silence. Barristers did not take early retirement. They worked till they dropped. The man must have a private income.

'Michael?' asked Adrian. 'I realise this puts you in an unenviable position.'

What did they expect him to say? Why had he even bothered to come?

'I'll need to consider my options.'

'Of course.'

He sat out the rest of the meeting with little sense of what was discussed or decided. There were two votes. He abstained on both and left chambers without saying goodnight to anyone. What was there to say?

A walk might clear his roaring head and he set out for the station on foot. His options were few. He could hang on at Great Court, pick up what little work arrived in his field, while starting a new practice in family and crime. Family and crime. The bottom of the barristers' pecking order.

Option two. Resign and look for another tenancy. He might try commercial or company law, but legal Bristol was a small place and any failure to get into another set would soon become public knowledge. There was only one decent Legal Professional Partnership and they had already poached his colleagues and failed to invite him. There might be something in London, but he'd never get Kate to move.

One other option drifted into his tired mind, as soothing as the summer breeze that softened the gritty traffic-fumed air. He could give up the lot.

A drink would help. Or two or three. In the station bar, he gulped down a double G and T. He picked up a can in the shop, sipping the over-sweet mix as the train rolled through the dull towns and suburbs of North Somerset. He imagined the comforts of home. Kate would be waiting for him with a plate of something tasty and a glass of decent wine. They'd sit out on the terrace in the evening light, and she'd ask about his day with genuine interest and this time he would tell her everything. He'd tried to tell her that evening after the art fair, but she'd been distracted as usual, not really listening. Though she was keen enough for him to listen to her when she had a point to make. Like that business with Immy. Her words still rankled: 'Women are not obsessed with sex like men are.'

It was a provocation and he'd done well to walk away. He couldn't imagine her turning away if he spent the night with a young woman. Or worse, heaven forbid, a young man. And she was the one who had the cheek to talk about double standards. But he mustn't let himself get riled up. When she realised what was at stake she would have to listen.

Then he remembered Immy was coming over. It would make it difficult to speak freely. He needed another drink.

The train was stationary on the westbound track at Weston-super-Mare station. Had been for at least ten minutes. He would be late for supper, though Kate would have kept something for him. His stomach was rumbling, and his mouth tasted stale from the G and T.

A voice sounded over the tannoy. Passengers raised their eyes from their screens. The train was being held here due to an incident at Highbridge. A few people pulled out mobile phones and began texting or speaking loudly to their invisible partners. There was no indication as to how long they would be stuck nor of the nature of the incident at Highbridge. No one was prowling the aisle to answer questions. Did they even have guards on these trains? You rarely saw a ticket collector after eight p.m.

The last thing he needed was a delay after the day he'd had. God knows what time he'd get home.

He rang Kate's number but there was no reply. He texted.

Train delayed. I'll keep you posted.

The train didn't budge. He had bought a paper in Bristol but by now he had read all he wanted to read. The woman in the seat opposite him, elegantly dressed and with blunt-cut blonde hair, was strikingly pretty, early thirties, plugged into a film or TV programme, smiling and laughing. Her hands were small and beautifully manicured with pale pink nails. She wore two gold rings, one plain, one diamond and sapphire. Unlike Kate whose hands were broad and strong, whose nails were short and unvarnished, who preferred not to wear her wedding ring as it got coated with clay dust. The woman must have sensed him looking at her because she glanced up and smiled. He smiled back and she lowered her eyes. You didn't speak to people on trains in the twenty-first century. You just fantasised about their lives. He opened his Sudoku.

–

It was past eleven o'clock when he reached the farmhouse. A single light had been left on in the studio, but the house was dark. And where was Kate's car?

He parked and stepped out into the wide beam of the security light. He stood awhile, waiting for the light to go out. When his eyes had adjusted he looked up as he always did when he came home late. There was only a sliver of moon in a coal-black sky studded with glittering stars. After the worldly concerns of Bristol, it was soothing to look out on the infinite. Perhaps Kate had been tempted out. He remembered her telling him she had once gone out in the evening to listen to nightingales, how she knew a place where you could see glow worms. He tried to imagine her with Immy, scrambling along in the dark seeking out the little creatures in a hedgerow. Nature rambles didn't sound much like Immy. And they would have ended up in the pub.

He unlocked the front door and walked into the empty, silent house. No welcoming bark. So, Timba was with them.

Half a loaf of bread had been left on the counter. Next to it, a lump of Cheddar, butter in its foil wrap. Crumbs. A dirty knife. Nothing decent for his supper and she hadn't even bothered to tidy up. He'd told her he might be late. It wasn't his fault the trains were messed up. She might have waited. Glow worms or no glow worms. It felt like a deliberate slight.

He sliced bread and cheese and looked in the fridge. Behind the ageing leftovers, he found an ancient jar of pickle. He slopped a spoonful on his plate and sat down at the table with a glass of water. His appetite had vanished. He gulped some water and called Kate again. After a few rings it went to voicemail. He tried Immy and the same thing happened. He stared at the bread and cheese and contemplated going to the pub, walking into a room full of locals he didn't know, looking for his wife and daughter. He would feel like a fool.

He went into the sitting room and turned on the TV, scrolling through iPlayer for the latest episode of the predictable thriller he and Kate had watched together a few nights ago. He sat through ten minutes, realising he was taking nothing in. Then, just as he was about to give up, the protagonist opened an app on his mobile phone. A road map flashed across the TV screen, flicking a switch in Michael's tired head. It was obvious. Why hadn't he thought of it before?

He reached for his laptop, opened the Google search bar and typed, *how to track a mobile phone*.

Chapter 29

Something was wrong. Seriously wrong. Kate stood in the kitchen doorway staring at him out of redrimmed eyes. Her long, curly hair was sticking out around her head where it had come out of its clasp, and there were muddy marks on one cheek as if she'd been gardening and wiping her hands on her face.

'Jesus, Kate, what happened?'

'I lost Timba.'

'What do you mean you "lost Timba"? Where?'

'I was out in the woods with him. Up near the Ministry of Defence range. You know how he likes to chase scents. He always comes back. Only this time he didn't.'

Her voice sounded forced, rasping, as if she had swallowed something rough. It was then that he noticed her jacket was torn and there was dirt on her trousers. She hadn't moved from the doorway. It was as if she were waiting for the right words from him. He had no idea what those words should be.

'Aren't you going to say anything?' she asked.

Under the bright kitchen lights her face looked so pale it was almost transparent. He could see the cheek bones, the jaw bones, realised how thin she had become. She would be looking for words of comfort but all he could say was, 'Where's Immy?'

'She came over on the bus and there was no one here. I was still out looking. She called me and I came back to pick her up. We had some bread and cheese and set out to look again. I've just dropped her home. She was upset.'

'Why didn't you answer your phone when I called? Why didn't you call me back?'

'I knew you were in a work meeting and... I was scared what you would say. I thought we'd find him. Or maybe he'd just come home.' She walked over to the table, reached for his glass of water, took a long gulp and sat down.

He said, 'I'll come out with you. He might have got trapped somewhere. Or hurt himself. There's corrugated iron near the path, old sheds and water-tanks. Remember when our neighbour's dog fell down the well?'

He was shocked when she said, 'I'm completely exhausted. I should just go to bed.'

He stood up to fill the kettle, waiting for her to say more, but she was silent. When he turned back to face her she was staring down at the table, tracing small circles on the wood with her finger. She had taken off her jacket and he noticed a large plaster stained with blood on her left forearm.

'What happened to your arm?'

'Oh that. Stupid. My hand slipped. I was using one of those metal tools. I wasn't thinking.'

'Shall I look at it?'

'No, it's fine. Not deep or anything. It'll heal.'

He was unconvinced, though he wasn't going to argue. Kate was left-handed, so it was surprising she would injure that arm. And it was unlike her to hurt herself at work.

'Did you call the police? The RSPCA?' he asked.

'Of course.' The words came out sharp, clipped, as if he were accusing her of something.

'What did they say?'

And now her voice sounded flat, mechanical. She spoke fast. It was as if the words had been pre-recorded, rehearsed.

'They took my mobile number. I gave them a description. Apparently dogs go walkabout all the time. Sometimes they disappear for months. Mostly they just go home... I thought I'd see him waiting outside the door.'

There was a dislocation between the content of her speech and the expression on her face. This might be the effect of trauma. But would trauma explain her inability to meet his gaze? She was staring at the wall, everything about her taut and strained, and he found himself thinking that for a beautiful woman she could, on occasion, look quite ugly. Was she waiting for him to open his arms? It felt more as if she was pushing him away and he heard himself say, 'Why didn't you keep an eye on him?' Her features stiffened further, and he turned back to the mugs and poured boiling water on the tea bags. 'Sorry. I shouldn't have said that. I'm not blaming you.'

He returned to the table with the tea and set hers down in front of her. She said, 'Don't think I haven't been beating myself up all evening.'

He didn't know what to think. She still wasn't meeting his eye.

'Are you sure you're all right?'

She touched the plaster on her arm. 'It's fine. It's nothing.'

'I don't mean physically. I mean is something on your mind? You don't usually slip up at work. And losing Timba. I thought you'd been feeling better...'

'Don't start on me, Michael. I'm all over the place. I've just lost the one thing I really…' She stopped.

'OK. We won't talk any more. We'll go out together tomorrow. I'm not in court. We'll ask around at the big farms. Someone must have seen him. There's a phone number on the notice board at the MOD. I can see you don't want your tea. Go to bed. I'll check Timba's not waiting outside and then I'll join you.'

'Forgive me, Michael. I know I've been difficult.'

'I knew when I married you. We can both be difficult.'

She stood up, paused for a few seconds as if waiting for something. Then she turned away and left the room.

He continued to sit at the table, staring ahead of him, a crushing weight across his shoulders. His head was pounding, a jagged pain running through his eye, his cheek, his teeth, his jaw. He sat with his head in his hands, waiting for it to pass. Occasionally he took a sip of water. He'd had no other drink since the G and T on the train, no food apart from the corner of cheese and bite of bread. He had no urge for alcohol. When the pain eased sufficiently for him to ask himself what he wanted, the word that came to him was 'peace'.

He raised his head and remembered he had promised to check for Timba. As he had anticipated, the dog was not there. If he had been, he would have barked to be let in. But Michael was glad to get out. The air smelt pure and soft, and when the security light faded the carpet of stars appeared even brighter than before as night reached its darkest hour. The single light in the studio was still burning and he crossed the drive, intending to switch it off.

As he opened the door and walked in, he felt like an intruder in a private world. Yet he had paid for every pane of glass, every inch of green oak flooring. Everything. Because she was his wife. And because she was his wife, there should be no private world.

The studio smelt of incense. He even knew the name, Oriental Opium. She'd bought it from one of those hippy shops in Glastonbury, telling him it reminded her of her misspent youth. The truth was she used it to disguise the smell of dope. And though she knew what he thought of drugs, she continued to smoke when he wasn't around. Her silent protest. Kate's insistence that she wouldn't be controlled.

Near the entrance stood the dog she had mentioned, ears and tail flying. It was detailed work, but he would not want it in his living room and was glad she was selling it. He scanned the heads that lined the shelves. Mostly student work. Something jolted inside him as his gaze lighted on the full-size human skeleton dangling from a beam in one corner. Then he remembered. It was a teaching aid, along with the replica male and female skulls.

He was about to turn out the lights and leave when some impulse took him through the narrow opening into the storeroom. The shelves, here, were crowded with Kate's own work; a reclining nude that he suspected was Immy, though the face was indistinct; small horses and dogs which Kate had been unable to sell at the art fair, a few cracked heads on their armatures. Eventually the heads would be smashed with a mallet and dropped in the recycling tub which was squashed in the corner next to the miniature kiln.

One unusual object caught his eye, a broken male head leaning against the wall. The ragged edge ran from the temple, through the eye and cheek to the jaw, a visual expression of the way he had been feeling in the kitchen.

For a moment he wondered if the face could be his own. But no, this was a younger man. Probably one of those stray youths she had spotted in the street, who were all too happy to pose while she took their photographs from different angles. It was a dangerous habit. Michael had warned her. One day it would get her into difficulties.

He turned off the lights and stood in the drive for a few seconds. The sky was dark enough to make out the Milky Way, the constellations. He creaked his neck, momentarily calmed at the thought of his insignificance.

He slept fitfully, waking just after three a.m. Kate was sleeping soundly. For a while he lay awake, staring into the darkness, ruminating. The pain across his head had returned, like an axe in his skull. After a few minutes, he picked up his phone and padded to the bathroom.

He swallowed a couple of ibuprofen and sat on the edge of the bath. Then he opened the tracker app and tapped in Kate's number as Target. He was presented with a stylised map of white roads, wooded areas in green, rivers and rhynes in blue. His own location was indicated by a black arrow. His Target was a red arrow immediately beside his own. That would be Kate's phone, sitting on the bedside table a few metres away.

And there was another feature to the app. He hadn't noticed it earlier. By opening a different page, you could see not only the current location of your Target, but your Target's movements over the last forty-eight hours.

He followed Kate's progress through the day. She had been out in the morning on a short walk around the village. But she had spent the rest of her day in the house and the studio, and there was no record of a drive to the MOD range. She had left the house at about 9:40 p.m. and meandered around Lower Moor for about twenty minutes before stopping on a drove road near the riverbank. Here she had remained for more than an hour before passing through the town, presumably to drop off Immy, if indeed she had been with Immy. He was beginning to wonder if he could believe a word she said.

As he stared at the record of her day, so different from the story she had told him, he realised the pain in his head had lifted. In its place came a pounding in his chest, a new constriction in his throat. Timba had disappeared and her grief for the dog was genuine. But unless the app was faulty, almost everything else she had told him was wrong. He sat on the edge of the bath, staring, wondering. He would confront her. But his barrister training was never far away. Never ask a question if you don't know the answer. Before he confronted her, he would find out why she had lied.

Chapter 30

The following day they searched for Timba in the woods on the hill. Michael said nothing about the app, only watched Kate's face as she suggested different paths, telling him she had crossed into Ministry of Defence land in the early evening. If it hadn't been for the app, he would have believed her. And for the first time he began to wonder if the app itself was faulty. It was just a bit of free technology. He had no assurance of its accuracy. There might have been some difficulty in connecting in this woodland area. The MOD itself might have created deliberate interference to prevent unauthorised persons mapping the range.

A storm was rising, and the canopy swayed and creaked in the wind. After a break for lunch in a pub, during which neither of them said much, they drove to the moor. The river was still tidal here. Work on the downstream barrier was not yet complete and even in summer the water could break its banks at high tide. Remembering the location on the tracker, Michael deliberately led them towards the spot where the app indicated Kate had stopped the night before. A caterpillar digger was piling up silt on the raised bank. Kate walked past it and stared towards the muddy, swirling river. He studied her face, trying to remember when she'd last looked so sad. Then it came to him. It was the morning he'd woken beside her on blood-soaked sheets and realised she'd lost another baby. Something moved inside him, and he had an urge to reach out for her but then with a horrible jolt he remembered the lies she'd told. His arm stayed rigid by his side.

They knocked on the doors of farmhouses and spoke to the occupiers. No one had seen a lone brown dog. They posted messages on local Facebook groups, stuck notices on trees and telegraph poles, received several false alerts.

Timba had been neutered so would be no use for breeding. But he was a handsome beast and an unscrupulous passer-by might be tempted to hang onto him.

'Pikeys,' muttered one of the farmers. 'They'll take what they can find.'

Kate looked like she was about to take issue. But this was not a moment for principled discussion. Michael quickly thanked the man and led her out.

'Maybe someone decent will find him. The number's on the tag isn't it?'

She said, 'It might be hard to decipher. It's pretty old and worn.' Michael didn't ask why she hadn't replaced the old tag. 'Anyway,' she added. 'It could have slipped off. You know the way he burrows in the undergrowth. He's lost several that way.'

On the second day it was raining. Kate said she would go to her studio to take her mind off things. She had a class tomorrow and stuff to prepare.

'I haven't given up. I just don't know where to go, what to do. Work seems the only thing.'

'I'll make another call to the dog warden,' said Michael. The man was encouraging.

'Nine times out of ten they come back. Better to stay put at home. Don't worry. I've got the picture and the description. I'll let you know if he turns up.'

Kate looked doubtful. 'Sometimes it feels like we'll never find out.'

'We're doing what we can.'

'I bet he's been stolen.'

'Maybe.'

'You're not very encouraging.'

'What the hell am I supposed to do? You lost him.'

'Michael, that's all I need. Can't you see what this is doing to me?'

He could. And that was why he went into his study to be alone.

For over twenty-four hours he hadn't looked at his emails. Most of the messages were dispiriting. No work had come in. There was an email from the woman with black fingernails, asking if he proposed joining the chambers' relaunch in the new premises. Each member was asked to put £5000 towards the deposit. Thereafter there would be monthly rental payments. He would be very welcome. No mention of where the work was coming from or how he was supposed to pay.

He pulled up websites of other chambers in Bristol. There were no advertised vacancies, though a couple of places stated they would always consider applications from senior barristers with established practices. A shiver ran through him as he realised this no longer applied to him.

How had it happened? Jack did his best to bring the work in. But clients had turned their back on him. True there had been one or two shoddy performances, a couple of poorly managed conferences. But that was all. And even then he had done well for his client. Wasn't that what it was about? The truth was, his area of work was too specialist. Protracted cases were expensive, and the NHS was finding other ways of resolving complaints. Plus, and this was the worst of it, he'd been superseded by a new generation of quick-thinking, digital-savvy youngsters. Until now he'd not even considered how precarious it all was. He'd have to sell Bristol. Maybe even the farmhouse.

And yet as he stared at another dispiriting bank statement he realised none of this mattered. What mattered was Kate. Michael and Kate. If he and Kate were strong, they would manage on what they had. They would never be destitute. They wouldn't need a large house and a fancy kitchen to hold them together. But as he looked through the columns of meaningless squiggle, he knew what he had known for months, he had already lost the Kate he had fallen in love with.

He thought about the moment he first saw her in the gallery. Tall and striking standing out from the crowd with her mane of red hair. He was about to ask the gallery owner to introduce them but there was no need. Kate approached him herself. Later he reminded himself it was her job to approach potential buyers, but she'd made him feel it was for other reasons. He remembered their jokey banter about the artworks. How their different opinions felt like the start of a game he needed to win. And, looking back, he realised she had let him win, luring him in with her wide green eyes and attentive listening. And he'd been happy to be lured. Over the years the listening diminished. But the game never stopped. Kate always played games. And he would find out what game she was playing now.

He jumped as he heard her calling out across the hall.

'Miiiiichael.' He hated her shouting like this. Just as he hated her barging into his study. Her head was round his door. 'I'm going to Waitrose. I need to get out and take my mind off things. I'll stock up the freezer and get something nice for dinner. Buy some decent wine.'

'OK.'

'Might stop at a few pubs on the way and put up posters.'

'Fine.'

'Oh for God's sake, Michael, is that all you can say?'

'Good luck.'

She made a face and shut the door. Why had she decided to drive so far? She could have gone to the local Tesco, two miles down the road. Waitrose was a forty-five-mile round trip down the motorway. Timba could easily run forty-five miles in a day, but would he really make a beeline for Waitrose?

They had an account. It hadn't been paid for two months. The shop would surely stop her payment. Good. She would find out what he had meant to tell her months ago. By the time she confronted him, the truth would have sunk in. There was nothing left.

He heard the front door bang. Suddenly hungry, he went to the kitchen and made himself a peanut butter sandwich, opening World of Warcraft and eating in front of the screen. After about an hour he had started to develop a headache. He closed the game, stood up, walked out of the study, and down the hall. The big house felt empty without Timba. The dog's familiar presence had been a comfort.

Standing by the front door he opened the tracker app. Kate had gone straight to the motorway and had stopped in Wellington, presumably in the Waitrose car park. It would be at least forty minutes before she returned. He crossed the drive through spitting rain and re-entered her studio for the second time in two days.

Chapter 31

He went straight to the storeroom. As he entered, he glanced again at the fired and broken head. The expression was arresting. One of the eyes was missing, but she had captured a look in the other that was rare in figurative sculpture where eyes could easily appear blank, even dead. This one was alarmingly alive. What was left of the face was vaguely familiar, but he was unable to place the model.

He opened the cupboard. Sculpting tools, glazes, chemicals, pieces of metal for constructing armatures. What had he expected? He pulled open a drawer. More tools. The next was stuffed with photographs printed on ordinary A4 paper and sorted into transparent folders. Animals. Heads. Miscellaneous.

He flipped through the animals. Mostly Timba. Running. Sleeping. Standing. He held one up and looked again. Timba was a stunning dog, with long legs and large soft eyes, a gentle soul in a tall, strong body. To his surprise he found his eyes were pricking with tears. How long was it since that had happened?

Horses, more dogs, cows, foxes. He moved on to heads. Miranda, the model. Kate's students. A couple of himself that she had taken without permission. There were several photographs of a young man. Strong-featured. Good-looking. Where had he seen him before? Then he realised.

This was the full face of the severed head balanced on the armature. Who was he? She had done this before. Spotted someone in the street and persuaded them to let her take photographs for her work. The background was blurred. It could have been anywhere. The guy could be anyone. She probably found the photos on the internet. Was he perhaps a well-known actor? There was something familiar in the striking face.

Next, miscellaneous. More portraits of unknown faces. He flipped through, unsure what he was looking for. One of the pictures jumped out at him and he paused, holding the paper up for a better light. It was a young woman, naked, long and lean with well-developed muscles, a bit like Kate. But Kate could not hold herself like this: leg raised behind her, arms outstretched like wings, head held high and proud. The face was turned away, but as he carried on looking, the old suspicions returned. Only this time his doubts were dropping away to make space for a new clarity. It was a dancer's body. Leaping, flying. And as he rummaged through the pile, even before he saw the lovely face beaming towards the camera in the final picture, he knew whose body it was.

His daughter was posing in the studio, chairs and tables stacked to make space for her private performance, natural light pouring through the skylights onto her shining skin. And as he studied the photograph, something collapsed inside him, and everything that was solid seemed to melt away until his body was a gaping emptiness but for the enormous lump that lodged in his throat.

Hadn't he always known? The hush as he entered a room when they were speaking. The tender hug. The earring in the bed. Their obvious intimacy. Immy's sudden departure. Kate's perpetual excuses. Even the story about Timba. He couldn't imagine what possible connection that might have with Immy. All he knew was that something was going on and his wife was lying to him. He had tried to delude himself that she was innocent. He was wrong. She was a liar. Her whole life was a lie. Their life was a lie.

His heart was banging against his chest as he opened another drawer. More sculpting tools, mostly wood, a few bits of metal. He didn't know what else he was looking for, only that he would know when he found it and would carry on until he did. He yanked open the bottom drawer. Scraps of paper. Sketches. Animal and human heads, detailed anatomical drawings of musculature. They were good, but of no interest to him. Then something prompted him to tug the drawer out a bit further. What he saw made his banging heart stop and swell inside him until he thought he would choke. He had to shut his eyes. Breathe. Open his eyes and look again. Behind the papers, stuffed into the furthest corner of the drawer, lay Timba's collar.

He reached in and lifted it out. The sturdy woven fabric had faded, the leather lining was cracked. There was a metal loop for the lead and another one for the ancient tag with the worn engraving, the mobile number only just decipherable. The collar was dirty. It usually was. Kate washed it occasionally, but it soon became discoloured with mud in wet weather. But this dull brown stain was not mud. The colour was too vibrant, too heavily tinged with red. It could only be blood.

He took the collar into the studio. He would be very calm and ask her to explain. As he crossed the room to one of the tall stools he felt a splat of water on his sleeve and looked up. It was dripping from a crack in the ceiling, pooling on the wooden floor. A dark patch of damp had already spread through the plaster. He moved the stool away from the leak and sat down at a worktable, listening to the rain as it drummed against the skylights. Louder and louder. He waited.

Chapter 32

The door of the studio flew open and Kate stood on the threshold, shaking the rain out of her hair.

'What are you doing in here?' she demanded.

'Waiting for you.'

'Strange place to wait.'

'I thought I'd look at your work.'

'I wonder you can even see it.'

Clouds hung heavy in the afternoon sky and the studio was veiled in a pale grey light. Kate flicked the switches next to the door, illuminating the space with dazzling brilliance. She carried on talking, words spilling out like water.

'I spent a fortune in Waitrose. There was a mess up with the account, so I paid on my card. Wiped me out.' She was smiling, a bright, fake smile, brittle and fragile as blown glass. 'We're having duck with star anise and blood orange. Quinoa and red cabbage. Plus, I found the Merlot you'd noticed in the Sunday Times Review. Come and have a drink.'

Her babbling poured out from another world, the false world she had created for them and which he had trusted for too long. She was trapped so deep in her fantasy that she hadn't even noticed the bloodstained collar on the table in front of him.

'Come here,' he said.

'Why?' She didn't like to be told what to do.

'I want you to look at this.' He gestured to the collar.

She looked and her expression froze. It took a few seconds for her to emerge from her trance, but when she did the bright smile melted, the mask collapsed, and in front of him he saw a frightened woman.

'Well?' he asked. She had bowed her head in her hands, and he couldn't see her face. 'Why don't you go back to the beginning and tell me what really happened?'

Her hands slid down. She raised her head and opened her eyes. 'The beginning...' She faltered, closing her eyes again, her face screwed hard and tight.

'Or was that so long ago you cannot even remember? Have you been lying to me ever since the wedding, ever since we met? I think you have. I think you like lying. I think you get a buzz out of it.'

She looked up at him in silent pleading, then away. He grabbed both her arms. She was wearing a short-sleeved T-shirt, and he dug his fingers into her bare flesh as he shook her hard. He would get the truth.

'Stop it. You're hurting me.'

He stopped shaking her, still holding her arms.

'Let go of me.'

Her eyes were wide now. The fear and hurt had switched to anger but he wouldn't let go.

'First, you tell me what happened on Wednesday. Timba was still here when I left for Bristol.' He let go of one arm and held up the collar. 'And as far as I recall he was wearing this.'

'I'll tell you everything, if you let go of my arm.'

He released his hold and dropped his hand, but he did not take his eyes off her. He had glimpsed her lies before. Now he saw them clearly. And he would discover the truth that lay behind them. He spoke in a low voice, accentuating every word as if she might not understand her own language.

'What happened to Timba?'

'Timba's dead,' she said. He felt no shock. In his heart he had known from that moment when they stood on the riverbank and he saw her sadness. He waited for her to speak again. 'A woman called Tamsin killed him.'

'Go on.'

The name sounded familiar. He wasn't sure why. He was standing close to her now. If she tried to move away, he had only to extend a hand to stop her – she would tell him everything.

'Tamsin came to the studio.' She stopped, gulped, carried on, the words coming out in little bursts. 'She accused me of killing her husband. Timba must have picked up on her aggression. He just went for her. I doubt he would have hurt her, you know what he's like...' she paused, '...was like. But he was growling and jumping up.'

Anger rose inside him. It was throbbing, spreading from his stomach through the furthest reaches of his body. Yet he kept his voice calm, as if he were speaking to a difficult child.

'You'll need to tell me why she came. Why she believed you'd killed her husband. You realise that, don't you, Kate? You're going to tell me every fucking detail.'

And she began. Tamsin's husband was the man in the photos. His name was Steve. Michael flinched when she said the name. But he didn't touch her, let her go on.

And the story she told him almost hung together. It was the kind of daft thing she would do. Invite a stranger into the house. Take photos of him. Give him cups of tea. Let him have her card. Her phone number. Then turn shocked when the stranger read more into it. But there was a flaw.

'So, if her allegation is all bollocks, why lie to me? Why not tell me about the guy? Why keep quiet when you heard he was dead?'

He glared at her, waiting for the reply which didn't come. He had kept the fury out of his voice, but he could hear the volume rising as he continued.

'...then his wife comes in and kills your dog. That's a criminal offence. Even you know that. Why not go to the police like any normal person?'

'I was scared what you might think. I didn't want to worry you. I knew you were having problems at work.'

'Bloody hell. Now it's my work. That's a good one.'

'I was trying to protect you.'

'From what?'

She didn't answer. He could prompt her, but he needed it from her.

She was silent. Her right eye twitched as it sometimes did when she was nervous. He waited until he could wait no longer and grabbed her arms again, looking hard into her eyes. So hard it seemed he could see inside her, into the chaos and lies behind that once beautiful, calm exterior. And the Immy pictures started to feel irrelevant. There may have been something there, a flirtation, perhaps even intimate games. But Immy had left and was living with Jo. There was something else. Something that had led to the death of their dog, and which would expose the truth behind all these lies. He needed the truth, and he would get it from Kate herself.

'Forgive me, Michael. I know it was wrong. I was going through a bad patch. We both were. Losing the baby...'

'Jesus,' he snapped. 'I don't believe I'm hearing this. First my work then the baby. Are you totally incapable of taking any responsibility for your own actions?'

'I'm really sorry. I was trying to stop it. Only he kept pestering me. The last time he came he was drunk. I told him to piss off. He drove off like a mad thing. The next thing I heard he'd been killed. You remember. At the dinner party. That's why I was so upset.'

'Because you had lost your lover.'

'Because a man had died.'

'The man you'd been screwing.'

'It meant nothing, Michael. It was a casual thing. It's you I want.'

'You are so full of crap.'

And the thing he had been damping down since he first arrived back in the empty house, that he had been trying to bury, deeper and deeper with every new assault of information, surged up inside him. Even now, even when she had pushed him to the limit, he wouldn't hit her. He pulled her close. The wonderful face he thought he had loved was inches away from him, cheapened and fouled by her actions.

'Take your hands off me,' she screamed.

He did. But not before he had spat in her face. Then he tossed her to the floor like the piece of trash she was. Her side hit the edge of the table as she fell. He thought she may have bashed her head. She lay very still. Curled into a ball, eyes closed, her breath coming in quick, short pants. He wanted to kick her. To destroy her. And he knew he needed to get away.

Back in the house he grabbed his keys, wallet and jacket, drank a long glass of water and looked around him. The polished floor, the comfortable sofas, the abstract paintings, and small sculpted figures, all screamed at him under the bright recessed lighting. So carefully selected. They'd even employed a lighting designer. And now he wanted to smash everything she had ever painted or sculpted, everything they had ever chosen together.

He left the house, leaving the front door unlocked. As he walked towards his car, he stopped. No sound came from the studio. How badly was she hurt? Images crashed through his throbbing head and he realised he didn't want to know. He already knew too much. He opened the driver's door and started the engine. His heart was thumping, his hands trembling as he released the handbrake, engaged the clutch, and roared up the lane towards the main road.

Chapter 33

She was staring at a low shelf and the dusty floorboards that ran beneath the counter. A woodlouse crawled away from her, inches from her nose. Rain pattered gently on the skylight above her. She didn't try to move her head. It was enough that she could breathe, though breathing hurt, and she wondered if she had cracked a rib. If he had cracked a rib. He. Him. The scene spooled through her mind, over and over like a film on a loop. His flushed face, his eyes narrowed in rage. Where was he now? In the house? The car? She focused again on the woodlouse, travelling towards the wall. Small felt safe. Would she ever be safe again?

He hadn't hit her. Her face felt sore where she had grazed the floor. But he hadn't hit her. He had never hit her.

The roar of an engine cut through the quiet. The crunch of tyres on gravel. Loud, then fading. He must be driving away. Where to? Would he come back? Of course, he would. When? She tried to move. Toes, hands, an arm, a leg. All worked. But her head and neck ached, and when she ran her hand gently across her face it came away wet with blood and saliva.

The pain in her side was local. Bearable. Maybe it was only bruising. But as she heaved herself upright it was as if someone had thrust a dagger between her ribs. It was hard to stand, but she could stand. Just. If she leant on something.

The lights were still blazing. She dragged herself into the storeroom. Steve's smashed head was balanced on the armature. She took it down, then reached for the dog and the horse, winding each piece in bubble wrap, packing them all in a large carrier bag. Then, bending to a drawer, pain shooting through her side, she picked out a pair of long-bladed scissors.

Leaning on the counter and then the door frame for support, she edged her way out of the storeroom into the studio, the carrier bag dangling from her arm. At the place where Timba had fallen, her heart gave a jolt. She wouldn't come here again.

Her bag was on one of the tables. Amazingly, her phone was still inside. She should ring for help. Family? What family? A friend. What friend? She hadn't spoken to Jen since the encounter with Tamsin at the art fair. Kate had been waiting for Jen to call, but there'd been only silence. It wasn't like her. But Kate knew the reason. Jen was a friend of Tamsin's sister, perhaps now a friend of Tamsin. What if Tamsin showed her the marks on her neck, told her how Kate had tried to strangle her? Who else was there? The police? Not the police. They would ask too many questions. It was inconceivable to speak to anyone. She had brought all this on herself.

Outside the studio door she stood in the rain and looked back. There was nothing else she wanted from this place. She would like to douse it in petrol, set it alight and watch it burn.

Hobbling like an old woman, she dragged herself over the drive to the house. It took her so long to get there that she was drenched when she arrived. Clinging to the banister, she heaved herself upstairs. In the bathroom, she towelled her hair and swallowed four ibuprofen, stuffing the rest of the packet into an overnight wheelie, along with toothbrush and toothpaste, underwear, a change of clothes and shoes. In the mirror above the sink, she could see that her right eyebrow and cheekbone were grazed, but there looked to be no serious damage; she could still open and shut her eyes and move her jaw. She dabbed the wounds with a clean wet flannel. They would soon heal. As to the pain in her side, her rib might be cracked but that too would mend. Pulling herself up straight and telling herself to stay strong, she made her way slowly down the stairs one at a time, bumping the wheelie bag in front of her.

In the kitchen she went straight to the sink, gulped down a glass of water, and looked around. Two Waitrose bags were sitting on the floor still unpacked. The Merlot was on the side counter, other wines lined up ready to go in the cellar. The fridge was stuffed with fresh food: duck breasts in their plastic wrapping, an assortment of expensive cheeses, vegetables in the cooler. There were leftovers in Tupperware containers. The sight of it all made her nauseous. She filled up a plastic water bottle, picked up a banana, dropping both into the carrier bag with the scissors and the sculpted objects.

Through all the pain and throbbing around her eye she was still capable of thought. There was one more thing. Money.

There was no credit in her account. She was running on overdraft. What she hadn't told Michael, what she'd intended to mention after a tasty dinner and a bottle of good wine, was that there was nothing in the joint account either. Even the overdraft was exhausted. But the world of joint accounts had been shattered. She would have to manage alone.

She glanced around the sitting room. In addition to the sculpture, there was a large oil landscape she thought she might sell. But her body ached and she could hear the wind whistling and the rain hammering on the windows. This was not the night to start transporting art works. Michael might return at any moment.

She crossed the drive through the relentless rain. Then, just as she was about to get in the car she had another thought. It was unfinished. It hadn't been cast. But Jason liked the flying dog. Might he also like her flying dancer? She unlocked the studio door, holding her breath as if she couldn't bear to breathe the air Michael had polluted. Going straight for the dancer, she tucked it under one arm. For a second she closed her eyes, pained to be standing once again in this place of work that had meant so much to her, that she was now leaving behind. Then she opened her eyes and walked out, locking the studio door behind her and pocketing the key.

Even with the wipers at top speed it was hard to see the road ahead. She drove slowly, following taillights when there were any, until the car ahead of her sped away. Lorries whizzed by, crossing to the right-hand side of the road, narrowly missing oncoming traffic, blinding her with spray from enormous puddles. Flash floods arrived without warning and Kate would find herself driving through water, foot on the accelerator in the hope she would get out at the other side.

Without thinking about direction, she realised she was heading for the drove near the river, close to the spot where they had buried Timba. It crossed her mind that she might end everything now, swallow the painkillers, slash her wrist with the scissors, throw herself in the river. But it was merely a passing thought. The suicidal impulse was alien to her. Even at her worst, rebuilding after each successive miscarriage, in all her confusion and pain, the instinct to survive had prevailed.

She remembered the man sleeping in his car. Some people lived in their cars. People who had been excluded or had excluded themselves. The man had moved on, and she stopped and parked where he had parked.

The rain had eased into a faint mist, and her headlights illuminated pollarded alders and willows along the rhyne. She extinguished her lights and waited for her eyes to grow used to the dark. With so much rain, the river might have burst its banks. It might not be safe. Three days ago, the moon had been new, the time of highest tides. Fields close to the car might be sheets of water. And yet she could think no more, drive no further. Michael would never look for her here. She checked her phone. He hadn't called. No one had called. No one would know where she was. She took a swig of water and waited.

When the rain stopped she went outside to pee. There was a slight breeze and the air felt cool on her arms. The path was dotted with puddles and a few branches had broken off the trees around her. She was lucky not to have hit anything when driving, lucky nothing had fallen on her. The sky was clearing, and now the crescent moon was visible, casting a faint, silver light across the landscape, showing the outline of the willows along the riverbank, the distant line of the hills. She took out her phone and shone her flashlight across the fields. The dull shimmer was water, gleaming in the moonlight like a sheet of beaten pewter. But she was high enough to be safe here.

Her head still throbbed and her side ached, but her spirit felt strong. She was alone in the world, but she was free. The ibuprofen had clicked in and the pain had eased into a pleasing numbness. She climbed into the back seat of the car where she had left the old, grey blanket, the same blanket that had shrouded Timba and was still stained with his blood. She had meant to wash it, but everything had happened so fast. The seat was too short but with bent knees she could just fit across. Her head was jammed against a door handle, her hands tucked under her cheek. She pulled the blanket around her and under her chin. It had once covered Immy's shoulders. She and Steve had made love on it. It smelt of human and animal mingled with paint and chemicals from the days she had used it to transport artworks to the foundry. But it was all she had and it was warmth and comfort. She slept.

–

Through her good eye she watched the dawn rising. The sky was bright and the air fresh after the rain. It was five o'clock, too early to go anywhere. Her head was sore, but her thoughts were clear.

She stepped outside took a swig of water and cleaned her teeth. All around her the land was flooded. Her car was parked on a patch of higher ground at the end of the raised drove. She had been lucky not to have driven off the edge. And now she wanted tea and breakfast and ordinary things. But ordinary things had disappeared with the life she had abandoned. To start again she would need help. She opened her phone and switched on mobile data. She was £280 in the red and her limit was £500. There were no texts. No emails. Though there was a WhatsApp message. Photos. They were hard to make out in the light, so she moved out of the sun and looked again.

It was what she feared most, the photograph Kate hoped she would never see, the one he had promised to delete. She was lying naked in her own studio. The smile was drowsy, happy, stupid with sex in that split second before she had spotted the camera. She swallowed hard and looked at the others.

They were photos of Tamsin's head and shoulders, taken from the front, the side, the back. Her hair was tied back to expose her neck. And on the front of her neck, close to her windpipe, were two distinct red marks about the size of Kate's thumb. The photos from the side were taken from closer range and showed the smears of blood next to the marks. Timba's blood. The photo taken from the back showed a ring of faint discolouration, as if someone had brushed Tamsin's skin with a stripe of red-brown blusher.

Kate felt sick. She'd had no breakfast today and no supper yesterday. There was nothing to be sick with. Only some bitter tasting liquid that was rapidly filling her mouth. She bent over and vomited a thin yellow stream onto the grass. She reached for her water bottle, swilled out her mouth, took a deep and painful breath and read the brief message.

Call me.

She took another painful breath, holding the phone away from her, looking out across the flooded fields to the Polden Hills as if a fine view could blot out the shock of what she had seen. For one terrible moment she feared it could be Michael. But she looked again. The number was

Steve's. Tamsin. And as she watched the early morning sun glistening on the water, she contemplated her broken life.

Even if Jen were prepared to understand, Kate couldn't descend on her. Jen had a husband, a child. Azeem would have to clear out his office in the third bedroom to make space for her. A fuss would be made. Police would be alerted, doctors, lawyers. She would become a cog in someone else's machine.

There was only one person she could contemplate calling on. It might be the most dangerous place to go. But they could lock the door. And it would only be for a few days until she worked out where to go next. She would look for work. Cleaning. Gardening. The sort of work you could do around here. Maybe they would offer her something in the foundry. Moulding and casting, working with bronze resin and plaster and clay. Other people's clay. She might even change her name.

Immy would be asleep. The cafe opened at seven a.m., but Immy had bagged all the late shifts. Kate smiled as she remembered Immy's grumpy breakfast rule: 'Don't speak to me or expect me to speak before ten a.m.' Well, Kate wouldn't speak. She would wait a little longer and just turn up.

She walked around the car. It was cool, and she kept the blanket on her shoulders as she raised her face to the morning sun. Birdsong rang in her ears, and the air was pure and fresh after so much rain. Something stirred in the bushes and out jumped a young deer, perfectly poised head, long legs, graceful as a dancer. It splashed across the field towards her, stopped, stared at her. Should it not have escaped to higher ground? Kate was spellbound by its fragile beauty as she watched it leap into cover.

Hope ran through her. She would like to sculpt it, capture that magic encounter of beast and human. And with that thought came the image of Timba, leaping with equal grace through a field of corn. And as she remembered his horrible death, she felt a stab of anguish but this time the pain was different. This time there was no anger towards Tamsin. Timba had found the wolf in him and any human would have reacted that way. And then she remembered Immy's words, quoting Michael: 'There's always fault. Unless it's an act of God.' Poor Timba. If it was anyone's fault it was Kate's. She had destroyed everything.

But the moment of self-pity soon passed as the instinct to survive re-emerged. She thought, as she often did in moments of crisis, of her father. He was lost now, sunk in booze, but he had encouraged her once. When she'd been small, when it had mattered. And when she came through this, and somehow she knew she would, she would go to him, rediscover him, try to make things work again. Her mother too, in her quiet way, had tried to give Kate confidence. Somewhere, way back, she had been lucky with what they'd given her.

She straightened. Apart from the pain in her ribs, worse when she coughed or breathed deeply, she sensed no other serious injury, only tenderness around her eye and aching down the side of her face where she had fallen. She ate the banana, swallowed three ibuprofen, cleaned her teeth for the second time, and drove to the town.

–

Immy and Jo had the ground floor of a house on the same estate as Tamsin's. Steve had mentioned the name of the street and she'd already looked it up on Google maps. If she chose to visit his widow, it would be an easy walk between the two houses.

'Where the poor people live,' Immy had informed her with a meaningful look.

Immy and Jo had only one bedroom, but they had a sofa, and that sofa would be freely offered. Through them she would find a way forward. From her conversations with Immy it was clear that Jo had lots of friends; she knew young people on the move, people with few possessions who sofa-surfed and house-shared or lived in vans. They negotiated their way around the housing crisis by skimming the edges of society. Work might be casual and precarious, but they looked out for each other. A bit like herself in her twenties when she'd drifted from job to job. Galleries, waitressing, a bowling alley. She'd made good money working on a super yacht.

Her messy pre-Michael history tumbled in her head as she pulled up outside Immy's door. Art school had been fun, but it had been no preparation for the real world, the world of joblessness and overdrafts and sleeping on the back seat of her car.

She crossed the small, tidy front garden, rang the bell, waited, and rang again. Then, as she was about to turn away, the door slowly opened and Immy appeared in a long towelling dressing gown. Her hair was sticking out all around her face and her eyes were ringed with the make-up she had failed to remove the night before. Kate felt a wave of affection for her sleepy stepdaughter. But she remembered Immy's rule about speaking before ten, so she said nothing, only tried to smile, forgetting that smiling would hurt, moving her face as far as she could before everything got stuck. It was Immy who broke the rule.

'What the hell has he done to you?'

Chapter 34

'I'm not blaming him,' said Kate.

'How can you say that?' said Jo, her eyebrows high, her eyes round with incredulity.

'He didn't actually hit me.'

'Oh, for God's sake. Have you looked in a mirror recently?'

She had, half an hour ago, when she'd showered and changed, and what yesterday had looked like a minor injury had expanded overnight into a multi-coloured geological map. The pain in her side felt much the same. She didn't need to tell them about the rib. But both watched her slow, painful movements and must be drawing their own conclusions.

They were sitting in Jo and Immy's tiny kitchen area, hands wrapped around coffee cups, elbows resting on the small wooden table. Kate had thought she was hungry but after half a piece of toast she felt full.

'Swallow it down. I've got more in the toaster,' said Immy, watching her with what felt like motherly concern. The women were kind, attentive, though Kate could have done without Jo's forceful pronouncements on gender relations. There was a time for sexual politics. And it was not when you were stuck in the middle of them. When Immy had rung to tell her girlfriend what had happened,

Jo immediately asked a colleague to cover for her and scooted home.

'It was my fault,' Kate was saying.

'I don't believe I'm hearing this.' Jo's voice rose a notch and she covered her eyes with her hands. 'Have we learnt nothing from three waves of feminism?'

'Don't give her a hard time...' pleaded Immy. 'Lesbians get jealous too.'

'It was a bit more than...' started Jo. But then she smiled and shook her head. 'Sorry, Kate. I know I can come over heavy. Only... seeing you like this. It touches a nerve.'

At that moment Immy moved towards Jo, tilting her face and kissing her. When they separated, Jo spoke again and this time she sounded warm and welcoming. 'You can stay here as long as you like. There's not much space but...' and she waved her hand around the cramped ground floor flat, 'what's ours is yours.'

'Thank you. You've been so good to me. I hope it won't be for too long.'

She nibbled her toast and felt the scrutiny of two pairs of eyes.

'Are you going to the doctor?' asked Immy.

'No. I'll be fine.'

'You should, just for the record,' said Jo. 'That way if he tries anything again...'

'He won't.'

'You don't know that.'

Immy stood up, walked over to the sink, and began scrubbing her coffee cup. And Kate reminded herself they were talking about her father; it must be painful for Immy to hear him spoken of as if he were just another violent man. Then the young woman put down the cup and spun round with that balletic grace that was so wonderful to watch.

'What are you going to do, Kate? I don't mean about the doctor, I mean all the other stuff, your work, your students.'

Jo frowned. 'It's a bit early for those kinds of decisions.'

'It's OK,' said Kate. There was a directness in Immy that Kate had come to love. 'I can't go back to the studio. Not now. Too much has happened there. I'll tell the students something, I'm not sure what. Then I'll refund their fees and return their work. I'll need to find a job. I thought maybe cleaning.'

As soon as she said it, she thought of her own cleaner. Sally was due at the house today. She was honest and hard-working and would let herself in, unpack the Waitrose bags and give the house a thorough clean, expecting to be paid next week. Kate had Sally's address and phone number, but rather than ring, she would go and see her. She would pay her what was owing, then she would have to tell her, face to face, that they wouldn't need her any more. And with that came the horrible realisation that it wasn't just a grazed and bruised face, a cracked rib and a night in a car. Her whole life was turned upside down. Other people would suffer. Unless something could be salvaged. But it was too painful even to think of that.

'What about the gallery guy?' said Immy. 'You told me he was interested.'

He was. And at that moment her work seemed like the only true thing about her. She felt herself smile and nod as she answered.

'I'll call him.'

She looked in her wallet. The card was still there. Jason had made the first move towards a professional

248

relationship. It was time to take herself seriously. For too long she'd been busy creating the fantasy home, spending Michael's money on a fancy kitchen and an absurdly large studio. Creating a space that people could see and admire. As for her sculpture, she had destroyed most of it. The animals had been her first small successes. People had started asking for models of their pets. Now finally, a dealer had seen a spark of originality.

If he liked what she showed him, she might give him the keys to the house and studio, invite him to drive over and pick up anything he thought he could sell. He might like the oils. All she needed to tell him was that she and Michael had fallen out and she couldn't face going back to the house. Jo's voice interrupted her thinking.

'Are you going to the police?'

And at that moment, she wished there had been somewhere else to go, somewhere silent and private where no one knew her, no one asked what she intended to do next.

'I can't face it. They'd want to know everything.'

She thought of the photos she had seen a few hours ago and not looked at since. She didn't need to. They were printed on her mind, her naked body, the bloodstains on Tamsin's neck, the reddish-brown pressure points.

'At least call a solicitor. I can give you the number of a good one,' said Jo. 'She'll get you an injunction. Stop him coming after you. We don't want him sniffing around here. Sorry, Immy. It must be hard for you to hear all this.'

But going to a solicitor would be just as bad. 'I hear what you say, Jo. But I can't do that. Everything would escalate. I'd become a victim, passive. I don't want to lose control.'

Jo was studying her with hard, questioning eyes and Kate knew she was thinking… you are a victim. But she said nothing, and Kate carried on.

'I'll have to talk to Michael at some point. I'm aware of that. And I'm sure he's regretting what… happened.' She couldn't bring herself to say, 'what he did.' She'd told them about the shaking, even the push. But she'd minimised it, suggested she'd slipped on a piece of wet clay. 'He'll be sulking in Bristol. Watching movies, playing computer games.'

Immy was staring at her. The look was disconcerting. It reminded her of Jen, prompting in her that old need to pull away from the people who loved her, that old fear that they might see what lingered deep inside her. And when Immy spoke, there was an urgency and conviction in her tone which Kate had not heard before.

'Jo's right. You should get an injunction. Just in case. If you don't want to go to the doctor, we can take some pictures for evidence.'

Kate recoiled inwardly. Much as she loved Immy, she didn't like the way she was trying to organise her. In coming here, she'd hoped they'd let her be. She was wrong.

'Michael was in shock. Finding Timba's collar. Me telling him everything. But that was it. I don't believe he'll hurt me again.'

For the first time, she had acknowledged publicly that he had hurt her. Immy looked away, then at Jo, then back to Kate. Then, in a low, steady voice, she said, 'That's what Mum said.'

'What?' Kate's heart skipped.

'It was years ago. I was… like… too little to understand and I don't remember anything. Mum told me much later.

She'd done something he didn't like. I don't know exactly. There was another man. She wouldn't tell me more. Only that Dad hurt her, bashed her about. They were living in a rented flat. She left with me and found somewhere else. Only he followed her. He kept following her. That's why we went to Canada.'

Kate stared. Immy was looking away from her through the window at the drifting clouds.

'Why didn't you tell me?'

Immy turned back to face her with a pained expression.

'It was so long ago. I didn't want to freak you out.'

'So why did your mum stay in touch? Why did she let you come and stay?'

'He never hurt me. Plus, he changed. When he came over to Canada to see me, she said he seemed completely different. I guess she forgave him. She never thought he'd settle with anyone. He sounded so happy with you. His face lit up when he talked about you – that's what she said. Everything had worked out for him. He was doing well as a barrister. He was going to get married. He told her he'd been in therapy.'

Michael? In therapy? It was hard to believe. Why had he never told her?

'She said he sounded really sorry for what he'd done. It was a long time ago. They were both young. They'd grown up a bit. She wanted to meet you. I did too. You came to New York with him once, but you didn't want to come up to Toronto.'

Kate felt a lump in her throat so large she thought she might choke. She had wanted to come, begged him to let her meet Immy. Somehow, he had dissuaded her, and she had not pushed it. She had always been afraid to push it.

'Then when I had my... you know... my thing... Mum was in love with this guy in Paris. Still is. I don't think she'd been in love like that since Dad. There was no space in the Paris flat. Anyway, Dad begged her to let him take me. I didn't know what to do. I was pretty out of it. But I did want to meet you.'

It was not what he had told her. She remembered his exact words: 'She says it's my turn.' Did Simone ever say anything like that? It seemed unlikely. More likely Michael was wanting to make amends for pushing them both away all those years ago.

All the time Immy was speaking, Jo was holding her hand. Looking at them both, Kate thought for a moment that she might start to cry. Not because of what Michael had done or what Simone had suffered. Not for herself. But for Immy, the beautiful, vulnerable child of a broken home, who had found someone to love her. They were both waiting for her to respond.

'Thank you for telling me, Immy. I'll need a bit of time to take it all in. And no. I'm not going to get an injunction. At least not today. Right now, I just want to rest. I'm too exhausted to decide anything.'

There were so many things she wanted to know and was afraid to ask. How badly had he hurt Simone? What had Simone done?

'If we leave you alone, you must promise not to open the door to anyone,' said Jo.

'I promise.'

'There's food in the fridge. I better get back to work. Can you stay a bit, Immy?'

'I've got an hour.'

'Good. Look after her. Take it easy, Kate. Get Immy to make you cups of tea. And if you want to borrow our bed when we're out, that's fine.' She stopped at the door and added, 'Have a think about that injunction.'

Kate and Immy sat with their tea in the grey morning light. The girl's presence was a comfort. At that moment she was the stable one, open, honest. Someone to trust.

'I should have told you before, warned you,' said Immy.

'It would only have made me dislike you. It would have made no difference.'

Kate thought of those first meetings with Steve, alone in their magic world, untouchable. They'd lived in the present. Wasn't that what you were supposed to do? Afterwards, retribution, his fury, her terror. She saw again the blood on his arm, the shock in his eyes when she'd wounded him. Then she saw the marks on Tamsin's throat, captured for all to see. What would Tamsin do?

Immy said, 'Sometimes the most important things are the things you can't say.'

She was looking out of the window and Kate wondered if there was more, but she didn't ask. She didn't want to know more. Not now. Then Immy turned to look at her and said, 'I've been thinking about Tamsin.'

Kate felt herself nod. She hadn't told Immy about the calls, the photos, and she didn't intend to. Immy went on.

'What it must be like to lose the person you love. Like that. Suddenly.'

Kate cleared her throat and in as calm a voice as she could summon, she asked, 'Have you heard how she's coping? Has Jen said anything? She hasn't been in touch with me.'

'No. Only that there was a police report. About the accident I mean.'

'Do they know any more about how it happened?' Despite what Steve had done to her, she still cared.

253

Immy put down her tea. 'I don't think so. At least, if they do, no one's told me.' A curtain fell across her features and she jumped up. 'I need to get to work. Help yourself to anything you need.'

—

The front door slam behind her. Kate sat on, wondering at Immy's sudden departure as she picked up her phone and called Tamsin.

'I've seen the photos,' she said.

'Good.'

'What are you planning to do with them?'

'The pretty one is for your husband.'

Something was lodged in her throat. She swallowed, breathed, managed to ask, 'And the neck?'

'That one's for the police.'

Kate had already seen the rage in Tamsin. Nothing she chose to do would be a surprise. Then she heard Tamsin speak again. 'Unless…'

'Unless?'

'You can help me get to New Zealand.'

There was a pause. The question in Kate's mind was, 'How much?' The question that came out was, 'How can I do that?'

'£6000 would be a good start. Cash.'

Her heart tripped, but she managed to say, 'Give me your address.'

Tamsin gave it, adding, 'Come tonight. After the kids are in bed. Around eight thirty.'

'I'll need at least a day to get the money.'

'Tomorrow night then. Come alone.'

Kate rang off, conscious of a tingling through her body, a pent-up energy that cried for action. £6000. Blackmail was a crime, wasn't it? But, looked at from another angle, it sounded reasonable. If she could help Tamsin make a new start, why not? And if offering money could ease Kate's conscience, they would both benefit. Immy had said there was a police report. But nothing in the report would make a difference. Whoever was at fault in the pile up that killed her husband, in Tamsin's mind, the guilty one was Kate.

She stood up, stepping through the kitchen into a garden a quarter the size of their terrace at home. Cracked flagstones were surrounded by shrubs and climbers, choked with bindweed, everything lush and green from the heavy summer rainfall. It was warm with a soft breeze and Kate inhaled the scent of unknown herbs as she shut her eyes, letting the mingled sounds float in her head: the occasional purr of a car on the main road, the louder vroom of a motorbike on the estate, the lone piping of a bird from a tree behind the fence. Beyond all this there seemed to be a buzzing, whirring sound she could not recognise, but when she stopped her ears it was still there, and she realised it was inside her head.

What Immy had told her about Michael was meant as a warning. But she felt no fear, only pain and sadness that he had been unable to be open about his past. If he had, would she have listened? Would she have believed his protest that he had changed? Or would his words have alienated her? Right now, she had no idea. It seemed there was no consistency in anything. One minute she never wanted to see him again. A minute later she longed to hold him in her arms.

Then common sense kicked in, reminding her that whatever the chaos of her emotions, it would be sensible to go to a doctor. Sensible to avoid Michael. But no amount of sensible could stop the throbbing ache in her heart that had now dropped to her stomach. Something was strangling her guts, twisting them tight, tugging them out of her body. She couldn't move, could only sit on the low wall in the garden and wait for the sensation to pass.

She waited. And, after a while, the tugging eased, and she was conscious once again of the sweet herbal scents and the mild breeze of the afternoon, the hard stone of the wall beneath her. How quickly everything could change. When at last she was able to focus, she picked up her phone, bringing up Jason's contact details, tapping the call icon. He answered immediately.

'Kate. Hi. Of course, I remember you.'

'I was thinking about what you said at the art fair, about the flying dog.' Her voice sounded strange, as if it belonged to a different woman.

'Yes.'

'There are a couple more pieces I'd like to show you. I wondered if I could come tomorrow.'

He didn't reply immediately, and she thought she detected an intake of breath.

'I'd love to see them. But tomorrow's not great. Why don't you just send over a few photos?'

'I'd rather show them to you.'

This was crazy. He wasn't even that keen to see them. No way was he going to produce £6000.

'Please, it's really important.'

Madness. She was pleading with a man she had only met once.

'OK. How about three p.m.? You know how to find the gallery?'

'I've got your card with the map.'

'Great. I'll see you then.'

Having made her arrangement, she felt drained of energy. The buzzing was still there, but the tingle and the restlessness had gone. The torment in her stomach had faded. She wanted only to sleep.

Back in the flat, she drew the curtains against the bright sunlight, curling up on the hard sofa. Images of Michael floated into her head. His face screwed tight when he was upset, the way he walked suddenly out of a room when he was angry, as if he needed to get away from her. How it always felt as if he was ducking, avoiding confrontation. His inability to speak of Simone, of the intervening years. Her decision not to ask. Then another Michael, the softness in his eyes when they made love, the long, slow kisses. Even after seven years of marriage he'd been a good kisser.

She shut her eyes. Her breath was growing heavy. More images of Michael danced across her tired mind. And now he was joined by another, younger man. Steve. He looked as he had when she'd last seen him, desperate, anguished. And then the two images were dissolving into each other, and all she could see as she drifted into a restless sleep was a single figure, burning with anger. The face was blurred, unrecognisable, and yet she knew him only too well as he backed her up against the studio wall, one arm raised high, about to punish her for what she had done to him.

Chapter 35

After Glastonbury and Wells, the road to Bath crossed the Mendips. Kate's spirits rose as her little car climbed the wooded slope, leaving the low plain of the Levels behind. The sky was clear and bright, the view across the plateau magnificent. She remembered the last time she had driven here with Jen. It had been a couple of years ago. They'd been looking forward to a day of clothes shopping, punctuated by a good lunch and an hour in the baths. But Jen had been momentarily cast down by the sight of the dead ash trees on the slopes. Kate thought of her dear, compassionate friend, imagining sitting with her over copious cups of tea, telling her everything. This year the ash trees were almost bare.

But as she drew into the traffic-clogged streets of Bath her excited anticipation returned. It was always good to be in the heart of a city, surrounded by the buzz of other people. Anonymous. Armed with a plan.

She parked in a multi-storey on the lower side of town. Before leaving her car she checked the mirror, patting more make-up on the bruising which had spread down her cheek, pulling her thick hair into a tie, covering her head with a hideous red peaked baseball cap which she had borrowed from Jo. Immy had lent her a pair of over-sized dark glasses. Kate contemplated her reflection. She looked more like an eccentric tourist with bad taste than a professional artist. But anything was better than looking like a woman who'd been bashed about.

She crossed the river and walked uphill into the city's heart, pale ochre buildings rising high on each side. The air was full of the screech of gulls. When she came to the sweep of the Royal Crescent she stopped, momentarily thrilled by its timeless symmetry and classic proportions. Lightly clad figures were spread out on the grass in front, picnicking, drinking, chatting, looking happy, as groups of strangers always did. And now the pavements were filling, crowds of language students and tourists blocking her route, buoyant tour guides brandishing flags on poles. Frustrated by her slow progress, Kate checked Maps and found a backstreet route, cutting through to the pedestrian area which was home to the gift shops and galleries. Several had closed down in the last few years, artists moving their work online. But Horizon Gallery was still there. She took a deep breath, pushed the door open and walked in.

The walls were covered with charcoal abstracts. Small tables were dotted with glazed ceramics. Some might call it pottery, but the clay was so fine, the glazes so colourful and original, it was clear to Kate that this was art. You wouldn't eat or drink from these bowls. You wouldn't put flowers in them. They were meant to be looked at, touched, loved.

Jason was listening to a customer. The man wore a pink shirt and jeans. Solid, tall and loud, he reminded her of some of Michael's barrister pals. Or Michael himself in full flow. She stood waiting, clutching her bag of work, conscious of the pain in her side. She stared at the walls. The drawings were bold and arresting. But each was similar to the other. Should she be sculpting the same thing repeatedly? Was that how you found a style that was your own? Was she trying to do too many different things?

The customer left, looking past her as if she didn't exist. Kate felt a stab of irritation. Men usually noticed her. But why would he bother with a gawky woman in floppy clothes and a hideous baseball cap?

'May I help you?' asked Jason.

'It's Kate.'

She was aware that her voice sounded feeble. Was it the contrast with the customer, a man booming with confidence and smelling of money?

'Kate, of course.'

Jason seemed more polite than pleased. She wondered if he even recognised her. Had he forgotten the enthusiastic approach at the art fair? Or was that just his holiday demeanour? She removed the sunglasses, cap and tie, letting her hair fan out. His mouth curled into the beginnings of a smile, but the eyes behind the rimless spectacles were questioning. She felt like screaming. 'I am not what you think I am!' But she only said, 'I've brought some work to show you.'

'Yes, of course.' The smile shifted into a different gear and she detected a glimmer of professional curiosity as he cleared papers aside on his desk and gestured to the space he had made. 'Please.'

His manner reminded her of a male doctor inviting her to lie on a raised bed in a cubicle. Any minute now he would ask if she wanted a chaperone.

'This is the one you saw.' She put out the dog. 'These are two others in a similar style.' The pieces looked small and insignificant.

'Mmm.' It was hard to interpret his reaction though it certainly wasn't enthusiasm. 'Only three,' he said.

'I could do more.'

'We'll try these for starters. We have what we call Open Gallery once every two months. That's when we show a selection of less expensive work. Giving young artists a chance. Buyers can pick up a bargain. Yes, these might suit. Anything else?'

'Only this.'

She pulled out Steve's broken head. There was no stand, so she simply laid it on the desk, resting it on its side. He walked around, then squatted to get an eye level view.

'May I touch?'

'Of course.'

'I like this. I like it a lot.'

Her heart jumped. The ceramic pieces were labelled between £500 and £1000. Might she get the same for this? More?

'It would need to be properly mounted. A light metal stand might work.'

'How much do you think it would sell for?'

'Of course, you're unknown. And we'd need more than one head to make an impact. Buyers tend to be more interested if they see a developing pattern, potential for a collection. Casting would be difficult with this level of detail. It would be hard to capture that shattered edge. But that's the beauty of it.'

Something jumped inside her. People had liked her animals. Praised her technique. But this was the first time anyone from the art world had seen something original in her work. Even if, as she reminded herself, that shattered edge he so admired was Tamsin's work. The words stuck in her mind, '…the beauty of it.' She remembered Steve as he'd been in life, the penetrating eyes and perfect mouth.

Then the awful smash as the fired head hit the floor. Jason was still talking.

'I'm thinking different glazes. Bring me three or four more in this style and we might find a buyer. Let's say two hundred each for the animals, three hundred for the dancer. Maybe six or seven hundred for a head.'

She nodded. It was wonderful that he liked something. But at the same time, she was beginning to realise the absurdity of her expectations. She needed £6000. And she needed it now. What was she thinking?

'I'll keep the animals and the dancer, but I suggest you take the head back until you have a series, properly glazed and mounted.'

He went to sit at his desk, asked for her name and address. She thought quickly and gave Immy's address. Then he handed her a receipt for the three sculptures.

'I did wonder,' she faltered, 'if there might be some kind of advance?'

He smiled. It was biggest smile of the afternoon and she was not sure if it was kind, or patronising, or whether he was just amazed by her naivety.

'My dear girl. You have to understand that's not how we operate. The art world is on a knife edge. Galleries are closing all the time. I take in some unknown work. I do it for love and because I want to support aspiring artists. Very few dealers do that. I also sell online. I will certainly put your pieces on my website. But I can't offer anything until I have a buyer. My terms are good. I give 40 per cent. It might be helpful if you could send me a short biography. Not too much detail. Where you trained, location of your studio, inspiration for your work, what you're trying to say. You know the sort of thing.'

40 per cent. Her heart sank. And nothing until the pieces were sold. What a fool she was. She thought back to those years in the Bristol gallery, moving art works, serving drinks, chatting to visitors. She'd never been involved with the money side. Still, she ought to have known better. How could she have dreamt he would give her anything before a sale? The truth was she had latched onto Immy's suggestion without thinking it through. Thinking things through. She was finding that more and more difficult.

She thanked him, promised him the biography, wrapped the head in its old pillowcase and left. Jason's interest was encouraging, but she needed the money now. It was not simply the fear of what Tamsin might show Michael. There'd been a promise.

She crossed the river, following the map on her phone towards a shop with several five-star Google reviews.

Paula couldn't have been more helpful.

Takes the sting out of borrowing.

–

Musical instruments, electronic gadgets, jewellery and watches were spaced out behind the plate glass. Like an undertaker's, it was the kind of place you only noticed when you needed it. She pushed the door, a bell pinged, and she took a couple of steps forward to a high desk and a middle-aged man with a welcoming smile.

'How can I help you?'

This was not the loan shark she expected. He looked like everybody's favourite uncle with his tousled reddish-blonde hair, lightly freckled face and sticking out ears. She twisted her mother's emerald and diamond engagement ring off her third finger and unclasped a thin gold chain from her neck. As he inspected the items, she fingered her wedding ring, knowing she wasn't ready to remove it. There was another gift from Michael in her bag. For her thirty-fifth birthday he'd given her a watch. He'd produced it over a special dinner, nervously pushing the small parcel across the restaurant table. It was large for a woman's watch, housed in steel, 100 per cent waterproof. He'd hinted that it was expensive. But she found it heavy on her wrist, too cumbersome to wear when sculpting. After he'd picked it up lying around the house a couple of times, she'd put it back in its case, telling him she would keep it for special occasions. She'd sensed his disappointment. And now she was about to hand it over. She felt a twinge in her stomach as she laid it on the counter next to the jewellery. It might produce a few hundred.

'I'm afraid I do have to ask. Where did this come from?'

'I'm not sure where my husband bought it. I believe he has papers. But I'd rather he didn't know. It's just temporary. I'll redeem it as soon as possible.'

He must have read her story in the cap and sunglasses, the purple stain that ran down her cheek. His smile was kind.

'I can offer £120 for the ring and chain. £3000 for the watch.'

The sum astounded her. She almost said, 'No, I've changed my mind.' It pierced her heart that Michael should have spent so much on a luxury gift she had never worn. But she nodded and said, 'That's great. Take the watch. I'll hold onto the ring and chain for now.' She clasped the chain around her neck. It felt cool on her skin and she realised how loathe she had been to part with it. Then she picked up the ring and twisted it back on her finger. She and her mother had never been close. But it felt right to keep something that had been so important to her.

She left the shop with cash in her wallet and her head swirling. *Just breathe. In, out. In, out.* She stared at her feet. One step at a time. Step after step after step. The clouds had gathered while she was in the shop and, sensing the first drops of rain, she stuck on the silly cap. It wasn't far. She was in a side alley. According to Maps, this would take her to the back of the multi-storey car park.

She walked past locked garages, rolled down doors daubed with crudely painted numbers. Then a line of overfull dustbins, rubbish spilling out onto the street. Where the garages stopped there was only the back of what looked like small workshops, edged with a thin pavement mostly blocked by cars. This was the side of Bath the tourists didn't see.

The sky was a heavy grey mat and the rain was thickening. She was tired and hungry and wanted to be home. Home? Immy and Jo would house her for a while, but she could never go back to the farmhouse. *Don't think. Focus on now.* She had money. She could pay Tamsin, at least some of what she wanted, perhaps enough to quieten her. Somehow she would get through this. She stepped off the pavement to avoid another car, glanced at Maps. One more minute. She was practically there. But as she pocketed her phone and walked on, the rain was growing so intense it was stinging her face and she could only stare down at the wet street as she ploughed on through towards the back entrance to the car park.

She sensed rather than saw the shape of a man drawing near her. She tried to step aside but he blocked her path, and when she raised her eyes, shock jolted through her body. Michael.

'Hello, Kate.'

He looked flushed and unshaven. His shirt was crumpled, and even in the rain she could see his hair was greasy and unwashed.

She almost said, 'You look a mess.' But that would be the start of something intimate and she quickly stopped herself and said, 'How did you know I was here?'

'Let's get out of the rain. We could go and have a drink.'

'I don't want a drink. I need to get back.' He was still blocking her path.

'Back where? You've not been home.'

He must have gone back to the farmhouse. Must have waited for her.

'Michael, I can't talk to you just now. Please let me pass. I need to get to my car.'

'We can sit in mine till the rain stops. It's just here.' He was holding her arm now, his fingers pressing into her flesh.

'Please let go of me.'

'I need to talk to you.'

'Fucking let me go!'

But he continued to trap her, gripping her arm.

'You're being ridiculous.'

He glared at her with hard angry eyes. Five minutes ago, she had felt like a traitor in handing over the watch he had bought for her. Now she felt only rage at his arrogance.

'You all right, love?' It was a young man, one of a couple passing by with hoods pulled low over their heads. She could barely make out their faces. The kind of young men she would cross the road to avoid.

'We're fine thank you,' said Michael, obstructing the youth with his body. But there were two of them.

'This guy bothering you?' said his friend.

'If you could just let me talk to my wife,' interposed Michael before she could answer. It was the posh barrister voice, the voice of the customer in the gallery.

The young men ignored Michael but stood very close to her. She felt herself shivering with cold and wet. In a quiet voice she said, 'Please let go, Michael.'

He loosened his hold but didn't drop his hand.

'She said let go,' said the youth and at the same time his friend placed a hand on Michael's shoulder.

She heard herself say, 'My car's in the car park. Would you escort me there?'

The words were clear, but her voice was trembling.

'Come on then,' said the taller of the two. They were both skinny. Neither of them much over twenty. But between them they could easily hurt Michael. His arm dropped away. He must have known he wouldn't have stood a chance in a physical confrontation because he stepped back, both hands limp and dangling by his side. She caught his eyes again, and now the glare had faded and anger had softened into pleading. How could he change so quickly? This was the look that spoke of an emptiness inside him that only she could fill, that it was her duty to fill. And part of her wanted to tell the boys to disappear. To go with Michael to a warm pub, sit over drinks at a corner table as they had done so often in the past, tell him she was sorry, wait for him to forgive her, hear herself forgive him.

But there was no further word to Michael as she walked with the two young men towards the back door of the car park. When they reached the door and she turned round,

Michael was still in the same spot, head uncovered in the pouring rain, arms dangling by his sides, watching her. The boys escorted her to the car.

'You all right now?' said one.

'Fine thanks. You've been very kind.'

'Not a problem,' he replied.

'Any time!' laughed the other.

She drove home with her head pounding. She was exhausted, but she would visit Tamsin. If not tonight, tomorrow, pay her the cash she wanted. Eventually she would talk to Michael. Maybe in front of a mediator. She would not be forced. Would not be followed.

Back at the flat, Immy and Jo were both home from work, waiting for her.

'I thought you were staying in,' said Jo.

'I needed to go to Bath. To see the gallery guy.'

'Is everything all right? You look kind of weird,' said Immy.

'Michael was there. He must have followed me. How else did he know I was in Bath?'

Immy glanced at Jo, who was looking out of the window and now turned back to face Kate, her face set and determined.

'Two things, Kate. One, you need to change your mobile number. Two, you need to get that injunction.'

Chapter 36

Jo took pictures of Kate's bruised face and the small red marks where he had gripped her arm, three hours earlier. Immy looked on in silence. When Kate caught her eye, she detected only sadness and wondered how it must feel to witness the damage your own father has caused. After the photo session, Immy disappeared into the bedroom. Jo then contacted her solicitor friend, Petra, who promised to meet them at the Family Court the following morning.

Kate crashed out on the sofa at ten p.m. As she drifted into sleep she heard Jo and Immy murmuring on the other side of the partition wall. She imagined their whispered conversation. However supportive they might appear, whatever Immy had said about not judging, they would surely find fault in Kate's actions. Anyone would. Most of all herself.

Eventually she slept. At three a.m. she was awake again with swirling thoughts. No job, no safe place to live. She needed to speak to the bank, her students, her cleaner, Jen. Accusing faces whirled around her in the darkness. Overshadowing them all, huge, angry, fixing her with sharp hazel eyes, was Tamsin.

Petra was a plump middle-aged woman with a low, calm voice, thick brown hair tied back off her face and kind, intelligent eyes. Kate told her what Michael had done while Jo waited outside the small conference room. It was easier talking to an outsider and she even mentioned the spitting. Petra hesitated a moment, looking as if she might say something. But after a short pause, she continued tapping notes on her laptop.

She explained that the hearing would be private. It was important that Kate should tell her everything, including, if she felt able to do so, any actions of her own that could have provoked her husband's violence.

'We need to pre-empt what he might say when he comes back to challenge the order. That way it won't look as if you've been hiding anything.'

'He'll be coming to court?' Kate was shocked. 'I thought it was just me.'

'You're trying to exclude him from the family home. That's pretty major. The judge will give him the chance to attend and answer the allegations.'

'I wish I'd never started this.'

'We still don't have the order, so theoretically you can pull out now. But you should know that in 90 per cent of cases where there has been more than one incident of violence or harassment, the pattern continues.'

'So, when does it stop?'

'An injunction is some protection. If he doesn't comply it can lead to an arrest. You may decide to move away.'

Kate thought of Simone. She still didn't know what Michael had done to her. It couldn't have been that bad or she wouldn't have agreed to meet him again. And Michael had changed. But she remembered his eyes when he'd gripped her arm in the back street in Bath. She had seen something then that she had never seen before. Something that had frightened her.

Petra carried on talking. 'The non-mol is not much use alone. It's hard to enforce. Much better if we keep him out of the house.'

'Will it be forever?'

'It's usually for six months. Until you can sort things. It doesn't affect ownership. It has nothing to do with divorce.'

Divorce. The word cut like a knife. How had this happened? How had everything escalated so fast? They had been happy, hadn't they? But then she remembered Steve's face. The scent of his breath, the touch of his lips. She'd been a fool. A weak fool.

It all seemed so abstract. Legal rules. She knew how Michael loved to seek out loopholes, challenging judges' orders. She imagined him confronting her in court, cross-examining his own wife. He'd done it in the house, when he'd been checking on her whereabouts the night Timba disappeared. Now he could do it in front of a judge. He'd revel in it. A chance for him to rip her to shreds in the way he knew best. It would all come out. Steve, Timba, the lost babies. Perhaps even those smiling naked photographs. She felt sickened, horrified that she had let things come this far. She told Petra some, not all, of what had provoked Michael's actions.

—

Jo remained outside when they went into the courtroom. Kate was terrified lest she be asked a lot of questions. But the judge, a brisk, efficient-looking woman in a crisp shirt and jacket, only looked at the statement which Petra had printed off in the court office. Then she asked how many rooms there were in the house. She would make the non-molestation order, but Michael would have the chance to return and challenge it.

Everything happened very fast and they were out in the lobby with its buzzing air conditioning and glaring artificial light.

It all seemed so abstract. So little to do with her life. Her man. Her relationship. She wanted that solved. None of this would solve that.

'What happens now?' she asked.

'He gets served with the order.'

'He'll go mad.'

How had she let it come this far? She could have talked to him. She would have talked to him in Bath if the young men hadn't turned up. However angry he might be, she could have talked him down. And now she had become a cog in the legal machine, the very machine Michael had spent his working life learning how to master.

She was asked to fill in a form for Legal Aid. Michael would be handed a copy of the order later today, if he could be found. She gave them both addresses plus details of his chambers. Until she knew he had received the order, she was advised to stay somewhere safe. If she left Jo's flat, she should not go out alone.

Immy was at work when they returned from court. Soon after, Jo left for the gym and Kate spent the day on the sofa, watching telly, playing games on her phone, conscious of a slew of things she needed to do. When the others came home she was itching to get out of the house.

'Come with us tonight if you want,' replied Jo. 'There's a folk night at the pub.'

'We'll look after you,' said Immy.

'Lots of jolly people singing. I don't think I can face it.'

'In that case you need to stay here,' said Jo. 'Until Michael has received the order it can't be enforced.'

'I don't think he'll do anything. He followed me. He didn't hurt me.' Did she even believe what she was saying?

'Tell her Immy.'

'It was the same with Mum. He didn't hurt her. Not at first. Just followed her. That's when we moved. We kept on moving. It got more difficult then. She couldn't get an injunction. It was different in those days. He didn't touch her, so she had no evidence. Then he did. Touch her I mean. That's why she left the country.'

The old questions ran through Kate's mind. What had he done to Simone? And why had Immy come back? She didn't need to put the question. Immy read her mind.

'He's my father. I wanted to know him. I thought he had changed.'

Petra called to say the process server had been to the farmhouse, but there was no car outside and no one answered the door. There was no reply to the buzzer at the Bristol flat. He'd tried Michael's chambers and was told that Michael had not been in for two weeks. He would try again early tomorrow morning.

'Can't they just send it electronically?'

'He needs to receive it in person.'

Kate imagined how he would react on being handed an injunction preventing him from seeing his wife. It was supposed to keep her safe, but might it tip him over the edge?

After Jo and Kate had left for the pub, she sat for a bit staring at the wall. Then she called Tamsin.

'I've got the money.'

'I've been trying to call you. You were supposed to come yesterday.'

'I got stuck. It's complicated. I had to change my number.'

'Interesting.' Kate wasn't going to tell her why. 'Are you coming then?'

Tamsin's house was two streets away.

'Give me ten minutes.'

The wallet containing £3000 in £50 notes was zipped into the side pocket of her bag. She wondered about taking the car. But muggings were unknown in this small town and she felt a powerful urge to breathe fresh air. It crossed her mind that Michael might be lurking in the area. But she would not live her life in fear, would not let him make her a prisoner. And Tamsin's house was only a couple of hundred metres away. She threw a jacket over her T-shirt and set off down the narrow alley behind the back gardens that would take her to the end of Tamsin's road.

Chapter 37

She entered the small garden through a rusty gate and walked over a patch of uncut grass. Straggly shrubs struggled for space with clumps of thistles and dock choked with bindweed. A large, neglected garden could look wild and picturesque. She had always imagined her own did. This one just looked sad.

She pressed the bell and stood back from the front door. A dog barked. Maxie. Kate had forgotten about Maxie. Did Tamsin find him a consolation? Had she changed her views about dogs after what she did to Timba? It was too painful to think about and Kate wished she were somewhere else. But she had the money, at least some of it; she had promised to come and the meeting would soon be over.

The door was flung open. Maxie rushed up, still barking. Kate stood still, offered a hand. The dog ran in circles around her and back into the house. His bark faded. And now Tamsin was standing in front of her and it was as if Kate were seeing her properly for the first time. At the art fair, she had been unaware of her identity until seconds before Tamsin had rushed away. On their second meeting Tamsin had been drenched with rain and incandescent with rage. Now, at the third meeting, she appeared calm, normal, even pretty. Her streaked blonde hair was freshly washed, framing delicate features emphasised with subtle make-up. As they exchanged glances, Tamsin's sharp hazel eyes narrowed in apparent concern.

'You look a mess.'

'I'm OK. I fell over in the studio.'

Tamsin threw back her head and snorted. 'Come in,' she said. 'Shut the door behind you.'

Kate did as instructed, following Tamsin down the narrow corridor towards the kitchen. A large, framed, colour photograph of Steve and the twins was hanging on the wall close to the front door.

It was obvious from the ages of the children that it was a recent shot. He was sitting on a bench, one child on his shoulders, the other balancing on one leg on the bench beside him leaning into him for support. There was no background landscape, no horizon, only a vast blue sky behind them. All three pairs of eyes were screwed up from the sun and the boys' curly hair was blown out around their little heads. They might be on top of a hill, or perhaps a cliff near the sea. Yes, the sea. Looking at them sitting there she could smell the salt, hear the seagulls. The child on Steve's shoulders appeared to be tugging at his father's curls as if to stop himself being blown away. The other boy was clutching his arm, grimacing for the camera. It was a typical family snap and Kate's gut was turning inside her.

Tamsin had walked on ahead to a kitchen that smelt of fish fingers. Kate followed her, quickly absorbing her surroundings. A small bookcase on one wall contained a couple of cookbooks and a row of misery memoirs. Maxie was curled up in his basket. Four stools were wedged under the breakfast bar, but there was no invitation to sit so Kate stood with her back to the bookcase. Tamsin shut the door behind them.

'You been to the police about that face?' she said. It was more statement than question.

Kate shook her head.

'You should do.'

'I'd have to tell them everything.'

She wouldn't mention her morning at court. Didn't want to talk to this woman about Michael. She just wanted to give her the money and go.

'You mean how you slept with my husband and tried to kill me?'

'I brought you cash,' she said, unzipping the side pocket in her bag, removing the £3000. Tamsin counted the wad of notes.

'That's not enough. I need £6000.'

'It's all I've got. I might get more. I'm trying to sell stuff.'

'People like you can borrow money.'

'It's not that easy.'

'You saw the photos then.'

'You know I saw them.'

Kate felt herself being studied, judged. But as she turned away her gaze halted at the purple-brown marks on Tamsin's neck.

At that point, the kitchen door flew open and the small boy who was grimacing in the picture by the door, the one who'd played with her clay animals at the art fair, ran in, arms outstretched pretending to be an aeroplane. He screeched to a landing on seeing Kate.

'Your face looks funny.'

'Bed,' snapped Tamsin, stepping to reach him.

'We're going to Nu Theeland,' he squealed, evading her arm, taking off again around the tiny room, bashing into cupboards with his wing-tip fingers.

'Bed,' repeated Tamsin, bringing her hand down sharply and catching the little boy's bottom, causing him to laugh loudly as he disappeared out of the room.

Kate's throat felt thick and her eyes were pricking with tears. 'I'll try to get the money...'

'So, how did he find out? I never sent him the pictures. Was it the dog?'

'I told him.'

'You are one crazy lady.'

'It got difficult. I needed to explain.'

'You could've gone to the cops. Given them the lies you told me. They might have swallowed that, you being so respectable and everything.'

'I didn't want to lie. The truth was the only thing I had left to give him.'

'And he lost it.'

'Yes. So, I guess...' No. They were not square. They would never be square, however much she paid Tamsin. 'I'll try to get you another £1000. I'll bring it as soon as I can.' She paused, still standing against the bookshelves.

'Are you going to the police? About your neck?'

'Dunno. Sit down for Christ's sake. You're making me nervous standing up there.'

Tamsin didn't look remotely nervous. In Kate's short acquaintance with her, she had only looked nervous once. Tamsin must have read her mind because she said, 'I honestly thought your dog was going to kill me.'

Kate sat. She wasn't going to argue. She had never seen Timba like that before. But she wasn't going to apologise on behalf of her poor traumatised dog. Tamsin carried on talking. 'I'm not crazy about the police. Me and Steve had one or two run-ins. Only I did speak to them. Not about what you did to me. Not that. I'm not standing up in court to be pulled apart by some pompous arse lawyer. No. I spoke about Steve. I was hoping for a bit of dosh. Jen said I should speak to your husband only that didn't sound like a good idea, so I got some free advice.'

'But you still think it's my fault?'

'He was there 'cos of you. He was drinking 'cos of you. He drove too far into the road 'cos of you.'

Kate wasn't going to argue. Everything Tamsin was saying was true. 'I need to go. I don't want my step-daughter knowing I've been out.'

'Looking after you, is she?'

'More or less.'

'That's good. Nice to have someone to look after you.'

Tamsin was studying Kate's face. 'Hang on a minute.' And she ran upstairs, returning seconds later with a small aerosol canister. 'Just keep that in your handbag.'

'What is it?'

'Spray. It stinks and it'll cover him with purple dye. Gives you time to get away. Or find a proper weapon.'

'Isn't it illegal?'

'No. You're talking about pepper spray. This one's what the bouncers use. It's fine. Steve got it off the net. Never been used. He made me take it if I went out without him. I can get more. Not that I go anywhere now.' Kate took the spray, touched. 'I can get the pepper spray too if you want. Only that's painful. Could get you into trouble.'

'Thanks. This will do fine. I'm not expecting to use it. I'll bring you the cash as soon as I can.'

'Sooner the better. Steve's cousin's waiting in New Zealand. They're tough on migrants but he reckons he can sort it. We'll get there.' And her face broke into a smile and for one moment it seemed to Kate she was about to take her hand. But she took a step back as if having second thoughts.

'Listen, it wasn't just you. He was a bugger, my bloke. Too young when we got together. The twins were a shock. He loved them to death, but everything changed after they were born. He started going for other women. He said I'd changed. 'Course I bloody changed. I guess you got to him more than most.'

There was nothing she could say.

'You better get out.' Tamsin walked down the corridor to the front door, opened it and stood back for Kate to leave. 'Don't go down the alley. Take the main road. You'll be safer with the streetlights.'

'Thanks for the spray,' said Kate. It had started to rain again, and she wished she'd brought the car. Then as she walked out into the dark she turned and asked, 'Did you see the police report? I mean about Steve.'

'They told me what they had. They haven't finished the report. The lorry driver had a dashcam and the police let me look at the footage. You couldn't see much, everything was going so fast. It wasn't just Steve and the lorry on the road. There was a car too. A silver car. Heading in the opposite direction and going like the clappers. The lorry had to swerve to avoid it.'

'Did they say what sort of car it was?'

'They weren't 100 per cent sure. But they reckon it was definitely a saloon type. Probably an Audi. Silver.'

It was a warm evening, but Kate felt herself shiver. 'Did they get the registration number?' she asked.

'No, they couldn't make it out.'

She felt Tamsin's eyes on the back of her head as she crossed the scruffy garden in the dying evening light. Her thoughts swirled. Silver Audis were common enough.

The make and colour of the car would be pure coincidence. Michael had been in Bristol that day. But what if, and as the what ifs poured through her mind, they spun and multiplied like the darkest midnight fantasies.

She told herself the supposition was ludicrous. There were plenty of silver Audis around. Her imagination was running away with her. But even as she convinced herself that Michael couldn't possibly have anything to do with Steve's death, she found herself quickening her step.

Chapter 38

There was no one around. Not even a dog walker. It was that hour when everything was about to fade into darkness and what you had thought were large trees became strange beasts with mad hair.

Kate crossed the empty road and set off down the pavement along a line of bungalows tucked behind a patch of grass. Only a few had lighted windows. Most were dark. Their elderly inhabitants must have retired early to bed.

After her momentary wobble in the front garden, the visit to Tamsin's had gone better than expected. In her forthright way, the young woman had been considerate, and her parting gift was touching. The silver car was a momentary shock. But it was absurd to imagine Michael could have been involved, wasn't it?

After the bungalows, the pavement ran along a line of high fencing, bordering the no man's land that stretched along the mainline railway from London to the West Country. The station had long been closed and trains now surged through the cuttings and over the viaducts, leaving the sleepy town unvisited, untouched. There was no pavement on the opposite side, only a steep bank of vegetation topped with high trees, screening the grounds of the care home behind them.

A car drove slowly past. She had the uncomfortable feeling she was being checked out and stepped up her gait. Had she just been mistaken for a streetwalker?

The sharper pace set off her rib and she slowed down as she passed under a streetlamp. But the rib was only a minor irritation. Overall, she felt better, calmer after the visit to Tamsin. Immy and Jo had called it blackmail, but it felt more like an attempt at recompense on Kate's part. All she wanted from now on was to do the right thing. And as she passed out of the light and carried on along the line of wooden fencing, her body felt easier, as if it were coming back to her and would soon become her own once more. Within days she would be running again.

Jo was right about the injunction. It gave her some security. And once it had been served on Michael she would go back to the studio. She would keep her phone close, lock the door and if she saw his car she would call the police.

Rain was falling in a fine mist and she pulled up the hood of her jacket. It was the wettest summer she could remember. Flooding was forecast and occupiers of low-lying homes were advised to vacate their ground floors and leave their properties if possible. The fields were already saturated, some of the lowest land was already under six inches of water. If the river burst its banks at the next high tide those same fields would become lakes. The bottom of the farmhouse garden would flood, though the house was high enough to be safe. Not that it mattered any more. And Jo and Immy's flat was too high to be affected.

Another car was moving slowly behind her. Perhaps Tamsin knew something about her estate at night that Kate didn't know. Was that the reason for the spray canister? Could this be the town's red light district? But this one didn't drive past to check her out. It stopped. And when she swung her head around, she was dazzled by a pair of undipped headlights. She turned back and carried on, her body tightening as she heard the purr of the car edging forward.

She clutched her bag tightly under one arm, trying to open the zip with her other hand to reach the canister. Typically, the zip had stuck. She needed a light to see where it had jammed, but the flashlight was on her phone, and her phone was in the bag behind the useless zip. And then she heard a car door opening and shutting. Better to keep moving. It wasn't far now to Jo's flat. She could just see the end of their street and was beginning to increase her speed again when she felt a light touch on her shoulder.

'Get in the car,' he whispered.

His hand was on her arm, pushing it behind her back. She struggled to release herself, but he only pushed higher and there was nothing in front of her to grab or bite or kick. When she tried to scream, no sound came out. Even if it had, who would hear? They were about fifty metres from the nearest house, and everything looked shut up. As he walked her towards the passenger door she managed to croak, 'Are you mad?' Though she already knew the answer to that question.

With her good arm she was clutching her bag, but as he opened the passenger door and threw her down on the seat, he tugged it off her, breaking the strap and hurling it over the fence to the railway line. Tamsin's gift, the one thing that could have helped her, gone. And now he was walking around the bonnet to the driver's door. Her body was shaking, but she could still think and plan. She was wearing trainers. In normal times she was a fast runner.

Even with a cracked rib, adrenalin might get her to safety. If she made a spurt as he was getting into his seat, she might make it to the trees. Tensed for flight, she tugged at the door handle. The door refused to open.

He drove fast down the hill. His fixed expression gave no flicker of acknowledgement as he passed the end of Jo and Immy's road. As they left the town behind them she leant forward and opened the flap of the glove compartment. A small packet of tissues. An old map. Half a packet of wine gums. No pencil, no biro, no screwdriver. Nothing useful. She pulled out a tissue.

'Disappointed?' he asked, laughing, his eyes never veering from the road ahead. The car swung around the turning onto the main road towards Kilver.

There were few other cars. Nothing on their side and coming towards them only the occasional pair of headlights, their beams heavily flecked with rain.

'Are we going home?' she asked. There was no reply, and she realised he would speak only when he chose. His actions answered her question as he sped past the turning to their house. They carried on along the ridge, high above the twinkling lights of the next village below them.

'You can turn round at the Vere Road triangle,' she suggested lamely, as if he didn't know the route and had mistaken the way on a pleasant outing to the seaside.

At the Vere Road triangle, where the road dropped towards the moor, he drove on into the rain-soaked night, wipers at top speed; volley after volley of tiny droplets splattering the windscreen.

'What the fuck are you doing, Michael?'

Again, no answer, and she glanced sideways, taking in that steely focus that seemed to come over him when driving. She thought of all the times they had argued about speed, coming to a compromise at ninety miles per hour on the motorway.

He appeared to be heading for Bristol. But before the motorway fork, he turned onto one of the bigger drove roads that crossed the moor. This road was often flooded after heavy rain, and in the glare of their undipped headlights, on the narrow verge to the left, she could see the yellow triangular signs warning Road Closed. Someone had pushed them out of the way. The road was raised above the fields on both sides, but still below sea level, little used except by farmers with huge tractors.

He drove on fast. At least if they crashed on this smaller road they would hurt only themselves. And then, because she could no longer bear passivity, she tugged at the steering wheel, causing the car to veer onto the verge, only to bounce back onto the road as Michael righted its course. He pulled to a stop, turned to look at her and placed his hands on her shoulders. In the light of the dashboard, she could make out his features. They looked sharper, harder, than the features she knew, with an intensity of purpose she could not fathom. He hadn't been drinking. His breath smelt sweet from the wine gums. He would have been eating them for comfort, and the thought was reassuring. If she could offer him some other comfort, they might come through this together unharmed.

'Don't try that again,' he said.

It was a trick. A trick to exert power. He wanted to scare her by driving too fast, taking her to some secluded place. Michael liked to tease. She remembered the time they had hired a canoe and paddled out to sea and he had stood up and rocked the boat, so fiercely they had nearly capsized. Or the times he had called her out publicly, telling the assembled company how lovely she had been when they first met, 'before she lost her looks'. Or flirting with other women in front of her, carrying on until he knew it hurt. Teasing could become bullying. Looking back now she could see that's what it was. And he had driven out here for the same reason, he enjoyed frightening her. He would drive to the edge of the flood, intimidate her with his silence until she came out with some grovelling apology, some promise to be a better wife. Then he would drive her home. But it could never again be her home.

'Why are we here?' she asked.

Again, no reply. He restarted the engine and drove on, turning down one of the unpaved tracks that crossed the flooded field. And soon the track itself was flooded, marked only by the silhouettes of stunted willows jutting out of the blackness. He stopped and turned off the engine. She waited for him to speak, explain, but he said nothing. The floods had been bad on their first winter, and she remembered someone telling her that two feet of water could take a car off the road, less than a foot could knock out the engine. It felt suddenly cold and she pulled her jacket tightly across her chest.

'You'll have to back out,' she murmured.

'I don't have to do anything.'

He turned off the inside lights, took out the ignition key, flipped the blade and squeezed it into a back pocket.

She said, 'Let me drive. I'll get us out of here.' He shook his head slowly. 'Why don't you call Immy? Jo's dad has a tractor.'

He laughed, picked his phone out of a compartment in his door and put his hand through the small gap above the partially rolled down window. She heard a splash as he let it fall. By now water had seeped into the car and had already penetrated her trainers. Her socks were wet, her feet cold. He'd said nothing about the injunction. He probably hadn't received it and she wouldn't tell him. What would be the point? The whole notion felt ludicrous.

'Why are we here?' she asked.

'Who took those photos?'

'What photos?'

'You, naked, smiling. The ones I just dropped in the flood.'

She couldn't pretend they were fakes. Michael knew her body. And now he had his hand on her arm. A light touch. But it felt like a warning, 'Don't mess with me, Kate.'

She felt herself stiffen. How did he know?

'I see all your pictures. Remember? We used to share stuff. I still have the password. Not just stuff you take. Anything anyone sends you. Who sent them? Was it him?'

Of course. Michael must have accessed her Google drive.

'Please, Michael. Don't make me talk about this. Not now. We need to back out before the water gets too high. Is there a torch? I can stand behind the car and guide you.' He made a scoffing sound. In the growing dark she could barely make out his expression, but some instinct told her she needed to connect with him, needed to waken his heart. 'You already know who took those pictures. Forgive me, Michael. It was a terrible time for me. I think I was slightly mad. What can I do to make it up to you? Like I told you, it meant nothing.'

How pathetic she sounded, how lame every attempt at explanation. His answer picked up the hollowness of what she was saying.

'Nothing? Didn't look like that from the smile on your face. Where were you? On the studio floor? I thought I recognised that blanket.'

She was silent. His hand was still on her arm. He had swivelled in his seat to face her. And now he was holding her, digging his fingers into her flesh.

'So where were you tonight? Some new bit of rough?'

He repeated Tamsin's address. He must have followed her there.

'It's Tamsin's house. She wants to go to New Zealand. She had nothing when Steve died. I was helping her.'

'You make me sick when you say that name.'

'I'm sorry. I won't say it again.'

'Some poor kid you picked up in town.'

'When did you find out, Michael?'

'Find out what?'

'About Steve.'

Her eyes had grown accustomed to the dark and she could see his face, just well enough to read the incredulity.

'You told me. Remember? Like you told me it meant nothing. At least I know what to believe.'

She wanted to believe him. And what did it matter anyway? Steve was dead. In that moment, all that mattered was getting out of there. The water had covered her shoes now and was rising fast. Could the river have burst its banks? Would it be possible to even start the car?

'We need to get out, Michael.'

He was staring at her, hard. She couldn't see the fine detail of his expression, but she sensed him studying her, appraising, considering his next move.

'Please, Michael. For Immy's sake. Don't do this.' Do what? A new fear ran through her... 'I wanted to help. Tamsin lost her husband. She was broke.'

He was staring at her hard. The light was dimming, but she could still detect the madness in his eyes.

'You were a beautiful woman once. When I met you, I thought you were a goddess. That cool detachment. I thought you mysterious. But there's something wrong with you, Kate. You know that, don't you? You knew when you decided that you weren't meant to be a mother. You don't have feelings like ordinary people. You don't know how to care. All the lies you told me. Sure, they meant nothing. It all meant nothing. You have no heart. You're callous. But you're worse than that. Deep down you're rotten, filth.'

Both hands were on her arms now. His words were tiny darts, peppering her skin, the final ones, the sharpest, reaching deep inside her, stabbing her guts. She couldn't speak. And when he started again his voice rose in pitch, as if he too couldn't bear the dreadfulness of his accusation, needing to mock her to make it endurable.

'So, where else did you do it? The studio? Our bed? What was he like? Good in bed? Better than me? No wonder you were so down on Immy coming to stay. Cramping your style. Then you try out your witchcraft on her. Poor kid. Not surprising she needed to get out.'

His voice rose from a whisper to a shout, accusations coming one after another like a hail of gunshots. Her arms ached where he was squeezing, and his breathing was getting louder, more like panting, harsh and jagged. Her mind whirled as she remembered what she had done to Tamsin, how easy it was to squeeze a woman's neck. There would be no handy metal tool with which to defend herself. Her heart was pounding as she tried to conceive of potential escape routes. But with every attempt to pull away his hold tightened. And then, suddenly, his arms dropped.

He swung away and now he was staring through the windscreen. Instead of gripping her neck, as she had feared he would do, he was gripping the steering wheel. She waited as her heart began to settle.

'What do you want, Michael?'

'I only want to talk to you.'

'Like this!'

'You used me,' he said, still staring ahead of him.

'If I did, I didn't mean to. I'm sorry. Can you forgive me?'

'I should beat you up. Only I'm not that kind of man. You know I'm not that kind of man.'

The water at her feet was rising.

'Please, Michael. Get us out of here.'

He turned the key. The car spluttered and died. They needed to get out fast. At any moment, the tide could reach its peak. The river might trickle over the raised banks. Or it might spill over in an unstoppable wave. She had seen it happen from the safety of a bridge. And when it did, the water in the field would rise suddenly and fast.

'We need to get out of the car.'

'I think you'll find the doors are locked.'

'Give me the key.'

He didn't respond. And it dawned on her that this was what he had intended; to drive out here to die and take her with him. He didn't need to kill her. The water would do it for him.

Even if she could open a door it would be unsafe. Water pressure could turn a car over. The only way out was through a window. She thought fast, planning, calculating. There was a jack in the boot, a wrench. If she could get to either of them, she might manage to smash the glass. In the half-light she could make out the shape of his head, though not the features. He was immobile, waiting. She took in a silent breath, let it out, and in a single swift motion, swung her body around, pulled herself up and into the back seat.

Her movement roused him, and he turned and leant over the seat and grabbed her right arm. But adrenalin was pumping through her and without thinking how badly she might hurt or maim him, in a single fierce motion and before he could reach her other arm, she veered around and punched his face as hard as she could with her left hand. She heard a strangled gulp as his head whiplashed back against the side of the car.

She gasped stale air. Breathing out seemed impossible and for one long moment she felt as if she were being suffocated. A voice in her head was saying, over and over, *This is how it is. This is how it is.*

She touched her hand. She had been wearing the engagement ring since she came back from Bath. The cut stone had a sharp edge, and her fingers were wet with Michael's blood.

He was groaning and whimpering, reminding her of her dying Timba. But she would not think of Timba now.

Her rib screaming, she leant into the hatchback boot and pulled up a corner of the cover. The jack was there, wedged into a tight cradle next to the spare tyre. She manoeuvred herself into a better position, tightening her lips at the pain in her side, managing to unscrew the fixing and lift it out. Then she climbed into the boot.

But with all the strength she could muster she was unable to smash the back windscreen. The jack was too heavy, the space too small to get enough leverage, the glass too heavily reinforced. The side windows would be easier though they were small. She might bash one out, but it would be tricky to get through and she would never get Michael out. And though the water seemed to be rising more slowly now, there was no way they could afford to wait. The inside of the car was beginning to smell; river, rain, and ground water, all mingled with the effluent that filled the rhynes and ditches. At any moment, the car could be swept off the track.

She tried, tried again. At the third blow she succeeded in smashing the side window with the wrench. She looked behind her. Michael was climbing over the seat. Part of his face was dark with blood. He was in the back with her now and she held up the wrench in front of her.

'Don't come any nearer.'

But he said nothing, only stared at her as if in a trance. Then in a low, hoarse voice, he said, 'Go.'

She took the wrench and pushed out the remainder of the glass where the pointed shards lined the window frame. Then she took off her jacket and laid it across the ledge. It was too dark to see the level of water. All around her was the flood, glistening in the faint light of the moon. When she splashed down, the water was above her knees. Her legs were jelly and she needed to steady herself on the body of the car.

It was just light enough to see and from the pale glow in the sky she could make out west. To get back to the road she would need to head east and what would be the rising sun. Her feet stumbled on the uneven tussocky ground. The water was cold through her summer trousers, and the tide was pushing her to one side. But she pushed back against it, forcing herself to stay upright, reminding herself she had come this far and soon would be on higher ground.

At first she couldn't bear to look back, couldn't bear to think that she had left her husband wounded in a flooded car. But when, eventually, she turned, she saw Michael's tall, stooping figure moving slowly behind her through the dark water.

Chapter 39

It was a mile to the village, but she walked fast and in under half an hour she arrived at the flat, soaked to the skin, numb with cold. At least Jo and Immy were still out. She couldn't have faced explanations. She ran a hot bath and lay in the steaming water as the events of the evening tumbled through her mind. Something had flipped in Michael. He needed help. But it was not for her to help him and from now on she would look after herself. An hour later, dressed in her change of clothes and sipping a hot chocolate, she was still shivering, still seeing the fury in his eyes as he grabbed her arm, then the sadness as he faced her at the end, blood running from the wound she had inflicted, murmuring, 'Go.'

She had seen him walking behind her through the water, but she had moved fast and quickly lost him. Where would he go? She suspected he knew nothing about the injunction.

Immy and Jo returned shortly before midnight, giggling and boisterous from large quantities of local cider. No questions were asked about her evening.

The following morning, she stayed in the flat. In the afternoon, she drove to the supermarket to buy a new cheap phone. Contrary to her earlier resolve, she made a quick detour to the farmhouse on the way back. There was no car outside. She wondered if the Audi was still stuck in the field. The studio and the house were dark. If she were to produce more work for Jason she would need to get back inside her studio. There were good locks on the door. And she could bolt it from within. She would not be controlled by Michael. Once the injunction had been served, she would go back there.

Immy came back from the cafe with news. Michael had stayed with Jen and Azeem the previous night. He'd had some kind of accident, but he was fine. He'd driven the car into a flood by mistake and the car had to be towed out. As soon as it was fixed he planned to go back to Bristol. Kate wondered how he had explained the injury to his face. Jen would have got the truth, or something close to the truth. But for some reason she had decided not to pass it on to Immy.

'Jen said she's been trying to call you.'

'I lost my phone. I think I must have dropped it on the way back from Tamsin's. I got a new one, a new number. You said I should.'

'Tamsin?' queried Jo. 'I thought you weren't going round there.'

'I wanted to give her the money. She wasn't exactly grateful. I didn't expect that. But she was fine. Almost friendly.'

Jo made a face and went to fill the kettle. Immy looked from one to the other as if wandering what she ought to think.

Kate added, 'She told me about the police report.'

'And?' Immy's eyes widened.

'There was another car.'

She wouldn't mention the make of car, her absurd suspicions about Michael. But Immy was curious.

'Was that all? Another car? What sort of car? Did they get the number plate?'

'I don't know,' said Kate, wishing she hadn't mentioned Tamsin, the phone, the police report. But her body ached from holding things back. She felt like an instrument with over-tuned strings. Eventually the tension would break her. From now on she wanted only openness, trust, honesty. Jo looked unconcerned as she set out mugs for tea, but Immy seemed determined to mine every nugget of information.

'And what are the police doing? Did they interview the driver? What did the guy in the lorry say?'

'I've no idea. I didn't ask. Does it matter now?'

'Of course it matters!' Immy's voice was raised, cracked. 'A guy died.' The other two women stared at her.

'Why are you so wound up?' asked Jo. 'You didn't even know him.'

But Immy didn't answer, only saying, 'I'm going out,' – then, turning back at the door – 'Do we need anything from the shop?'

'No,' said Jo, staring in amazement.

'I'll go anyway. I fancy a walk.'

And she left the flat.

Kate asked, 'What's up with her?'

'Maybe it's all getting to her. All this stuff about her father. You know what she's like. Susceptible. Thin-skinned. It's what we love about her.' But Jo looked unconvinced.

'Do you want me to leave? I mean I'm just a reminder of everything that's gone wrong.'

'Don't even think of it. Like I said. What's ours is yours. Stay as long as you need to. I'll talk to Immy. She's not angry with you. It's not like you've hurt anyone.'

Kate thought of all the people she had hurt, physically, emotionally. She said nothing. And then Steve's tortured face rose in her mind and she heard again his words, 'I love women too much.' And then she saw Immy's face, her obvious distress when she'd heard of his death, her sudden disappearance from the dinner party. And now, her sudden departure from the flat. But such speculations were ludicrous. Immy was gay. Immy was loyal. And how would they have found the time? But a flirtation? A flirtation that had gone too far? And now the idea had struck, it was impossible to scrub it from her mind. Hadn't he described Immy as 'the sexy one'? Didn't he say he recognised her from the reclining nude?

'Give us your new number,' said Jo. 'And don't forget to call Jen back.'

'I won't.'

Another lie. She had no intention of ringing Jen, much as she might wonder what Michael had told her. They settled to watch a film, eating a take-away from the freezer.

It was more than an hour later when Immy walked back into the flat. Jo didn't press her about where she had been. They retired to bed early, and Kate stretched out on the sofa, haunted by images of Steve and Immy, their perfect bodies guiltily entwined.

Chapter 40

Petra rang to tell her Michael had been served with the injunction. He'd returned to Bristol and the process server had found him early in the morning.

'So, I can go home.'

'I wouldn't. There's an order protecting you, but some men flip when they see it and try to put pressure on their partners.'

Kate couldn't help wondering what the point was if that were the case, but she only said, 'Michael's a lawyer. He knows the score.'

'I wouldn't be so confident. Don't go anywhere alone until you know how he's reacted.'

Kate wasn't as confident as she sounded. But she needed to make those heads for Jason. She still had no money, no work. And she couldn't help feeling that the touch of clay might restore her sanity.

'Keep your phone to hand. Don't drop it this time. We'll come and check on you after work,' said Jo. 'What time do you finish today, Immy love?'

'Five.'

'Right. We'll be over around five to see what you're up to.'

It was wonderful to return to work. Despite everything that had happened there, the studio was still her private space. She was worried for Michael. But he had good friends in Jen and Azeem. People took sides when couples split. Women usually sided with the woman. Men were usually the ones in the cold. Not this time. Jen and Azeem were a team and as a team they would offer Michael sound advice. It hurt. But Kate should have realised that if she chose an affair over fidelity, she would need to sacrifice her closest friendship.

It was very quiet. Normally she worked with music, but she wanted to stay alert to the crunch of tyres on the drive. The studio door was locked, her new phone on the table. If he appeared, she would call the police immediately. She doubted he would try to find her now. Not after reading the injunction. More likely he'd be sitting in his flat with his head in his hands.

The clear light was perfect for sculpting. Kate's focus had returned, and she was creating the head of a young athlete, using one of her blown-up postcards. For three uninterrupted hours her mind was engaged. No thoughts of where or how she was going to live, no worries about court orders or what Michael might do next. But by mid-afternoon her concentration was dipping, and she decided to take a break.

Walking into the house, she was hit by its cool stillness. In the past there had always been the tick of the clock, the welcome bark or companionship of a dog. Now it was as if she were entering a show home. As if all this belonged to someone else. Which it probably did. She remembered Michael talking about the bank and the mortgage. She should have listened better. If only she could pick up her studio and drop it down in some other place. But if this went, everything would go.

The kitchen was spotless, tidy, gleaming. She took in the shining parquet floor and granite worktop. Sally had been in as usual and Kate felt a pang of guilt as she remembered she still hadn't paid her.

The milk was sour, so she made a cup of herbal tea and carried it along the corridor towards the sitting room, unsettled by the alien hush. No voices, no traffic, no distant birdsong, no sound of wind or rain. All she could hear was a faint hum which must be coming from one of the light fittings. It could be chilly here in summer, the thick stone walls keeping out the heat. She shivered, wondering whether to take her tea back to the studio. But she lingered, as if by wandering through the different rooms, she might bring the place to life. She glanced into Michael's study. It was at once crowded and tidy, the creamy yellow walls lined with old books and legal prints. She'd teased him that it looked like a gentleman's smoking room.

'What's wrong with a gentleman's smoking room?' he'd retorted.

Looking at this place that was wholly his, she felt a wave of nostalgic affection. Michael's old-fashioned tastes and qualities had been part of the appeal. She'd yearned to rip away that veneer of public-school detachment. After months of slow courtship during which they'd circled each other warily, she had succeeded. And what she discovered had delighted her. But with every miscarriage she had retreated further to her private world. Finally, she had done him wrong. Walking down the empty corridor now she was suddenly aware of how she had longed for him to call her back. But he had not the language and he too had turned away. She sipped her tea and stopped, breathing in the scent of dry stone and woodsmoke that lingered in the walls even through the summer months. Everything around her spoke of their gradual separation.

She carried on towards the sitting room, her least favourite room, the coolest, darkest room in the house. It faced north-east, overshadowed by a vast yew tree that grew in the corner of the drive. Despite the wood-burning stove and the comfortable sofa, the room never felt welcoming. She pushed open the door.

He was sitting in one of two upright chairs, hands dangling over the squared arms, long legs stretched out in front of him. He looked relaxed but poised, ready to jump up at any moment.

'Hello, Kate.'

She couldn't respond. She wanted to tell him to get out, but the words wouldn't come.

'Not speaking?' he said.

'You should go,' she said.

'I needed to see you.'

'You've seen me. Now leave. Please.'

'More importantly, I wanted you to see me.'

'I see you, Michael.'

'I mean really see me.'

He stood up slowly and she turned quickly away and moved down the corridor to the kitchen. If he wished to catch her, he could do so easily. Unless she ran into the toilet and locked the door. But she wouldn't run from him. She would simply make her wishes clear. She would walk out into the garden and to the studio. Then she would lock the door behind her and call the police.

He shouted after her, 'Don't walk away from me.'

She froze.

'Come back in here.'

In the past he'd lost control. This was different. What she heard was the voice of cold command. She started to run, spilling her tea, chucking her mug on the floor as she sped past the toilet into the kitchen and towards the back door.

'I'm not going to hurt you, Kate,' he shouted. 'I just want to talk.'

'That's what you said in the car,' she shouted back.

'It was true.'

'We could have died.'

'Don't exaggerate.'

'There's a court order. You're not allowed to be here.'

As she spoke she was struggling with the glass door into the garden. It was locked. Of course. Sally would have ensured that. The key was nearby but opening it was not simple. Two levers and two separate keyholes. There was no quick way out.

'It wasn't your idea, was it?' He took a step towards her. 'You can drop it you know. You only have to tell the court you're withdrawing your application. The order runs out next week. That's it. No more hassle.'

'Don't come near me.'

'I suppose you think I'm some kind of monster.'

She made no reply.

'Look at me, Kate.'

She was staring at the floor.

'I said fucking look at me.'

She looked. His right eye was swollen, the eyelid a purple-brown colour. There was a small plaster on the eyebrow. Even without the disfiguring wound he would have looked exhausted. There were dark circles between his lower lids and cheek bones, the flesh of his face was stretched across his skull and muscles like the illustrations in her anatomy book. His voice was hoarse. But the words were clear. He wasn't drunk, just taut with pain, as if at any moment he might shatter into thousands of pieces. She was torn between running away from him, though there was nowhere to run, and embracing him as if that would make him whole.

'I see you.'

'No, you don't. You have never seen me.'

He was wrong. But she would not contradict him. Something told her it was best to let him talk himself out. He was breathing hard and there were beads of sweat across his face.

'There was always something else. You were always somewhere else. Finally, there was someone else. I should have known from the start. You were never really mine.'

Sounds and images flashed through her mind. The early days. Their banter and flirtation, the unspoken sexual current that surfaced every time they met and culminated in that weekend when they hadn't left his flat, had barely left his bed. She had seen him then. Seen nothing but him. Their first date was the Sunday pub lunch when they had emerged blinking into the sun like a pair of night creatures. And so it had continued. Every time they met, they ripped off each other's clothes. Even after marriage. They started to seek out different places, the landing, the car, the bathroom floor, hotel bedrooms. Until the first lost pregnancy, the second, the third, when she had begun to drift away.

His words floated past her.

'You wanted a house, a studio, a baby, an income. I gave you all those. Then, when you couldn't keep the baby, you turned away.'

It was cruel. Everything he said was cruel. Because he knew that the truth of it would pierce her heart. Yet she had seen him. And now she saw the pain she had caused him. He was still talking.

'Where did you pick him up? In the street? You told me it meant nothing. A casual thing. Go on, look away. It's what you do. Nothing? Don't you see that makes it worse? That you would betray me for nothing!'

She was standing by the window now. Words were his weapons, and she was battered by them. He still hadn't touched her. He was like a sparring partner, waiting for his opponent to act.

'Aren't you going to say anything?'

He was very close. She had her back to the glass, trapped by his anger. She wanted to push him away, but she sensed that if she touched him he would react, and it wouldn't take much for him to hurt her. So, she stared into his burning eyes as if her stare could hold him. Her breath caught in her nostrils as she inhaled the dark scent of his sweat. There was nowhere to run, and fight was futile. Suddenly his hand grabbed her shoulder, his fingers digging into her flesh.

'Speak to me,' he said.

There was nothing she could say. But he barked the command for a third time and before she could stop herself, she had blurted out the question that had been lodged in her mind ever since they met.

'What did you do to Simone?'

Her body tensed and her heart was banging in her chest. Her words had cut a thread in him. Whatever had been holding him back, snapped. She shut her eyes, waiting for the pain of impact, wanting it, longing for it, anything to end this uncertainty.

It came with a crash across her eardrums and a strangled cry. His grip loosened. When she opened her eyes, he was staggering backwards. There was glass all around them and blood was pulsing through the gaps between his fingers where he was clutching his right wrist. Everything seemed to be running at half-speed as he slowly crumpled, backing up against the island and sliding down to the floor.

For a moment she was immobilised by shock, feeling the cool air from the broken window on the back of her neck. She glanced down. Her clothes were splattered red and the blood was still coming. He lay curled on his side at the base of the island, groaning. Instinct kicked in and she ran to the drawer for a clean tea towel. Dropping down beside him, she wrapped the towel around the gaping wound. It was soon saturated. Nothing would stop the bleeding. His face was screwed up in pain and he was making little moaning noises.

'Hold this,' she ordered, grabbing another towel from the Aga, not even sure if it was clean. 'I'm going to ring the hospital.'

He grunted something that sounded like, 'No.'

She ran to the landline and punched in 999, running back with the handset to hold the towel. When the emergency service answered she gave the address and postcode, asking for an ambulance and explaining in some detail how to find the drive and the house. The voice asked whether she could bring the patient herself. Michael's moans were growing faint now. Blood was pulsing out on every failing heartbeat. It had soaked through two towels and was pooling on the floor around them. She replied she thought it unlikely. He was losing a lot of blood and could they hurry. It was fifteen miles to the nearest A and E, ten miles to the minor injuries unit. Ambulances were in short supply and she had heard of cases in the village where patients had waited forty minutes in an emergency. The woman on the other end was still speaking, asking questions, but Kate could not follow her.

Michael's eyes were closed now, sweat glistening on his grey-white skin. Suddenly, a memory kicked in. She flung down the phone and jumped up, reaching for the kitchen scissors and a wooden spoon. Then she tore off her T-shirt, snipping the hems, ripping it down the middle and tying the strip once around his upper arm. Next she wound the ends around the spoon, twisting it like a corkscrew, pulling the T-shirt tight, so tight that Michael screamed. The scream was good. Her first-aid training was coming back to her. You needed to cause pain. That way you might save a life.

She wedged one end of the spoon between his upper arm and chest and held onto the handle, as she pressed the towel against the wound with her other hand. She watched him. Waited. Prayed. It was working. Within seconds his breath was easing. The blood flow was slowing. His eyelids flickered.

'Stay with me, Michael. The ambulance is coming.'

He closed his eyes. She started to speak. Random musings. Anything to keep him awake.

'Remember that first time I saw you in the gallery.'

He said nothing.

'You didn't think much of the installations. Called them a waste of space.'

His eyes opened a crack. He moaned. Some impulse kept her talking.

'We were happy then, weren't we? Remember how we laughed at the artworks? The stuff with writing all over it? I tried to explain it, but I knew no more than you. Then when we went to Rome. Remember that? The Bernini and Canova in the Borghese Gallery. We talked about form and muscle and beauty, and how I was going to be a sculptor.'

She talked and talked, and his eyes opened and closed as she rambled on, disconnected rubbish about long walks through European cities. Anything to stop him drifting away. No one came, and the dark blood was seeping through the tourniquet onto the floor, Michael's damaged life seeping from his damaged body. She had no idea how much time passed. It felt like hours, as she repeated the same stories, watched each flicker of an eyelid, each twitch of his twisted lip. Finally, when his breathing had grown so weak and shallow that she thought the end must come in seconds, she heard a car in the drive. It didn't sound like an ambulance. *Hang on Michael, hang on*, she prayed.

Immy stood in the doorway, her eyes wide with horror. She rushed towards them and dropped to her knees.

'Dad!' Then, turning to Kate, she stammered, 'How do I help?'

'I've called an ambulance. But I don't know how long it will take. We need to get him to the hospital. Is Jo here?'

'No. Just me. She was stuck at work. I was worried about you when you weren't back. I borrowed her car.'

'Hold these. I need to stand up.'

Immy took the spoon and the bloody towel and Kate pulled herself up by the counter. Her legs felt stiff and weak from crouching for so long.

The girl began speaking to her father in a low voice.

'You're all right, Dad. You'll pull through. I'm here. I'll always be here.'

A whisper came out in reply, the words barely audible but sounding like, 'My girl. My own girl.'

'Keep holding the spoon,' said Kate. 'Never mind the towel. Put your arm under his. I'll take his left side.'

They heaved him up. He was a big man, heavy and unresponsive, but they managed to get him to his knees.

'Can you walk?' she asked.

He couldn't answer, but she sensed the effort in him as they raised him. And now his body was slumped over the worktop.

'We've got you,' said Kate, as she and Immy attempted to straighten him. 'Lean on me.'

He was still moaning and his breath was growing short again as he fell against her. Immy held him upright on the other side. Together they dragged him along. He could barely hobble, but somehow he managed to move his legs, helping them as they helped him, a trail of fresh blood marking their path over the shining parquet floor to the still open front door.

Chapter 41

'So, are you going to report it to the police?'

Jo had her serious, justice-must-be-done look. Kate wondered why she hadn't thought of joining the police. She'd make a good police officer.

'What am I going to tell them? He breached his injunction. So? He nearly died. Anyway, the hospital will inform the police. They're keeping him in as a suicide risk. It'll all come out.'

She didn't want to talk to anyone about anything. All she wanted was to rest. Immy understood.

'Why don't you take our bed? We can put the sofa cushions on the floor.'

'You're very kind,' said Kate, wondering what Jo thought of this unilateral offer.

'Yes,' said Jo. 'Do that.'

And Immy added, 'We need to be kind. Kindness is the important thing.'

She looked so earnest. Kate was dismayed to think that even for a moment she could have conceived that this lovely girl had been in any way involved with Steve. There was something untouched about Immy. Even her offering to Kate had felt like a further instance of lack of guile. Kate hoped Jo would be good to her.

'And you're right about the injunction,' said Jo. 'The police will find out what they need to find out. You need a break from it all. It's easy for me to judge, I'm not involved like you two.'

'So, what shall we do?' asked Immy. 'It's a bit early for bed.' For one dreadful moment Kate feared she might suggest a board game. But when Jo said nothing she added, 'How about a nice movie? Something cheering.'

'*It's a Wonderful Life?*' ventured Jo.

Kate had vague memories of the Christmas film. Wasn't it all about suicide and angels, and ludicrous notions of what would have happened if everything had been different? But the others were keen, so she sat through it with her mind elsewhere, disappearing into the corridor every half hour to call the hospital and check on Michael.

Afterwards, Jo and Immy disappeared into the bedroom to sort out the duvets. They were gone a while and when Kate spread-eagled her limbs across the double mattress half an hour later, she realised she was lying on freshly ironed and laundered sheets. Once again she marvelled at the kindness of her stepdaughter and her girlfriend. And as her eyes grew heavy with sleep she saw Michael's face, grey turning to white as the blood drained from his helpless body. The she heard his voice, croaking and weak, 'My own girl. My own girl.' And she realised that if anyone could bring him back to life, it would be Immy.

Chapter 42

Immy was getting ready for work when the doorbell rang. Twice. She ran to open it. Kate heard male voices and put her head into the corridor. Two police officers in uniform stood just beyond the threshold.

'Miss Imogen Leonard?'

'Yes.'

'We're investigating the death of Mr Stephen Peppard. We'd like to ask you a few questions.'

An electric jolt raced through Kate's body. The name still had the power to unnerve her. And what had Immy to do with Steve's death?

'Come in', said Immy, sounding strangely calm.

The two men followed her down the corridor. Kate stood back to let them into the sitting room, breathing a mixture of sweat and aftershave as they passed her. Behind her, she heard Jo coming out of the bedroom.

'What's this about?' demanded Jo. She was ready for the gym in track suit and lycra. Both men were tall and bulky, and the room felt very small and crowded. Kate wondered if she should invite them to sit, quickly remembering this was not her house. Anyway, there was only the sofa where Jo and Immy's bedclothes were still bundled up near the arm.

'We could speak at the station if it's easier,' said the older man, ignoring the question and looking past Jo to Immy. He had sparse sandy-coloured hair and bored eyes, and Kate wanted to shake him for his rudeness. The younger man explained that they were here to ask about the circumstances around Mr Peppard's death. Not accident but 'death'. The word rang around the walls of the crowded space. And why would they want to question Immy?

Immy glanced at Jo and then at Kate. There was no hint of surprise or outrage in her expression. She looked almost apologetic.

'That's fine. I'll come with you,' she said to the men.

'That would be helpful,' said the sandy-haired one, still sounding bored.

Jo said, 'How can she possibly help? It was a car accident. She doesn't even drive a car.'

But Immy knew how to drive. She'd driven Jo's car yesterday. Had she driven other cars? Michael's Audi? Kate couldn't recall him ever lending it to her. On the day of Steve's death, Michael had the car in Bristol. A thought struck her. What was the day of Steve's death? No one had given her a date. She'd assumed he'd been killed on the day he left her. But what if he had used the same road on another occasion? It was Michael who told her about the roadblock on the day he was late back. Had she been making crazy assumptions? And why did the police want to talk to Immy?

'We'll explain all that at the station.'

'Then I'm coming with you,' declared Jo.

'No, Jo. I'd rather go alone.'

'I'll call you a solicitor,' said Jo.

'It OK, Jo. I don't want a solicitor. Just let me do this.'

Jo ripped a bit of paper off a pad, opened her phone and scribbled down a number.

'Take this anyway. You may change your mind.'

Immy took the paper and looked at Kate with pained eyes. Kate could not speak as her stepdaughter followed the older man into the corridor. The younger man nodded at the two women and stepped out behind them. Kate shut the door.

Jo was standing by the window. Kate walked over to join her, and together they watched as Immy climbed into the back of the police car. What had Immy done? What had she witnessed? It felt as if disaster touched everyone Kate had ever loved.

Chapter 43

Immy came back on the bus. Jo and Kate were waiting for her.

'Well?' said Jo.

'I thought you'd be at work.'

'No way. I needed to know. I swapped shifts. Kate and I have been going crazy.'

While Immy was at the police station, Jo had gone for a run and on her return home had made two loaves of bread and then played on her Xbox. Kate had spent the three hours lying on the sofa either dozing or staring at the wall.

'So?' demanded Jo. Immy threw off her jacket and sat on one of the hard chairs, looking at Jo as if hoping to be released.

'You have to tell us everything, Immy. Not just me. Kate too.'

Immy picked at her lip then dropped her hand on her lap and started again.

'There'll be an inquest. I might have to give evidence.'

'Evidence of what?'

'It all happened so quickly. I was frightened. But I should have stopped.'

'You're making no sense,' said Jo. 'Start at the beginning.'

'I'm not sure about the beginning. But I'll start with you, Jo. I'd only known you about two weeks. But that morning, the day of the crash... it was the day after you and I...'

'Made out?' suggested Jo with a smile.

'Yes.'

Kate felt a twinge of embarrassment.

'I remember that day. It rained in the morning, then the sun came out,' said Jo, still smiling, a pink flush spreading across her cheeks. Immy carried on.

'We didn't sleep much. I went into the cafe at midday, but I was useless. Kept muddling up orders and drifting off. Luckily, they weren't that busy. Jen could tell something was up. She asked if I was feeling OK and I said, "Not really," and she told me if I was ill I better go home. She didn't want all the customers catching it. I managed not to laugh. In a way I was ill. Not in the way she thought.'

The twinge had turned to a pang, but then Kate remembered their kindness in letting her stay and told herself not to be ridiculous.

'I came back here. But you were at work and I didn't know what to do with myself and my head was spinning. After the rain there was sun and a rainbow. It was a beautiful afternoon and I decided to go for a bike ride. Sometimes movement is the only thing that can stop me thinking. Since coming down here it's all been so crazy.' She caught Kate's eye. And Kate wondered if she had told Jo what had happened between them. Or was that another secret? 'I was missing dance. I still miss dance.'

'You'll get back to it,' said Jo. 'We looked up the Somerset colleges. You never lose something like that.'

Immy looked doubtful.

'Go on,' said Kate.

'I set off up the main road. I would have taken one of the droves, but I wanted to do the big hill. I needed to work up a sweat. It was hard work. There was blue sky, wisps of cloud, but for a long time all I could do was stare at the tarmac, feet hard on the pedals, standing in the saddle. Everything was pumping, pushing, no space for thought. It was like I was straining to get rid of something. Don't look like that, Jo. Not you. Something else. I should have been happy. I was happy. But sometimes happiness is too painful, too scary. The thought you might lose it. Or maybe I was just determined to get to the top without stopping and walking like some people do. You know that hill. How it starts off gentle and doesn't seem too bad and you think you've made it but there's more and more, another hill to climb. Only it's worth it because when you get to the summit, there's this amazing view over the fields to the river and then this insane run down. That's when I let go.'

Kate wondered if she had told the police about letting go.

'I was flying. It was like that moment in dance when you're weightless, free, only now I wasn't flying across an empty stage I was flying down an empty road.'

She paused.

'Only the road wasn't empty.'

Paused again, took a breath.

'This car overtook me. It was silver grey, like Dad's, and for a moment I thought it was Dad and I might have wobbled a bit. It swerved past. I should have put the brakes on then, pulled over to the side, but I was going too fast, and anyway, I was heading to the dip where the road rises again. Only there was this lorry. One minute it wasn't

317

there. Then it was. Like, coming straight towards me. I should have crashed into the bushes but that would have meant a decision and I couldn't make one. All I could do was carry on. I thought the lorry would hit me, only it veered across the road and I sped past. I was just starting to slow where the road levels out when I heard a squeal of brakes and a smash.

'Eventually I stopped. When I looked behind me. I saw the lorry blocking the road. That was all. I knew it must have hit something, but I couldn't see what.

'I should have gone back then, but I just stood there watching. Then the passenger door opened, and someone stepped down. I saw him leaning against the side of the vehicle. He turned back and must have seen me. I told myself he was all right, so I didn't need to stop. Even though I'd heard a crash. Even though the driver must have hit something.'

She stopped. Her face was screwed up and Kate thought she might be about to cry.

'There's a loop round over the hills so I didn't need to go back to the spot. And when I got home, I knew I would never bike again. Then I heard the man had died. I kept meaning to go to the police. But each time I set off something stopped me. I mean, what good would it do? Plus, I was afraid. I was just getting my life back. Only I couldn't forget that sound. The squeal and then the smash. When they came for me, I was relieved.'

'So how did they know it was you?' asked Kate. 'Tamsin didn't say anything about a bike on the dashcam.'

'They didn't pick me up on the dashcam. Or if they did, they didn't mention it. But the guy from the lorry saw me. When I turned around he was glowering at me. He told the police he knew me, but he wasn't sure where from. Then last week he came into the cafe. I remember this guy staring at me. Guys often stare at me, so I didn't think much of it. But I reckon he knew right away. I look a bit different from most people around here. Even when I'm sweaty and hot and frightened. So he told the police and they called Jen, and she must have told them where I lived.'

'Jen!' Kate was shocked.

'Don't blame her. If she hadn't told them where I was staying, they'd have asked to see her records.'

Of course. And Jen would have records. She was always scrupulous, law-abiding.

'Did you tell them what you told us?' asked Jo.

'Pretty much. They told me someone would be in touch about the inquest.'

—

Jo called the hospital. Michael had already left. Kate took the phone from her and explained she was Michael's wife and needed to know where he was. They told her a woman called Gillian had turned up. She and her husband had promised to take care of Michael, and he had persuaded his doctors there would be no more suicide attempts. The voice on the phone was unable to help further.

Kate called Petra.

'I'll see what I can find out.'

An hour later Petra called back.

'We need to go back in front of the judge. The police were informed of the suicide attempt, but they don't seem aware there was a breach of the injunction.'

Two breaches. Kate hadn't told anyone about what happened in the car.

319

'And what are we supposed to tell the judge?'

'He came to the house. That was forbidden by the order. There's a power of arrest. The police need to act on it.'

'Now? Michael nearly died. He's staying with this couple. I don't see how arresting him will help. If he does anything again, I'll let you know.'

'It's not what I advise, Kate. But it's your choice. I'll note everything you say. And I advise you to write it all down. Exactly as it happened. Just in case.'

'So, what will you do?' asked Jo, 'Will you go back to the house?'

'I don't think I can bear it. Is it OK if I stay a bit longer? Just until I find a room?'

'Of course you can.'

She had no idea what would happen to the house. Couldn't face sleeping in any of those cavernous bedrooms. But for now, the studio was hers. She would finish the heads for Jason. She would try to find a job. She would take it slowly, stage by stage. She would write down everything Michael had done. She would take control of her life at last. And she would be there for Immy.

Part Three

A year later

Chapter 44

The elegant Georgian house had a grey stone façade and large sash windows, open to the warm afternoon. The solid blue front door stood beneath a square, pillared porch and Kate's knock was met by a fresh-faced young man of around thirty with cropped hair and a ready smile just visible behind his Perspex shield. When she explained she had come to visit Michael, he invited her in, pointed to the dispenser of hand sanitiser by the door, requesting her to refrain from touching anything on the way to the garden.

'Do I need to keep this on?' she mumbled from behind her mask.

'Only inside the house. You're fine outside as long as you maintain a distance.'

She followed him through a spacious hall into a narrow corridor; he indicated a small cloakroom where she could wash her hands. When she emerged, he led her a little further on and then flung open a door to the garden, standing back as she stepped out onto a wide terrace that ran along the top of a lawn that sloped down to a wood.

'You can wait here,' he said, pointing to an empty bench. 'You'll see people wandering about. Some of them might walk quite close. They won't speak to you and I'd ask you not to greet them.'

He gave her his easy smile and left her.

She tugged off her mask and took a deep breath as she gazed towards the woods. The view was peaceful, yet she was conscious of an accelerating heartbeat as she prepared for the encounter. Immy had said her father was well, calmer, at ease with himself. It was hard to imagine. But he had asked to see her, and she had agreed. There were people around. There was nothing he could do to hurt her. She was steeled against anything he might say.

The sun was warm, the yew and lime trees that fringed the lawn barely moved in the still air. Through the quiet Kate heard the distant rumble of a tractor, the intermittent cry of a buzzard, the cooing of a wood pigeon. Occasionally a human figure would glide slowly across her field of vision. He or she would be staring at the ground or straight ahead, wrapped in a world of private meditation. After a few minutes, Kate's heartbeat slowed and she felt her body growing lighter, as if she were suspended in time.

And now Michael's tall, thin figure was ambling towards her across the terrace. He looked different. More than a year older. His hair was completely grey, the lines on his face more pronounced and the face itself seemed to have shrunk. But there was strength in his movements and his eyes were clear and bright.

'Hello, Kate.'

She struggled to keep her voice steady as she answered, 'Hello, Michael.'

He offered a cautious smile, nodding his head in acknowledgement and sitting on the other end of the bench.

'It's good of you to come,' he said.

'I wanted to see you. I needed to know how you were.'

'As you see, I am well.'

The cautious smile broke open. It was almost the old smile that had so entranced her all those years ago, though quieter, more contained, as if he asked and expected nothing. And then he said, 'You?'

And her heart turned as she sensed he really wanted to know, and she felt afraid of letting him know too much as if she might let him get too close. 'I'm well too. Thank you.'

The polite discourse felt absurd, but it was all she could manage. His presence four feet away from her was over-whelming. She was grateful for the rules on distance. Had it not been for those rules, she would have found it hard to sit on the same bench.

He started to speak.

'It was Gillian who suggested this place. I don't think you know her. She's from my chambers. Well, what was my chambers. At first it was just a weekend retreat. Then a week. Then another. I liked the silence. But then stuff started to come up. It's been tough, brutal even. But it's been good, like shedding an old skin.'

He was staring out in front as he spoke. She couldn't remember him ever talking about himself so openly, with such apparent honesty. He turned to look at her.

She asked, 'So what do you do here?'

'Gardening, mostly. Some maintenance, slipped roof tiles, plumbing. Whatever they need.' She said nothing, but he must have read her expression because he added, 'Yes, I know it wasn't my strong point at home. But I'm learning. I prefer the garden. As you see there's plenty to do. Also, I meditate.'

She paused. She was teaching herself not to react so quickly. Better to respond than react.

'Are you OK, Kate?'

'Yes. Fine. I was just thinking. It's a surprise. I mean Immy told me a bit, but you're so changed.'

'I would hope so. I wasn't that great before.'

A jumble of images flashed across her mind. Michael's profile, rigid against the dim light as he drove into the rising flood. Blood dripping down his cheek as she struggled to escape the mud-locked car. Eyes burning as he pushed her against the wall. More blood spurting from a self-inflicted wound, his body crumpling to the floor. His ashen face.

She jolted herself into the present, focusing on the man before her, no longer ashen but bronzed from the sun.

'Thanks for sorting the house,' he said.

With help from Sally and Immy, she had done it. Michael's things were boxed and stored. Mostly books. He'd told her to auction all the furniture she didn't want. Most of it had belonged to his parents and he had never much liked it. The sale brought in a few hundred, enough to pay for storage. As for her own stuff, she kept a few pictures, but the rest went to charity. How could a woman ever imagine she would need so many clothes?

'Immy told me you didn't like staying there.'

'I tried a couple of nights, but after that I went back to Jo's sofa. Then I got the job and found a room of my own. It felt better that way, cleaner.'

The only wrench had been the studio. It had been impossible to resume teaching without it, even if she'd had the strength for it. And it pained her to abandon all that equipment. Jason had found someone to look after most of it. She would never have a place like that again. Not with so much light and space. Like most artists, she would need to manage with a kitchen table, a garage if she were lucky.

He was sitting a few feet away. The man she had once so loved and later so damaged. She didn't tell him she was planning to leave the town. As she had feared, her affair with Steve had become public knowledge. Tamsin had kept to her word and said nothing about the injuries to her neck, and Kate stayed quiet about Timba and the request for money. But rumours multiplied and a sour taste lingered. Immy and Jo were moving to Glastonbury and had offered her their spare room. She had accepted immediately.

'What are you going to do? Will you go back to the Bar?'

'Not now. I doubt I'd survive there after all this.'

He threw his head back and she sensed his meaning. His own crisis had dovetailed into the world's crisis and everything had been transformed. 'There's no place for me there now. Even the court hearings are online. It's not what I was trained to do. Though I'm not sure the Bar ever suited me. I'm too much of a loner. I need something physical. Perhaps I always needed something physical and never realised it. Maybe because you were the one who made things.'

She thought about how partners created roles for each other. Like siblings. The beautiful one, the clever one, the artistic one. The difficult one, the angry one, the misfit.

'What about you?' he asked.

'Oh, the job's fine. I was never much good at teaching. In some ways, I'm better just working away alone. I guess we're both loners. Maybe that was the problem.'

If anyone had told her she would find a kind of peace in a casting workshop she would have been incredulous. Mixing chemicals, calculating areas for moulding, pouring in the resin, easing off the silicon. It was skilled work, transforming other people's art into something beautiful and long-lasting. You needed to be meticulous. The only hint of creativity was the choice of patina on the finished object. Sometimes she was given that freedom. It was enough. The longing to create her own art lay fallow. The workshop was struggling but so far it had survived. She had no idea for how long, but for now she was fortunate.

'We messed up,' he said.

'I messed up.'

He looked away across the lawn, and she sensed him tamping down the painful memory as he changed the subject.

'It's great that Immy's still got her job. And I guess I was wrong about Jo.'

She remembered how scathing he had been, about both the cafe and the relationship. Now Immy seemed to be the lucky one. The cafe had closed and opened again. The leisure centre too. And whatever happened in the world outside, however precarious their work, they were solid together. Immy was born in England and could stay. She wouldn't go back to dance performance, but she was thinking about teaching. According to Jo, she had got through the inquest with courage. Knowing Tamsin would be present, Kate had decided not to go. The conclusion was: Accident.

She said, 'Everyone's taking it very slowly.'

'I don't know how long this place will last.' For a moment he looked anxious as if this new security might be ripped away like the old one.

'We don't know how long anything will last.'

His hand was resting on the bench, a few feet away. She thought about touch. How they had all taken it for granted. They were both silent for a few seconds. And then he asked, 'What happened to the widow?'

'She went to New Zealand. Just after the inquest. Before lockdown. I guess she's still there.'

Kate had sold two more heads and raised enough for Tamsin's fare. At least she had kept that promise.

'Thanks for coming, Kate.'

'I'm glad you're OK, Michael.' She moved to stand.

'Don't go.'

She hesitated.

'Sit a little longer,' he said. 'We don't need to talk.'

She looked about her. There was no danger here. What harm would it do to remain? She had faced him and survived. They had both survived. She could give him ten minutes.

She sat down. People were still wandering around the lawn. The slow movement of their separate bodies was quietly mesmerising, and she closed her eyes. The sunlight warmed her eyelids as she took in the sound of distant farm machinery, the call of birds, the buzzing of insects on the wall of lavender that lined the terrace. Bathed in light and sound and smells, she felt not simply relieved, but released. As if her trepidation had been the fluttering of a trapped bird and now the cage was open, and the bird could fly. She could sit on a bench with this man without fear or hatred or panic.

And then she heard him say, 'You saved my life.'

She opened her eyes. He was looking out across the lawn.

'That's OK,' she said, rising.

'I'm sorry for what I put you through.' He turned his head to face her again and stood up, taking a small step towards her.

'I'm sorry, too.'

Did that mean he had forgiven her? His next question answered hers.

'Will you come again?'

She couldn't answer.

He gave a cautious smile. 'It's OK. You don't have to say.'

She would not come again.

Two weeks after his injury she had followed Jo's advice, attended court and told the judge everything. There had been no arrest. Michael had offered an undertaking not to contact her for six months, and he had kept to the agreement. Through solicitors it was agreed that the house would be sold. The debts would be paid. There wasn't much left and what there was would be hers. Michael would keep Bristol. At least for now. They could never again live together, she was sure of that. He was still her husband but one day they would divorce.

'Goodbye, Michael.'

The cautious smile dropped. She turned and started walking slowly towards the house. Her stomach felt tight as if someone, or something, was pulling her innards, twisting them, just as she twisted the tourniquet on Michael's arm almost a year ago. His eyes bore through her back to her heart and everything inside her was turning. Was this what it was like to fall out of love? She thought it had happened long ago. But falling out of love was a slow process, and just when you thought all love had gone it could come back to wound you. She carried on walking. And as she walked, the churning slowed and faded and she was conscious again of the warm air on her skin, the buzz of insects and scent of flowers. She quickened her pace.

Acknowledgements

In a difficult year for all of us I was lucky to be writing a novel, and even luckier to have the love and support of so many good friends. My particular thanks go to the following dear people:

Maudie Bradie and Nina Cairns for introducing me to figurative sculpture, Steve Drury for talking to me about flood risk on the Levels, Dougal Jefferies for helping me to sever an artery, Maggie Steele and Tim Woodbury for explaining the struggles of the commercial gallery owner and Louise Smith for veterinary advice.

I would also like to thank Maggie Gee and Patrick McGuiness, and the other inspiring participants at Arvon's novel writing week at The Hurst.

As always, I am grateful to Chris Peachment for reading and commenting on early drafts.

Finally, my thanks go to my wonderfully patient agent Anne Marie Doulton and my brilliant editor Leodora Darlington.